War INC
Book 1

by
Toby Neighbors

War INC
© 2020, Toby Neighbors

ISBN: 978-1-952260-07-0

Published by Mythic Adventure Publishing, LLC
Idaho, USA

Copy Editing by Julie Duke

Books By Toby Neighbors

Toby Neighbors Online

www.TobyNeighbors.com

GOODREADS

www.GoodReads.com/TobyNeighbors

FACEBOOK

www.Facebook.com/TobyNeighborsAuthor

INSTAGRAM

Instagram @TobyTheWriter

TWITTER

On Twitter @TobyNeighbors

Chapter 1

Alex Chester Evans looked at the computer screen with a sense of dread. The message from the Gemini Technical Institute was a form letter—a rejection notice. His application had been denied, just as it had been by three other institutions in the space of a week. He wasn't what they were looking for, and he was going to have to tell his parents.

Shutting down the message app, he slipped his PIL —Personal Information Link—into his back pocket and stepped into his last class of the day. It was Cosmic Geography, but Alex wasn't in the right frame of mind to learn anything. As a kid he had dreamed, as most children do, of traveling through the tunnels from one star system to another and seeing wild, unexplored planets. But that dream had died. He was a mediocre student with no aptitude for trade skills. Like over half of humanity, his family was stuck on a backwater planet owned by one of the big five—an Epic Corp, as the news media called them. They were bigger than the governments, with more money and resources. They were the only entities with the means to open new space portals or explore and exploit new planets.

His father had taken a job with NanCo. The company had settled them on NP8261, a planet so pathetically boring that it didn't even have a name. It barely had an atmosphere—just a thin layer of helium. The only value to the planet was in the ore mined by the large rock-busting machines. Alex's father was a heavy mechanic, which had been a good job, but they were stuck on NP8261 and were virtually slaves to the company. NanCo owned everything: the city, their apartment, the entertainment complex, and even the grocery outlet. They were paid in company credits, which had no value off-world. They couldn't even afford transportation to another planet if they wanted to leave.

Alex had been banking on acceptance to a tech school. Most had relocation programs, and once he graduated he would have job opportunities on a variety of worlds. He might even be able to get on a named planet, one with atmosphere and vast cities that span continents. But it was time to face the facts. He wasn't even good enough to get into a trade program. He would have a short, difficult life, probably as a rock-buster deep in the mines. Maybe if they had lived on a real world, he could have found a career if he hustled hard enough, but the truth was that he was caught in the company net.

Anger began to build as he sat in class. Was he really supposed to care anymore? He had done the work his teachers assigned, but his teachers weren't the cream of the crop. Only the teachers with no other prospects took an assignment on a company planet. He'd been told all his life that if he worked hard enough, he could accomplish anything—but it was all a lie.

When the bell rang and he was finally free, he strapped on his rebreather, left his data slate in the dock, and pulled on his heavy coat. Alex was tall and thin, as there was never enough to eat, and the coat—which was second- or maybe even thirdhand when he got it—was almost too small. As it was, his arms hung out of the sleeves. He buried his hands as deeply into the coat pockets as they would go, but there was still a gap between his sleeve cuffs and the pocket—just enough to let the cold, blustery wind on NP8261 slip up his arms as he walked.

The school building was near the security hangar, and Alex often walked by the warehouse-sized building to get a look at the MP Defenders housed there. They were big, bulky warfare units. Some people called them "mechs," or battle suits. To Alex they were like walking tanks; they had thick armor, hydraulic piston legs, and no arms—just a variety of weapon mounts. He had tested for the defense force against his mother's wishes. It was the one company job that had a future, if a person could actually survive long enough. But of course, he was rejected from that program as well. The big hangar doors were closed, and Alex felt like it was just another rejection. His future was as bleak as the planet he was stuck on.

He didn't notice the disruptor drones dropping toward the town from orbit until the sound of their sleek, armored skin began to keen in the thin helium. At first Alex thought someone was whistling. He looked around, but there weren't many people outdoors. Most of the locals never went outside; they preferred the dimly lit tunnels and underground links that didn't require rebreathers or heavy coats. When Alex finally looked up, he saw six dark shapes hurtling down toward the grimy, industrial town.

The first thought that went through his mind was why anyone would even bother attacking NP8261. The ore mined was valuable enough, but only after it was sorted and shipped to the refineries. Yet there was no doubt about what was coming down. Alex had never seen more than one transport descending at a time, and they were bulky ships with roaring engines. The disruptor drones were sleek, like fat bullets shot from a cosmic cannon far away.

He dove into a gap between the atmo-converter and the thick steel beams at the end of the security hangar. Being outside during an attack was dangerous, but Alex had no intention of running away. The attack was the most exciting thing that had happened to him in weeks, and he wasn't about to miss it. Besides, what did he have to lose?

The disruptors landed with booming thumps like muted thunder. Even before they shed their heat shells, the doors of the security hangar rumbled upward. Chains slid through hardened steel sprockets, and the thin metal doors shook as they slid up into the overhead rails. Alex couldn't see what was happening, but he heard the whir of the MP Defenders powering up and starting to move, and then the big, mechanized fighting machines came lurching from their den. The ground seemed to tremble as their heavy, all-terrain feet stomped on the rocky ground.

From where he has hiding, Alex could see one of the disruptors if he leaned out a little and craned his neck. The Defenders were spreading out, moving quickly through the town and searching for the disruptors. One went lumbering straight past his hiding spot and was about to turn the corner toward a disruptor drone when a flash of super-focused laser light cut through the Defender's rotating autocannon and slammed into him. Both of the huge fighting machines went down with a crash and slid across the rocky ground. The Defender was quicker and only a couple of meters from where Alex watched in wide-eyed fascination. The disruptor was a drone, manned from a ship in orbit. Without the natural balance and feel of an actual person inside, it struggled to right itself.

The Defender regained its feet and aimed its remaining weapon at the drone. Alex thought it looked like a fat warrior who had lost an arm. Sparks flew from the severed weapon on its right side, but the left was intact and fully operational—yet it didn't fire. Perhaps the operator hesitated for a second before pulling the trigger, or maybe the weapon had to charge before firing—either way, that second nearly cost the operator his life. The drone, acting out of desperation, hit the Defender with some type of electrical charge. The blast scrambled the Defender's systems and sent him toppling onto his side. The large battle suit opened automatically, and Alex saw the operator lying unconscious inside the unit.

The disruptor drone got back to its feet and moved on, looking for better targets. Alex didn't hesitate like the man in the MP Defender. He could see that the system was rebooting, but the operator was out cold. Alex dashed to the man's side, shouting for help—but there was no one to hear his cries. Looking around and realizing he was alone, Alex did the only thing he could think of: he ripped off his rebreather and tugged the operator out of the mechanized fighter. The man was breathing; Alex could see his breath fogging the clear face mask of the rebreather. Still holding his own breath, Alex stuffed the operator into the space he had been hiding in just seconds before, rushed back to the Defender, and crawled inside. There was a button lit in red. The label on it said *Initialize*. Alex pressed it, and the suit came to life around him.

Chapter 2

Alex was lying on a padded control seat. His legs fit in individual slots, and there were pedals below his feet. Safety straps automatically slid around his waist and his shoulders. His hands held two control joysticks. The entire suit felt like a high-tech video game. The inside of the head section was transparent with messages scrolling across in letters that were easy to read yet also easy to see through.

A status bar showing the unit's power and system readiness were on the screen, and the armor closed in around him.

"Life support systems back online," a robotic voice said.

Alex turned his body, trying to get up. It was a little like being in clothes that were too big for him, but he managed to roll over onto the side with the ruined weapon arm. Moving in the battle suit took more coordination and strength than he expected. The armor and weapons were heavy, so the computer-controlled hydraulics needed to sync with Alex's movements. He tested the left joystick and realized that it powered the left side of his body, specifically the heavy piston legs. There were several thumb buttons as well as a trigger. Alex raised his arm and saw the laser mimic the movement. The urge to fire the weapon was strong, but there was nothing to shoot at. The last thing Alex could afford was to get in trouble for destroying company property after hijacking a battle suit. He pulled back on the joystick and felt his left leg stretch out. He pushed it forward, and the leg bent forward. After pushing the other joystick forward, Alex twisted his upper body and managed to get onto his knees. Straightening his back felt like he was in some kind of exercise machine doing an inverted sit-up. By pulling back slightly on both of the joysticks and flexing his back at the same time, he raised the battle suit up into a kneeling position.

He could look around more easily from this position, but he knew he needed to stand up and help the other operators. There were damage readings scrolling across the bottom of the battle suit's display. The power was down by a third, which seemed odd to Alex. The unit should have been fully charged as it had hardly been out of the hangar. He guessed the damage done by the disruptor drone must have sapped some of the unit's power.

"Run systems check," Alex said, hoping that the computer was voice-operated.

He pulled on the joysticks again and rocked against the cushioned backrest. The suit responded, and Alex felt a surge of confidence as the suit rose up onto its feet. It felt a bit like he was on stilts—not that Alex had ever tried walking on stilts, but he'd seen it done online and imagined that's how it felt. There was a bit of balance required to remain standing.

The systems on the screen showed that communications and navigation were both offline. The "thermobaric cannon" was disabled—Alex guessed that was the weapon on his right side, which the disruptor had sliced in half with a poorly aimed laser blast. His own laser weapon was fully charged and ready to fire.

Turning, Alex saw the open bay of the security hangar. He stumbled a bit as he took a few steps, but he kept his balance and stayed on his feet. Surely there were people inside who could repair and operate the suit better than Alex could. Before he could decide what to do, a huge explosion nearly knocked him off his feet. He stumbled forward and turned around. The disruptor drone had come back and blasted a hole in the school not far away. Alex reacted instinctively. All of his life, friends and teachers had scoffed at his being left-handed, but with no time to think, he raised his left arm as if he were pointing a gun and pulled the trigger on the joystick. A bolt of red energy shot from the weapon on the side of the battle suit and burned through the disruptor's armor. Sparks flew out, and the drone stumbled back.

Alex marched toward the drone and fired again. The second bolt ripped into the disruptor's control center. It trembled for a second, then exploded violently. Alex raised his arm to shield his face, even though the weapon his left arm controlled did nothing to protect the battle suit, and the thick armor wasn't affected by the blast or the shrapnel that rained down onto him.

He could hear people shouting and the reports of more weapons firing. He followed the noise. The entire city was laid out in a square, and the school and security hangar were on the southwest corner. He passed several workshops and equipment depots. The colony had dozens of buildings above ground, but the work on NP8261 was done underground. It was a mining colony, which required a variety of heavy machinery. The buildings were all old and covered in the dust that was carried by the planet's nearly constant wind. None of the buildings seemed to be targeted by the drones.

Alex trotted to the residential section in the center of the city. Several tall apartment buildings—all exact replicas—towered over the open communal space called the "quad." The four tall buildings, one at each corner of the square, made up an open courtyard of sorts. The area was paved, and company ground transports were kept there. Three disruptors stood like desperados in a bad holo-film, firing their weapons at a Defender that was pinned down behind the wreckage of several ground transports. Alex didn't hesitate. He raised his arm and blasted away. He had come up from the side of the three disruptors, and his laser blasts tore through them. Even when he missed the closest drone, the shots managed to hit one of the other two. The closest fell to the ground, and the second stumbled into the third before they both exploded.

Alex was walking across the quad to check on the other Defender, but the fallen disruptor wasn't out of the fight. It turned, trying to bring its weapons to bear. Alex swung his right arm around, flinging the remnants of the broken thermobaric cannon. Metal hit metal with a grinding screech. Then Alex dropped onto one knee right on top of the drone and fired point-blank into the disruptor. It shook violently for a second, and sparks flew from where its armor had been compromised—then it went still, the lights on its optical sensors going dark.

Alex got to his feet and walked over to where the other MP Defender was pinned under the wreckage of the ground transports. He had no hands, and his weapons weren't suited for grabbing or lifting, so he stomped around to the far side of the mangled vehicles, lowered his shoulder, and pushed. The hydraulic pistons had no trouble lifting the heavy wreckage. They squealed in protest as they slid off the downed Defender and across the pavement.

The fallen security officer got to his feet, and Alex stood aside. For a moment nothing happened, then a voice came out of the Defender's public address system. The voice boomed across the quad—much too loudly, Alex felt.

"Thanks for the help," the voice said.

Would you like to activate system speakers?

"Yes," Alex said, not sure if he was doing something right or something wrong.

"What's the matter?" asked the other Defender. "Is your comm system down?"

"Yes," Alex said, then jumped nervously as his voice boomed from the suit's speakers.

"The threat has been neutralized. Let's get back to the shop," the other Defender said.

The operator didn't wait for an answer. He just started walking back the way Alex had come. This time, Alex did hesitate. He couldn't help but wonder what would happen when the security members found out he had appropriated a battle suit. Still, he couldn't exactly just walk away and keep it. So after a few seconds, he followed the other Defender past the fallen disruptor drones and away from the quad.

The journey back to the security hangar felt long. They passed several buildings, and he couldn't for the life of him remember passing them to get to the quad. He had lived on NP8261 almost his entire life. The small town, which some people called "Moleville" since most of it was underground, was as familiar to him as his reflection in a mirror. He even spent more time outside than most people —yet somehow everything seemed new to him as he looked out through the Defender's view screen. Readings popped up showing the height of the buildings around him. Warnings of possible ambush sites were illuminated in a glowing yellow. Distances were displayed in orange numbers; for instance, Alex could see that he was three meters behind the other Defender and that they were moving at a steady ten kilometers per hour.

They passed the remains of the first disruptor drone. Techs from the security hangar were already gathering the pieces. Medics were helping the operator Alex had pulled from the battle suit. He felt another chill run down his back; soon he would be required to come out of the armored battle gear, and he wasn't expecting a warm reaction. He'd never heard of a regulation that a civilian couldn't operate company security gear, but he imagined it existed. He would be in trouble, and the company might even fire his father. Alex had no idea what would happen then.

"There's three more in the quad," the first Defender said, his voice echoing off the side of the surrounding buildings.

"Got it," one of the technicians said. "We'll head there next."

Alex wanted to run, but there was nowhere to go. They were almost to the hangar, and he had no choice but to turn himself in and hope for the best. They trudged into the hangar. Alex had watched from the outside but had never actually gone in. The MP Defenders each had their own dock. Plastic dividing curtains came down from the ceiling and created a barrier around them. A technician in a rebreather stepped in with Alex and pulled a lever on the wall.

"Give it a minute to equalize," the tech said, looking at the battle suit's damage. "Then you can push the button that says *Standby Mode*. That will open the unit."

Alex wanted to respond, but he didn't want to blast the technician's ears with the public address system. He just stood, waiting. A new reading on his screen showed the oxygen levels rising in the small bay. It went from red to yellow, then finally to green. A chime sounded and the robotic voice spoke again.

"External environment is now safe for human activity."

The tech pulled his rebreather down around his neck and gave Alex a thumbs-up.

"You can come out now," he said.

Alex hit the button marked *Standby Mode,* and the security straps slithered away as if they were living things. The armor cracked open, and Alex saw a ladder made of cargo straps hanging beside the mechanized fighting unit.

"Use the straps to pull yourself out," the technician said.

Alex grabbed the straps and pulled himself up, curling his legs and swinging free of the battle suit. Then he slid down to the concrete floor and looked over at the technician, who was staring at him.

"You're just a kid," the tech said.

"Be eighteen next week," Alex said sheepishly.

"Holy space dust, the sup is gonna flip," the tech said.

"I'm sorry," Alex said.

"Hey, don't be. Reynolds is alive because of you, kid. Actually, a lot of people are. That was a pretty selfless thing you did out there."

"I guess," Alex said.

"Grab that rebreather off the rack and follow me," the tech said.

Alex lifted the breathing mask and followed the technician out of the curtained-off area and into the inner building. Everything in the company town was old: the buildings, the equipment, and all the furniture and goods brought in for the locals. Alex had heard people complaining about the castoffs and the inferior-quality goods the company resold to their employees. When people don't have a choice, they have to take what they can get, and the only thing the employees on NP8261 could get was junk. But things were different in the security hangar. The tech showed Alex into a waiting room. There were chairs and sofas with plush upholstery that were stuffed thick with soft padding. The floor was some type of tile with a glossy finish, and a state-of-the-art display screen showed a top-down view of the town, with red blinking lights where the disruptor drones had been terminated.

Alex felt like he was on another planet. The waiting room was impeccably clean; he had never been in a room so clean. The dust and dirt on NP8261 were everywhere—the living quarters, the entertainment complex, the school—but by some miracle, not even a speck of it could be found in the waiting room except what had fallen from Alex's soiled clothes. Yet despite the opulence, there was a sense of importance in the waiting room. It wasn't a lounge; despite the plush furnishings, it was not designed for comfort. It was a place where the importance of the people in the other room was beyond question.

When the door opened, Alex felt like he might pass out.

Chapter 3

"You want to tell me what Zen Corp thinks they're all about?" Loman Haley snarled. "They dropped disruptor drones on our ore planet. How'd they even get to the eighty-second system?"

The hologram didn't respond. The woman glowing in Haley's office almost looked frozen in place, like the holo-call had lost connection and was stuck on the last frame. But Loman knew better. Ciara Prince was one of his finest security administrators. If anyone could get to the bottom of Zen Corp's attacks on Ahzco's planetary interests, it was her. But she was frustratingly patient—never wasting time or energy on unnecessary tasks like trying to answer rhetorical questions.

"That has to be our first priority," Loman continued. "Find out how they're moving between systems. Then I want to hit them back. I want to make those arrogant, back-stabbing phonies pay."

"I'll get right on it," Ciara replied.

Before he could end the holo-call, she vanished. Her lack of respect was frustrating. Loman was the Vice President of Ahzco's security division. Thirteen thousand people worked for him, and millions more depended on his security teams to keep them safe. His job was simple, with two main priorities. The first priority was to recruit the best fighters in the galaxy and equip them with the finest fighting machines that could be made. Ahzco had their own armaments and weapons manufacturing divisions. Developing and building could be regulated and oftentimes improved. But the best weapons in the galaxy were worthless without operators, and it took more than just a warm body to strap on twenty tons of armor and carry heavy weapons into a war zone.

The second priority was to make sure the portals between systems remained proprietary and safe. Knowing where the space tunnels were located and how they linked planets together was one of the most profitable resources that any corporation could possess. Finding new planets could be done from a distance, but committing the resources to travel through space to reach a new star system was incredibly risky. New planets didn't always equal usable resources. And since the corporation retained complete ownership of planets in their listed star systems, responsibility for keeping them safe also fell to the company. Unfortunately, that meant that attacking a rival's planetary interests was legal, so space had become the domain of big corporate interests like Ahzco—thus Loman Haley's job and subsequent power within the corporation.

He smoothed back his hair, took a drink from the mug of coffee on the corner of his desk, and cleared his throat.

"Connect me to NP8261, Security Chief McKinna," Loman said calmly.

There was a chime while his AI established a connection through the space tunnel system with a planet over four-hundred light years away from Arcadia, where Ahzco's universal headquarters was located.

Loman waited as patiently as possible. He had already read the initial report, but all that told him was that six disruptor drones had fallen onto the planet and been neutralized with minimal damage to company property. Even that was surprising, considering NP8261 was a minor planet with mostly older operators, many of which had suffered near career-ending injuries. It was supposed to be a quiet outpost on a relatively unimportant world. The ore mined there was of great value, but only after being hauled into orbit and across the galaxy, where it was refined into usable material. Ahzco had enough rare metals in storage that even if their supply to the raw materials was completely shut off, they could continue manufacturing at full capacity for a decade.

So why the attack? Was it just to prove that Loman's agents had failed to keep their trade routes secret? Was it a crime of opportunity? If so, it was an expensive failure. Drones had the distinct advantage of not requiring the operators to actually face danger, but they cost twice as much to manufacture as battle suits. And no one knew Ahzco's secret to their unparalleled control of their mechanical fighting vehicles.

Loman rubbed the back of his head, where the hair was long to conceal the scar where his own Implanted Neural Controller had been drilled into his skull. That had been a long time ago, but sometimes it still sent a shiver down his spine when he thought about the process of implantation. Fortunately, there had been improvements on that technology. New recruits were in and out of the facility in just twenty-four hours and filled with enough narcotics in the process that they hardly remembered the procedure afterwards.

A chime sounded and Loman stood up in the projection circle. The computer had made its connection and would begin recording his body and its movements to project a hologram of the vice president in Breck McKinna's office on NP8261. The air in front of Loman shimmered and then McKinna appeared, a glowing but nervous hologram.

"Tell me everything," Loman ordered.

"Not a lot to tell," McKinna said. He had lived on backwater planets so long he was starting to sound like a lifer. "They dropped six drones, and we deployed all six MP Defenders. We took some damage to ground vehicles, two compressor stations, and a hit on the school, of all buildings. Damn robots."

"That's all?" Loman asked.

"It is," McKinna said with just a touch of pride. "The compressor stations are repairable, as is the school. We'll have to replace the ground vehicles, but they were recreational-use machines, so there's no rush."

"Your people are on their game," Loman said, looking for something to be angry about. "Any casualties?"

"Well, that's a bit of an interesting story," McKinna said.

"This holo-call costs a thousand credits a minute— make it short and to the point."

"Grady Ulrich got hit close to the hangar. A shock weapon sent his suit into reboot and fried his INC."

Loman almost fell over. Was it a coincidence, or had someone discovered their secret?

"Fortunately, a local saw it and pulled him to safety before he sustained serious bodily damage. The kicker is, the kid that saved him then climbed into the suit, powered it back up, and destroyed the drone."

"With assistance?"

"No," McKinna said. "The comm system and half the weapons were offline. He'd even failed CFD training. We had no idea about this guy. And he didn't just destroy the one drone. Bradley Teague was pinned in the quad behind the land vehicles and under heavy fire from three drones. The kid took them all down."

"Impossible," Loman said.

"I'm telling you the truth. I'm going to question him as soon as we're done. He's in the waiting room and I've taken a look at him; he's a tall, gangly, pimple-faced seventeen-year-old. His old man's a mechanic. They've been on-world sixteen years. His mother works in the community hydroponics. One sibling—a sister, age eight."

"And you've been training him?" Loman said. "Off-book? You've got a soft spot for this kid or something?"

"No, I've never seen him before," McKinna said. "I've questioned all my operators. A few said they've seen him skulking around outside the hangar, but no one has ever even spoken to him before."

"That can't happen," Loman snapped. "We train the best candidates for months before they're able to operate a system like the Defender."

"Don't I know it," McKinna said. "I remember basic. I still have nightmares about it. This kid's a fighter. It's like it all just came naturally to him, and he didn't hesitate. We've got drone footage of him in action, sir. I've sent it through to you. Should be landing on your side any minute now."

"You find out how he did it," Loman said. "And if he really is a natural, you get him to sign. If he slips through your fingers, you'll be out on your ear. That clear enough for you, McKinna? And I want a full write-up of your interview with the kid as soon as you're done."

"Yes sir, Mr. Haley."

"And one more thing," Loman said, leaning forward. "I want you to run a back-channel investigation into all your people. If there's a leak in the department, we have to find it."

"Roger that, sir," McKinna said. "I'll be in touch shortly."

"See that you are," Loman snarled, then he switched off the call so that his hologram disappeared first.

A kid ran a battle suit, Loman thought. That should be impossible—not physically impossible, but mentally. Getting into a mech and making it work would normally overwhelm a person's senses, or at least frighten them half to death. But taking out four drones is no glitch, and it's more than just getting lucky. He would have to do his homework on the boy, but if McKinna was right, then they just might have an ace on their hands. Loman couldn't lose the chance to recruit an ace, and he was determined not to.

"Find me a transport going to NP8261," he ordered his AI. "Book me passage, no matter what type of ship it is, and clear my calendar for a week."

"Of course, sir," the sultry voice he'd assigned his computer replied.

He pulled out an old-fashioned metal flask he kept hidden behind some files in his desk and poured clear liquid into his coffee. He snapped the lid shut and screwed it tight, then replaced his secret libation. Liquor was a controlled substance on Arcadia, but Loman had his sources—and after a day like he was having, he needed a little something to calm his nerves.

He sipped the coffee, which burned pleasantly all the way down his throat and into his stomach. The heat spread through his entire body and brought a smile to his face.

Chapter 4

"Hi Alex, I'm Breck McKinna."

Alex shook the man's hand and walked into an office that seemed like it was right out of a holo-film. The walls were dark wood paneling. Alex couldn't tell for sure —he'd never seen real wood—but it looked real. There were leather-covered sitting chairs with big brass studs, and the desk was so huge that Alex guessed it must have been built in the office because it was much too large to fit through the doorways.

As impressive as the office was, Breck McKinna was even more impressive. He wasn't as tall as Alex, but the man looked like solid muscle. His tight shirt showed off an impressive physique that made Alex nervous.

"Have a seat, son," McKinna said, waving at one of the leather chairs. "Can I get you something to drink? We've got real soda. Imported from Arcadia and kept ice-cold."

"Okay," Alex said.

He was in awe. He'd lived his entire life on NP8261 —which his friends called "the Rock"—and thought he knew all there was to know about the mining colony. It was the only settlement on the planet, which was short on water and had no breathable atmosphere. They were on the equator, but it was always cold, and everything about the colony was dingy and poor. Yet little did he know that right in the middle of it all, in this security hangar, was an oasis of wealth and luxury. Alex had only tried real soda twice in his entire life. Both times had been on birthdays. Carbonated drinks were expensive to ship through space, so he had primarily lived on water and fruity drink powders.

McKinna pulled a can of soda from a cooler built right into the wall. He dropped chunks of ice from a leather-wrapped bucket into a heavy glass tumbler and poured the soda into the glass. It hissed and foamed. McKinna handed Alex the glass and then set the rest of the can down beside him on a polished wooden table. Alex was embarrassed that his hands were trembling, but he simply couldn't believe what was happening. He took a sip of the soda, and the sweet drink bubbled and burned its way down his throat. An involuntary grin spread across his face.

Everyone knew that the Corporate Defense Forces were some of the best paying jobs in the galaxy. And it wasn't just the pay; there were perks too, not the least of which being the respect CDF members got wherever they went. Alex could remember pretending to be an operator in the CDF as a child with his friends, so to him, the fact that he was sitting in the office of the colony's security chief was like a dream come true.

McKinna sat down opposite Alex and leaned back in his chair. The man had penetrating eyes that seemed as though they could see through any lie. It added to Alex's unease.

"Am I in trouble?" Alex asked.

"Have you done something wrong?" McKinna replied.

"No—I mean, I got in the battle suit without permission, but I had to."

"You *had* to fight the disruptor drones?" McKinna asked. There was a slight challenge to his voice. He thought Alex was lying or trying to use his circumstances to excuse what he'd done.

"No, sir," Alex said. "But I gave my rebreather to the operator and I had to get inside so I could breathe."

McKinna smiled. It was warm—almost friendly—but Alex could sense that the security chief didn't really believe him.

"Why?"

It was an understandable question, but Alex didn't have an answer. He'd been asking himself why he'd done what he did, and the only thing he could think of was that he *wanted* to do it. He wanted to see what it was like in the battle suit, and he was sick to death of being told no, of people implying that he wasn't smart enough or not suited do the things he wanted to do.

"I don't know," Alex said. "It all happened so fast."

"Why were you outside today?" McKinna asked.

"I was going home after school."

"You didn't know the attack was coming?"

"No," Alex replied. He was surprised that he was even asked the question. How could he know the colony was going to be attacked? It seemed like a ridiculous question.

McKinna's face twitched slightly. He didn't like the answer, Alex could tell, but he wasn't sure why.

"Do you always go outside after school?"

"Most days," Alex confessed.

"Why not take the tunnels?"

"They're crowded and noisy. No one bothers me when I go outside. Plus, sometimes I get a peek inside the hangar where you keep the suits."

"Ever get more than a peek?"

"What do you mean?"

"Have you ever been in the hangar, Alex? Ever gotten into a battle suit before? Ever run a simulator or just hung out with the operators?"

"No," Alex said. "I mean, I wish. No one's ever even spoken to me before today."

"Here's the thing, Alex: I pulled your testing."

Alex felt his heart drop. He couldn't say what he had been expecting, but it frustrated him to once more be pushed out of something he was interested in because his test scores were low. He wasn't stupid, and even though he couldn't say why his intelligence and aptitude tests didn't show it, he knew he was capable of more than people gave him credit for.

"You shouldn't have been able to do what you did," McKinna pressed on. "These aren't simple machines like ground transports or your data slates in school. Someone must have shown you how to work it."

"No, sir," Alex replied. "I've read about the CDF and seen some documentaries, but no one taught me anything."

"How did you manage not to get yourself killed?" McKinna said. "Disruptor drones are dangerous."

"I just did what came to me in the moment."

"You a southpaw, kid?"

"A what?"

"Are you left-handed, Alex?"

"Oh, yes sir, I am."

McKinna nodded. "That probably saved your bacon. The armor on that suit was degraded by half, probably from the shock that popped it open. They're not supposed to do that."

Alex just nodded. He really didn't know what to say. It wasn't his fault that the operator had gotten hurt or that the suit had popped open right in front of him.

"I think maybe you should retake CDF testing. Would you mind doing that for me?"

"I'd rather not," Alex said honestly. "It's humiliating."

McKinna smiled. "You don't like to lose, eh?"

Alex shook his head and took another sip of the soda. It seemed less acidic with every drink he took.

"Here's the thing, Alex: you've got a future in security. And I can tell you from experience there's not a better gig out there. But you don't fit our usual profile for a CDF operator, and maybe if you retake the test we can learn something that will help us recruit better candidates. I don't have to tell you that the security forces save lives. There are millions of employees—not to mention their families—who depend on us for their survival. We're looking for the best of the best. Maybe that's you. If so, we not only need you, Alex, but we need more people like you."

"All right," Alex said, "I'll take the tests again."

"That's great. How about tomorrow?"

"I've got school."

"I'll talk to your administrator. One of my people will come get you when we're ready."

"Okay," Alex said.

McKinna sprang to his feet and pulled Alex out of the chair. He walked him to the door of the office, and when it opened another technician was waiting for him.

"Show Alex out, and make sure his rebreather is in good shape," McKinna said.

"Yes sir, Chief," the tech said.

Alex finished the soda in one final gulp, then handed the glass to the head of planetary security.

"Thank you," Alex said.

"My pleasure, Alex."

The door closed, and Alex wasn't sure why, but he felt a sense of dread building up inside him. He followed the technician, who led him past a series of rooms. Alex told himself he had nothing to worry about—he had been expecting trouble and instead had been given genuine soda over ice. It was impossible to know what McKinna thought of him. The questioning had been one-sided, and Alex couldn't tell if the security chief believed him or not. Still, the day had been a complete adventure, and he doubted his parents would even believe him. But he had operated a battle suit, destroyed disruptor drones, and saved a man's life. No one could take that from him—even if he was forced to bust rocks for the rest of his life. For once in his life he had taken control of his future, and it felt great.

Chapter 5

"No," his mother said.

Alex's father was still looking at a rejection letter that had been sent to his personal correspondence account. It wasn't a physical letter, but rather a digital rejection notice. Nothing about it was any more personal than the one Alex had gotten.

"All they want me to do is retake the qualification tests," Alex said.

He was arguing with his mother, but his eyes kept returning to his father, who had been silent so far during the discussion.

"I think it's cool," said Jasmine, making shooting noises while she pointed at Alex.

"And what if you pass?" Alex's mother said. "What then? You're going to be whisked off-planet to who-knows-where. We'll never you see you again."

"I thought you wanted me to go to school off-world," Alex said.

"That's different, and you know it," she fired back. If his mother was anything, it was a passionate arguer. "Do you know what the life expectancy for the CDF is?"

"Twenty eight," Alex said.

"That's right," his mother retorted, her plate of food completely forgotten. "You're not even eighteen. I let you take their tests once, but not twice. They're trying to suck you in and ruin your life. That's not what you want, Alex, trust me."

Before Alex could reply, his father held up one hand. They all turned and looked at him. Alex saw the calluses on his palm and fingers that were dark from years of being covered in grease and oil. There was strength in that hand, but there were also scars.

"I think," his father said calmly, "maybe it's a good thing."

"No," his mother replied. "It's not good, Bruce. What are you talking about?"

"Have you seen this?" His father held out the Personal Information Link, and his mother took it. A pained expression crossed her face. "He doesn't have a lot of options left."

"You knew about this?"

Alex nodded. "I was notified today, same as you."

"It was the last one?" his father asked.

"Yeah, dad. I'm sorry. I really tried."

"I know you did. You don't have to apologize. You didn't do anything wrong. Not everyone fits into neat little categories. Some skills can't be shown on a standardized test."

"Did the man say why he wants you to retake the CDF test?" his mother asked.

Alex took a deep breath before he answered. "He said that I shouldn't have been able to do anything in the battle suit, and that by taking the test, it could help them improve the way they recruit."

"You're sure he didn't say anything about recruiting you?"

"No, mom," Alex said, trying not to let his disappointment show.

"But he didn't say he wasn't recruiting you, either," his father pointed out. "Hold on, Penny, don't blow a gasket."

Alex's mother's name was Penelope, but his father always called her Penny. Her face was red, but she didn't say anything.

"I just think we don't have a lot of options left on the table," his father continued, "and the CDF needs technicians just like every other division in the company. Maybe he could do that."

"Or maybe you could support me in this, Bruce. He's only seventeen years old."

"I know, and in a few months he'll graduate, and then what? Don't tell me you'll be happy with him working down in the mines."

"It's safer than combat," she replied.

"Not by much," Bruce replied. "And the pay is awful, there's almost no chance for advancement, and he'd be miserable."

"You don't know that," Penelope said.

"I've yet to meet a rock-buster that liked his job," Bruce said. "There's a chance for him here, and it may not be what we want, but we have to be open to the idea. He can tell them he wants to be a tech in the security force. That would be a great job for anyone."

Alex swallowed, trying not to let his discomfort show. The truth was, he didn't want to be a technician. He wasn't a natural mechanic like his father. Building things was stressful and frustrating to Alex. What he wanted was to be an operator, and he didn't care how dangerous it was.

"Fine," his mother finally gave in. "He can take their test again, but I want him to tell whoever is in charge that he wants to be a technician."

"It's settled then," his father said. "Now, let's finish our dinner. You worked hard on it, and we're all appreciative."

Alex stabbed his fork into a carrot. He didn't really like vegetables, but his mother was able to get them fresh produce from her job in the hydroponic gardens. It was one small perk amid a mountain of disappointing circumstances. Alex was well-practiced in looking on the bright side. He had his parents' permission to take the CDF tests again, and who knew what might happen? Only time would tell, and the truth was, Alex had nothing left to lose.

Chapter 6

There were only two months until graduation, and Alex had completed all of the necessary courses. His teachers seemed to have no interest in him anymore, especially Mr. Hobson, who seemed to know that Alex had been rejected from every technical institute in the galactic arm. When the office aid stuck her head into Hobson's class and asked to see Alex, the bored teacher looked up at him with a wicked grin.

"What's he done?"

"Sir?" the office aid asked.

"What is Mr. Evans wanted for? I assume he's run afoul of the rules again?"

"Actually, he's been requested by the CDF for special testing," the aid said.

Alex powered down his data slate and shelved it. Mr. Hobson gave Alex a sneer as he walked to the door of the classroom. It was clear that he was trying to come up with an appropriate remark, but being kind wasn't his specialty. He finally settled for a haughty "very well."

Alex tingled with excitement as he slipped on his rebreather and followed the technician who had been sent to get him out of class. There were no tunnels leading to the security hangar from the school, and it was quickest to go outside. Alex had spent the evening cleaning his coat and picking out his best clothes. Despite his efforts, his pants were too short, his shirt was tight across his bony shoulders, and his coat looked old.

They hurried across the dusty street, if it could be called that. Outside the quad in the center of town, none of the streets were paved. The surface of NP8261 consisted of rock and dirt that had once been rock. The soil was incredibly thin, but it seemed to be everywhere. The dust clung to Alex's clothes and followed him on the wind.

Inside the security hangar, he was taken to a small room and given a standard data slate—one that was much newer and nicer than anything he'd seen at school. Even his teachers didn't have slates as nice as this one. He was seated at a table in a padded office chair on casters. Against one wall there was a table with a coffee machine and snacks, including packages of dried fruit and actual nuts—not just protein substitutes.

"There might be some people coming in and out of here," the technician said, "but otherwise the room is yours. I'll come back for you at lunchtime."

"Got it," Alex said.

He had taken entrance exams before, but never without supervision. Usually he was taken to an empty classroom, watched over by a teacher or administrator, and given strict instructions about the test. Alex powered on the slate and saw that he was immediately guided to the testing portions. It was a strange exam with many questions he didn't understand. He knew the test would check not only his spatial intelligence but his psychological makeup as well. After picking out his clothes the night before, he had spent time on his PIL reading about Corporate Defense Force testing.

Time passed quickly, and Alex did his best to pass the test, but most of the questions were so strange that he didn't know if there was a right or wrong answer. When he finished, his stomach was growling, and the technician who had walked him over came back into the room almost immediately.

"All done?"

"Yes," Alex said.

"Good, let's grab some lunch. Then the Chief wants to speak to you."

"Okay," Alex said.

He was just happy to be there, rubbing elbows with actual members of the CDF. They were an exclusive group, and the rumors about them having the best facilities weren't exaggerations. They walked past large simulators and rooms full of exercise equipment. Everything looked brand-new to Alex, from the clothes he saw on the people around him to the building itself. Every surface gleamed, there were no out-of-order signs, and there weren't even visible signs of wear on the floor.

The security hangar even had its own cafeteria. It was small and automated, like most public food establishments, but the food was not at all what Alex expected. It was lunch fare—soups, salads, sandwiches, and a few hot options—but it was the quality of the food that surprised him. Almost every option had meat, and none of it was processed protein. It was real meat.

"Get whatever you want," the tech said. "The burgers are good."

Alex ate a hamburger with a thick patty of real beef. It was covered with actual cheese, too, and charred to perfection despite coming out of an automated vending dispenser. Alex ate it all, relishing each bite, and he felt a pang of disappointment when they had to leave the cafeteria for his meeting with Breck McKinna.

He was shown back into the waiting room. Half an hour passed before the door opened and the security chief waved to him.

"Come on in, Alex. Thanks for waiting."

Alex was used to waiting. Most adults treated him like a second thought, as though he didn't matter, and they never apologized to him for anything. McKinna's kindness only made Alex feel worried. When he stepped through the door and into the office, he was greeted by a heavyset man wearing a business suit. Alex didn't think anyone on the planet had a suit, but the newcomer looked important.

"You must be Alex Evans," the man in the suit said. "I'm Loman Hayley, vice president in charge of Ahzco's security division. It's a pleasure to meet you."

The man extended a hand and Alex shook it, embarrassed by the way his coat sleeve slid up to the middle of his forearm when he reached out. But Loman didn't seem to notice. He sat down in one of the leather chairs and waved at the other. McKinna sat perched on the edge of his desk.

"I want to thank you for retaking the CDF test," Loman said. "That's going to help us more than you know."

Alex nodded but didn't know what to say. He felt it was best if he said as little as possible. In the back of his mind he could hear his mother's voice warning him to be on his best behavior.

"I'm assuming you've considered a career in the CDF, since you had taken the exam already," Loman continued. "Normally, we have very rigid standards for acceptance into our ranks, but what you did yesterday—I saw footage—is really impressive. Four disruptor drones on your first outing would put you in the highest percentile of graduates from the academy. And you had never been in a battle suit before?"

"No, sir," Alex said, trying to keep his voice from shaking.

"Not even a simulator?"

Alex shook his head.

"Remarkable. Well, clearly you're a special case."

"The VP of CDF doesn't leave Arcadia on a whim, Alex," McKinna said.

"What you've done," Loman continued, "is the very embodiment of what we're all about. You saved an operator, put yourself in harm's way, and took out four drones that were programmed to kill anyone in a battle suit. If you hadn't acted, the damage to your colony town would have been devastating. People would have died, and not just security operators—civilians, like your mother or baby sister, Alex.

"I'd like to take you straight to our facilities on Helena Prime, if you're willing. Like I said, we have protocols for acceptance into the CDF, but we're going to fast-track you into the academy. We need to know what makes you different. Was yesterday just a fluke? I don't think so, but we need to learn as much from you as we can. It's vital to the security of people on dozens of worlds."

"You want me to join the CDF?" Alex asked. He could almost hear his mother and father saying he should tell them he wanted to be a technician.

"That's right," Loman said with a big smile.

Alex couldn't help but notice how perfectly straight the businessman's teeth were. They were white and glossy, just like the tile floors that led to McKinna's office.

"To be an operator?"

Loman sat back and chuckled. "That's exactly what I want."

"Not a technician?" Alex said.

"Do you want to be a technician, Alex?" McKinna asked.

It was the question he was hoping he wouldn't have to answer. He knew what his parents wanted. He knew what the safe answer was, but he couldn't bring himself to say it.

He shook his head. "No, I want to be an operator."

"Of course you do," Loman said. "Every red-blooded man and boy dreams of it. The most sophisticated weapons technology in the galaxy at your fingertips. Thousands of adoring civilians counting on you to keep them safe. Who wouldn't want to be an operator? But I'll be honest with you, Alex. Very few operators have done what you did yesterday."

"I was just lucky," Alex said.

"No, I don't think so. I think maybe you've got something that we've lost: an edge, an instinct that I want to identify that can help us recruit more people just like you."

Loman was very persuasive, but Alex couldn't help but worry about his family. They wanted him to leave the planet very soon, perhaps even before he finished school. He couldn't help but remember what his mother had said the night before: *You're going to be whisked off-planet to who-knows-where. We'll never you see you again.*

Alex decided to throw caution to the wind. He cleared his voice, forced himself not to look at McKinna, and looked Loman Haley straight in the eye as he spoke.

"What about my family?"

"What about them?" Loman asked.

"I want them moved to a different planet. A good one," Alex said.

Loman grinned. Alex felt like he might dissolve into a puddle of sadness and fear. His hands were on his knees, and he gripped them tightly.

"You see that?" Loman said to McKinna. "That's what I'm talking about. He has a knack for sensing his moment."

"That killer instinct," McKinna said.

"Exactly—like he knows the perfect time to act."

Alex felt sweat popping up on his forehead and down his back. He had never in his entire life been more terrified. He couldn't for the life of him figure out what had prompted him to make such an outrageous request. They would probably throw him out, and he would be right back where he started, staring down a bleak future with little to no hope.

"I think we can make that happen," Loman said. "Your father's a valued employee. Ahzco has a new plant opening on Skandia Seven. It's a level-one planet, right on the open trade route. You'll be able to visit when you have leave. There are only a billion people living there and there's plenty of room to grow. Your sister can go to a prep academy if she wants to. And I'll see to it that your father gets promoted."

Alex's jaw fell open. He couldn't believe his ears. Everything he'd ever dreamed of was suddenly coming true. He squeezed his leg so hard that it hurt, but he didn't wake up, and Loman Haley didn't blink. Loman stuck out his hand.

"What do you say, kid?" Loman asked.

"I'll do it," Alex said, shaking Loman's hand vigorously. "I'm in."

Chapter 7

Alex was home, packing a few belongings into an ancient duffle bag, when his father arrived. Normally, after at least ten hours, Bruce Evans came home to a full house. He was almost always the last person home in the evening. Seeing his father in the daytime was strange to Alex. He wasn't even supposed to be out of school yet, but Loman Haley had assured him that the school's administrator would waive his last few weeks of classes and give him an early graduation.

"Hi dad," Alex said.

"What are you doing here?" Bruce asked.

Alex could see the worry on his father's face and did his best to hide the good news.

"I could ask you the same question," Alex said. "Something happen at work?"

"As a matter of fact, it did," Bruce said. "They're transferring me. Just like that, without even checking with me first. Can you believe it? I work diligently for Ahzco for nearly twenty years, and this is the thanks I get."

"Maybe it isn't bad," Alex said. He had to look away from his father to keep from grinning.

"Oh, it's bad," Bruce said. "They don't transfer you and then refuse to tell you where you're going if it's good news. Your mother's going to be furious."

Before Alex could explain, his mother arrived home. She looked frightened. There was dirt smeared on her face, and her hair was tied up in a sloppy bun.

"What is it? What's wrong? Where's Jasmine? Is she okay?" His mother was asking questions so fast, Alex could hardly keep up.

"What are you doing home, Penny?" Bruce asked.

"I got a message that said to come home," she explained. "It said it was an emergency."

Alex raised both hands, trying to calm his parents down. "It was me, I'm sorry. But I need to talk to you both. Jasmine is fine. She's at school."

"Oh, thank goodness," his mother said. "I was worried something bad had happened."

"It has," Bruce complained. "I'm being transferred."

"What? Where to?"

"That's just it—they won't tell me."

"Oh, that is never good, Bruce. Did something happen?"

"No. I was just working, and my supervisor called me over, gave me the news, and sent me home."

"But you're not fired," Penelope said. "We'll survive. How bad can it be, really?"

"There are worlds that make this look like a level-one planet," Bruce said.

"Hang on," Alex said. "Please, just give me a second and I'll explain everything. You're not going anyplace bad. You're being transferred to a new plant on Skandia Seven."

"What?" Bruce asked. "How on earth could you know that, Alex?"

"Because I made it part of my deal," he replied. "The CDF asked me to join. They're making special arrangements, and in exchange I persuaded them to transfer you to a level-one planet, dad. You're getting a promotion, too."

"Skandia Seven?" Penelope said. "Isn't that on the open trade route?"

"Yes," Alex said. "New housing, free commerce, options for good schools for Jasmine—the works."

"Are you serious?" Bruce asked.

"Absolutely," Alex said with a huge grin.

"But why? What's so special about you?"

"I don't know," Alex said. "But I met Vice President Loman Haley of the security division. He came all the way from Arcadia."

"He came here?" Penelope asked. "What for?"

"To meet me," Alex said. "They checked me out of school, I retook the entrance exam, and they fed me lunch. I had a burger with real beef and melted cheese, dad. It was so good. Then I met with Security Chief McKinna and Vice President Haley. They asked me to join. Said it was really important. That they had a lot to learn from me."

Bruce had to sit down. Penelope had tears in her eyes.

"I can't believe it," his father said.

"It's true," Alex said. "I promise. We're getting off this rock, and you'll have a job you deserve, dad."

"Oh, honey," his mother said.

She stepped over and wrapped him up in a hug so tight he could barely breathe. When she let go, she looked him right in the eyes.

"Are you sure you want to do this?"

"Positive, mom," Alex said. "It's like a dream come true."

There was a quiet buzz, and Bruce pulled out his PIL. It was a simple, handheld device with a heavy, shock-proof case. He looked at the screen and then up at his wife.

"I can't believe it," he said. "It's all true. We leave tonight."

Chapter 8

The shuttle from the colony left at midnight. A liaison from Loman Haley's office met them and assured Alex's parents that their belongings would be packed up and shipped to Skandia Seven within the week. They were so busy researching their new home that they could hardly stand still. Jasmine fed off their excitement, until she realized that her big brother wasn't going with them.

The rest of the night she stayed right with Alex. He normally didn't have much time for her, but he gave her all his attention that evening. She fell asleep on the shuttle ride up to orbit leaning on his shoulder. NP8261 had a standard docking port with a secondary loading station for freight. They met Vice President Haley as soon as they stepped off the shuttle and onto the station.

"All right, Evans family, you're all here," he said with a grin. "That's good. We've got a short ride to the transit station in the New Wales system. From there, you all will take a transport to New Skandia. I hear it is absolutely beautiful there this time of year. You'll be working in a new plant right on the outskirts of the Waddington Metro area. The company has provided three first-class tickets to Skandia Seven, and all your moving expenses are covered. You'll have to stay in a hotel until you can find housing, but we've included a bonus with Mr. Evans' new promotion that will cover the down payment. And once you get settled, be sure to upgrade your PILs. Alex will be able to contact you in a couple of weeks once he's gotten through orientation and his first phase of basic training."

Their accommodations on the Ahzco freight hauler consisted of a metal bench in a tiny room that smelled like it had once been a restroom. Alex and his family didn't complain, and just as Loman Haley promised, it only took two hours to reach the transit station. The fact that they passed through a wormhole and traveled hundreds of lightyears to reach the transit station in only a few hours was completely mundane to the vice president of security. Alex had expected the experience to feel different, but it felt like any other form of transport.

The transit station was unlike anything Alex had seen before. It was a big space station shaped like a wheel with spokes spreading out in all directions for ships to dock with. Passengers hurried through the huge concourse. He saw people from a dozen worlds, heard different languages, and saw enormous display screens twenty meters tall advertising goods and services on a hundred different planets.

Once the shock wore off, his parents hugged and kissed them. His mother begged him to contact her as soon as he could. He promised he would. Jasmine asked when he would get to visit, but Alex wasn't sure.

"I don't know, Jas, but I'll write to you when I can. And I promise I'll come see your new home on Skandia Seven as soon as possible."

"I miss you already," she said tearfully.

He bent low and gave her a hug. She sniffled in his ear and gave him a tearful kiss on the cheek.

"Son, be careful, all right?" his father told him. "You don't have to prove anything to anybody."

"Okay, dad."

"And don't be a hero. You hear what I'm saying?"

"Yes, sir."

"All right. I'm proud of you. And thankful too—you could have asked for anything, but you thought of your mother and your sister. You've got a good heart, Alex. Don't let them take it from you."

"I won't," Alex said. "I promise."

"Good. Stay in touch now. And come home whenever you can."

"First chance I get," Alex said.

There were more hugs, more kisses, and more tears. Alex even had to swipe his eyes a few times to keep from embarrassing himself. Then the announcement for the flight to Skandia Seven was given, and his family had to leave.

"You'll see them again soon," Loman said. "Depending on your first assignment after basic, you might even get to visit them before you deploy."

"Yes, sir," Alex said, focusing on his excitement rather than the grief welling up inside him at being separated from his parents. He had known the day was coming when he would need to go his own way, but he hadn't expected it to happen so soon. It helped to know they were off on their own adventures, but part of him wished he could have gone to see Skandia Seven with them.

Loman Haley led Alex to a corporate transport. Unlike the freighter, it was built with passengers in mind. Loman and Alex were shown to a small cabin with reclining seats and a large window.

"We don't leave for another hour," Loman explained once they were settled, "and it takes about seven hours and three space tunnels to reach Helena Prime. Might as well get some sleep."

A stewardess brought them both pillows and blankets. Loman took a pill, strapped on a sleep mask, and was soon snoring softly beside Alex. But sleep wasn't even on Alex's radar. Outside the window of their cabin, a dozen starships were drifting past. In the distance he could see a glowing nebula—not to mention more stars than he had seen in his entire life.

He finally started feeling sleepy once the ship left the dock and began to move through space; his eyelids grew heavy and his mind sluggish after the excitement of his long day. He wanted to see the space tunnels, but there was nothing to see. It reminded him of going down a plastic slide in the recreation plaza back on the Rock.

Chapter 9

Helena Prime was a level-two planet, which meant it had a hostile environment but could support life. The entire system was volatile, and it had become the training ground for all of Ahzco's Corporate Security Forces. There were several moons that served as a variety of training bases, but it was Helena Prime, the third planet from the system's small, yellow star, that housed the Operators' Academy.

Loman woke Alex as they popped out of the space tunnel and into the system above the orbital plane of the planets and moons. When the transport banked into a long, arcing curve down toward the space station in orbit around the planet, Alex got his first look at a foreign world. The planet glowed a rusty red color.

"What's down there?" Alex asked.

"Sparta, your home for the next two months—if things work out."

"What sort of things?" Alex asked.

Loman shrugged his shoulders. "No one ever said that training to become a Corporate Warrior was easy, Mr. Evans. There are many variables at play."

"Like what?" Alex pressed. "A lot of running and that sort of thing?"

Loman shook his head. "No need for running—the suits can do that for you. But if you do what your instructors say, you'll be fine. Remember that. We're not in the business of wasting time or money. Bringing you here, relocating your family, and placing you in the training program—those are all investments that the company needs to get a significant return on. So don't let us down."

The transport docked with the space station. It was much smaller and calmer than the transit station in the New Wales system. People were busy. Many wore uniforms, but not all. Without exception, they all showed respect to Loman Haley.

"Is there a shuttle ready?" Loman asked a woman in stiff uniform.

She had chiseled features and short hair. Her hands flew over the computer controls at a console in the middle of the station.

"Yes sir, dock 8A," she replied.

"Thank you," Loman replied.

Alex had a thousand questions, but he was beginning to think that spending time with the vice president in charge of security was highly unusual. He didn't want to appear too friendly or give the impression that he was taking advantage of his proximity to the man in charge. So he decided to keep his questions to himself. He'd learn everything in time.

The difficult part was convincing his brain that the company hadn't made a mistake. Alex felt like he was sneaking in the back door and wasn't supposed to be there at all. But he had earned a spot, even if he hadn't passed the tests. The people in charge of the program knew he hadn't passed, yet they wanted him to be there. He would have to trust that they knew what they were doing and commit himself to being the best operator he could be.

They took a shuttle with big windows down from orbit. Alex stayed by the windows while Loman replied to messages on his PIL. The shuttle rocked as they passed into the planet's atmosphere. Moisture covered the shuttle's hull in ice, but as they descended, the friction heated the hull and vaporized the ice. The steam billowed up, blocking his view for several minutes, but finally the windows cleared and the ship stopped rocking.

Below them was a vast desert of rust-red rock and soil. Alex was disappointed. The only difference there seemed to be between Helena Prime and the Rock was the color of the planet. NP8261, Alex's home for sixteen of his nearly eighteen years, was dull gray. The ship flew over a deep gorge, and Alex saw a ribbon of dark water fall below. Eventually the desert gave way to a gnarly and twisted forest. The trees looked stunted and grew in dense clusters. The forest gave way to an open plain of yellow grass, and the shuttle circled over Sparta. It was a proper city divided into districts, and Alex felt his excitement growing.

"We'll be putting down at the airfield," Loman said, "and you'll be taken to the academy's intake facility. We won't see each other anymore."

"Yes, sir," Alex said. "I appreciate all you've done for me, Mr. Haley."

"Make us proud," Loman said. "And prove the naysayers wrong, huh, kid?"

Alex wasn't sure what to say to that, but he nodded as the shuttle came to a rest. The doors opened, and Alex grabbed his bag and followed Loman Haley out of the shuttle. For the first time in his life Alex breathed fresh air. It was cold and thin, but breathable. The sun was shining, which was a rare occurrence on NP8261. Alex basked in the warmth for a moment, then hurried to where a man in rusty red fatigues waved to him.

"You Evans?"

"Yes, sir," Alex said.

"Good, let's book."

The man was driving a transport with an open cab. Alex sat in the passenger seat with his duffle on his lap.

"First time on a level-two world?" The man asked as Alex gaped at the clean, well-maintained buildings they drove between.

The transport was a hovercraft, but the streets were paved with solar tiles. There were plants, trees, and patches of bright green grass strategically placed along the streets and between the buildings. There were people out; some were in uniform, but most wore casual wear with Ahzco patches on their shirts.

What surprised Alex most was the fact that everyone looked so happy. After a lifetime on a world that ground people down to hopeless husks just trying to make it through the dreary days, seeing people smiling and laughing was a shock.

"First time anywhere," Alex said. "Have you heard of NP8261?"

"Can't say I have," the man said.

"There's a reason. It's a mining world—just a big rock in space. That's all I've ever known."

"Well, just wait," the man said. "Once you make it through basic, you'll get a chance to visit a level-one planet. It will blow your mind."

Alex wondered what his parents were experiencing. He suddenly missed them so much that his eyes watered a little. They felt impossibly far away, and he could only hope that Skandia Seven was as nice or nicer than Helena Prime.

"All right, new recruit intake," the man said, pulling the hovercart over to the double doors of a nondescript building. "Good luck, man."

"Yeah, thanks," Alex said, standing up and closing the little door.

The man stepped on the throttle and the vehicle zoomed away, leaving Alex truly alone. He felt a weight on his shoulders, a sadness that he couldn't get out from under. He turned and went into the building. A woman in a uniform sat behind the counter. She stood up and looked him up and down. It made Alex feel self-conscious. He was still in his secondhand clothes that weren't really big enough.

"You must be Evans," she said.

"Alex," he replied.

"I know your name. My stars, you're a back-planet bumpkin, aren't you?"

Alex didn't know what to say, but his loneliness was quickly being replaced with rage. He didn't have a lot, but what he had he was grateful for. It made him angry to be mocked by someone who didn't even know him.

"Okay, let's get started," she said. "We're going to be going through a lot in the next few days, rook. Try to keep up. You've got a full physical scheduled, and you can just toss your clothes in the waste basket."

She opened a door to a medical exam room. Alex recognized the robotic scanner, although the one on the Rock was older and bulkier. There was a large waste basket just inside the door, and on a chair next to his were simple scrubs and what looked like shower shoes.

"You want me to throw my clothes away?" Alex said with a frown.

"The company will supply you with everything you need," the woman said, "including clothes that actually fit. When you're done with the exam, put on the clothes in the chair and come back out."

"What's your name?" Alex asked.

"You can call me Supervisor Purfoy. If you get through basic, you can call me Soup, but not until you're an operator. You got that, rook?"

"Yes, ma'am," Alex said, stepping into the room.

The door closed behind him with a thump, and Alex had to fight back tears as he pulled off his clothes. Maybe he had made a huge mistake. He was young, from a third-level planet no one had heard of, and he hadn't even passed their tests. It all seemed like too much at that moment, and he just wanted to go home.

Chapter 10

Loman was in an office in the tallest building in Sparta. The Ahzco administrative offices were on the top floor of the building, and his office had access to the observation cameras all throughout the Operators' Academy. He had a holographic projection of the intake exam room, where Alex was undressing. Loman watched long enough to ensure that his new recruit had no obvious physical defects.

Once he had done his own visual scan, he waved a hand to dissolve the hologram and focused his attention on the medical scan results that were being sent directly to his PIL. Unlike Alex, Loman had a large, flexible Personal Information Link. He could fold it in half and slip it into his coat pocket or slap it onto his forearm where it would stay wrapped like a cuff. For the moment, he was holding it one hand, activating the rigidity feature which kept it stiff like a data slate, as it displayed the information the vice president was waiting on.

Everything came back normal. Alex Chester Evans was healthy. All he needed was enough food and exercise to reach his physical potential. The kid still hadn't passed the entrance exam, and that was a mystery to Loman. He had spoken with Alex and gotten a feel for who the kid was. Somehow, the test was missing what made Alex special. It was an intangible quality—the ability to sense the right moment to act, which he'd displayed when requesting a transfer for his father. Loman wanted Alex in the CDF, and perhaps the fact that he'd gone to NP8261 was a mistake. He hadn't intended to offer the kid anything more than a spot in the program. It was a much better offer than anything Alex could hope for, yet in the moment, having committed himself by traveling to the level-three planet, he had given in to the kid's request.

Loman was rarely surprised by people, and he thought of himself as a master negotiator. He had lured the best operators from other corporations in the past, yet the kid had known just when to ask and had gotten his family a sweet deal. It didn't bother Loman—he didn't mind doing the kid a favor—and his father was a company man through and through. There was no harm to the promotion or even the funds given to help the family make the move —Ahzco made those types of deals every single day—and that one experience had proven to Loman that Alex wasn't just a flash in the pan. He didn't just get lucky by crawling into a battle suit and taking out four drones. The tests may not show it, and Loman's peers might not understand it, but there was no doubt in the vice president's mind that Alex was a superstar.

A message beeped on his PIL, and Loman saw that it was an update from Skandia Seven. The Evans family had arrived and were checked into the Excelsior Hotel. Someone from human resources was already setting up meetings with realtors and private schools. The Evans family would have a busy week as they settled into a new life, but that was important because it would build trust in the company—not that the father or mother needed it, but Alex would. If they took care of his family, Alex would be their guy for life—and if Loman was right, he had more than just a great operator. He had a poster boy for the CDF, a public relations dream come true. In time, Alex could be the face of the security division, and the company would reap the benefits all across the board. Workers would feel safer and be more productive. Recruiting in all divisions would increase; they could even use Alex to help persuade the best minds in every field to leave the other corporations and join Ahzco.

Of course, the next few days were extremely important. Alex still had to get through the intake process, and not everyone did. Being inside a battle suit could be claustrophobic. The ability to keep his head during a crisis was vital. And above all, the kid had to accept the Implanted Neural Control chip. They couldn't force it on him, and if he got nervous about the INC his body might reject it. That would be a real disaster. The kid had moxie, but he couldn't control the more sophisticated battle suits without an INC chip. Loman decided he couldn't worry about it and instead began focusing on finding Alex the right controller. He would need someone he could trust completely, someone whose voice in his head would feel natural. There were several veteran controllers available, but Loman's gut told him Alex needed someone closer to his own age, someone who could understand his strengths and weaknesses to help guide him in a fight.

He punched in a quick message to the head of controller training to request a list of all the current recruits. It was best if Loman picked Alex's partner himself, and then he just needed the right assignment once he passed basic training: something with enough action to get him accustomed to battle—but not so dangerous that they risked losing him.

Loman had other responsibilities as well. Running an entire division—especially one as important as security—kept him extremely busy, but he had learned to prioritize long ago. For the moment, Alex Evans was the highest priority of the CDF, and perhaps even for the company. Loman had no qualms about focusing all his attention on the boy. It was in the best interest of the company, after all, and Loman was himself a company man.

Chapter 11

After his physical exam, Alex was taken to a small, windowless room. It was barely more than a closet, with a single chair and an interactive display screen on the wall.

"Get comfortable, rook," Supervisor Purfoy said. "This is your orientation room."

"It's small," Alex said.

"Yes, better get used to that. There isn't much room inside a battle suit, so getting used to enclosed spaces is part of the training. You've got three introductory videos to watch. They're interactive, so you'll need to answer the questions to ensure you understand the material. It's voice-sensitive, so you can also ask questions. When you're done, we go to lunch, so try not to take forever."

"Okay," Alex said. "But I haven't had breakfast yet."

"Then you should be really hungry for lunch," Purfoy said with a sarcastic smile. "Hop to it, rook, we haven't got all day."

She closed the door, and the lights in the room faded. The only light came from the interactive display, and somehow the tiny room seemed even smaller. Alex told himself that it was just the power of suggestion. It only felt like the room was getting smaller because she had mentioned claustrophobia, but he couldn't deny that he felt a tightness around his chest. It wasn't from the clothes —they were light, thin, and baggy—yet it still felt like there was something squeezing him, making it hard to breathe.

On the display the video lessons were marked simply one, two, and three. He reached out and tapped the first lesson and did his best to ignore the feeling that the room was closing in on him.

"Welcome to the Corporate Defense Force!" The voice of the narrator was loud and unusually chipper. Alex had seen plenty of documentaries and training videos. It was a favorite tool used by his teachers on NP8261, but he'd never seen one in which the narrator didn't sound serious or just plain tired.

"You've been chosen to be part of an elite team of highly trained security providers. The CDF protects citizens on dozens of worlds and space stations using state-of-the-art battle gear, from military-grade carrier starships to the Titan Fast Strike mechanized battle suit."

There were scenes showing starships and battles on strange planets. It was exciting to see, but also a bit intimidating. Alex knew what the CDF was; he had no illusions about the danger of being in a battle suit and going into combat. Still, seeing it played out in graphic detail on the screen less than a meter from his face was a little shocking. Even though the Ahzco units were dominating whatever they faced on the battlefield, a worm of fear was working its way into the back of Alex's mind.

"There are six divisions in the CDF, and today we're going to take a look at them all. We'll start with operators: the men and women on the front lines of conflict. Next, we'll explore all things controllers do to coordinate efforts on the ground. Infiltrators are the shadow division, working undercover to help ensure the safety of company employees and assets as well as securing the future of Ahzco. The technical division oversees the functionality of the equipment used in the CDF, while the RDT is in charge of developing and testing new weapons, armor, vehicles, and more. Finally, the officers are the backbone and oversight of all military operations, from the vice president in charge of security right down to the supervisor who is showing you this video presentation."

The narrator droned on and on about the different divisions, but Alex's mind wandered after learning about operators and controllers. He had no idea that each operator was paired with computer expert who helped direct the operator in battle and played a vital role in the function of the battle suit.

When the video finally came to an end half an hour later, Alex was asked a variety of questions about each division. They were simple questions, and he felt as if he could have answered them even without watching the presentation. It made him wonder how he could have failed the entrance examination if the actual working knowledge they wanted him to know was so elementary. Perhaps, he thought, they were just easing him in—but he couldn't help but feel like he was missing something.

He tapped the second video, and a stern-faced man in a spotless uniform appeared. He had silver sea hawks on the loop of fabric between the shoulder epaulettes and his collar. A mass of ribbons and metals covered his left breast, and a name patch read "Douglas, Y." He stood rigid, and there didn't appear to be an ounce of fat on him.

"My name is Colonel Douglas, and I'll be taking you through the ranks of the CDF. Pay close attention, because rank and chain of command are vitally important to any military operation. We may be the Corporate Defense Force, but that doesn't make our jobs any less dangerous. You need to be able to recognize rank by insignia alone and give the proper respect to superiors, whether they are commissioned or enlisted.

Let's start with you. If you're watching this video, you're a recruit and nothing more. To become a full-fledged member of the CDF, you'll need to complete basic training. You may hear other members of the service calling you 'rook,' which is short for rookie. That common nickname applies to everyone at the beginning, even me. I was once just a rook, the same as you—but through diligence, hard work, and focusing on my strengths, I've risen to the rank of colonel, the highest military rank in the CDF.

Once you complete your basic training, you'll be a private, with the accompanying pay and benefits. You'll remain a private until you complete your divisional training. Graduate and get your first assignment to become a corporal. From there, promotion is based on merit and experience."

The colonel went through every rank, then covered them all again but focused on the insignias, starting with the sea hawk on his shoulders, then going down through the officers and enlisted personnel. Alex found it all fascinating. The video passed quickly, and at the end he was asked questions about rank and insignia. The testing was a little more thorough, and Alex knew if he hadn't paid attention during the video he would have failed to answer the questions. Before watching, he hadn't known the difference between a lieutenant's gold bar, a private's single stripe, and a supervisor's cross. But he did remember that the man who had driven him from the airfield had two stripes on the shoulders of his fatigues, which made him a corporal. And Supervisor Purfoy had two arrows in the shape of an X that signified that she was a supervisor on the admin track of officers.

It didn't seem like much, but just feeling like he could recognize the ranks made Alex feel more comfortable. He had been an outsider with absolutely no knowledge of the CDF beyond the company's promotional information and some articles he'd found on the company network back on NP8261. After watching the video, he knew how the CDF was structured and his place in it. He even knew when he would be promoted.

The third video was actually a tutorial in filling out the company information that would be used to keep track of his employment. It took half an hour to work through it all, from birthdate to setting up an employee compensation account in the Ahzco banking system. As a recruit he earned no money but would be provided shelter and food for the duration of his basic training, along with clothing and personal care items. Once he made private, he would begin to earn a monthly paycheck. It wasn't a lot of money, but it wasn't just company credits and could be used anywhere. The program gave him the opportunity to link to another account and automatically send a portion of his wages to that account. Alex typed in his father's name, found the employee link to Bruce Montgomery Evans, currently posted on Skandia Seven, and set the banking system to send a quarter of his monthly pay to his father's account.

Alex made a mental note to mention the money once he was allowed to contact his parents. Just the thought of being able to help them gave Alex a sense of pride. Things might be difficult at the CDF. He might be lonely—maybe even unhappy with the job, he couldn't say

—but he knew he could endure it if it helped his parents and sister.

When he finished the third presentation, the lights came on, and a few seconds later, just as Alex was standing up and stretching, the door swished open. Supervisor Purfoy stood there looking at him with a smirk.

"Well, you didn't start screaming about the walls closing in," she said. "I guess that's a good thing."

"You said something about lunch," Alex said.

"Oh yes, I haven't forgotten. You're a growing boy, I suppose. Let's get you filled up and ready for the afternoon."

Chapter 12

The cafeteria was in a separate building from the intake center. Purfoy led Alex out a rear door, and he realized he was on a campus with several other buildings. They went into the cafeteria, and to Alex's surprise, the food was being cooked and served by real people.

Purfoy led Alex to a counter and got them both a tray and silverware.

"Tell the cooks what you want," she instructed.

"I can have..."

"You can have anything they're serving, rook—as much as you can eat. Looks like you could use a good feeding. Just don't make yourself sick."

Alex stepped up to the counter. The cook at the grill was cooking pork chops, but there were chicken cutlets and fish as well. Alex chose the pork and added mashed potatoes, glazed carrots, a bowl of rice and beans, and a fist-sized slab of cornbread. Purfoy had a salad with a grilled fish filet. They both drank tea from large plastic cups. Alex ate with relish; it was the first time he'd ever had real pork. His mother had sometimes made pork-seasoned protein bars, and every once in a while they had canned meat that was just a glob of leftover bits of meat all packed together. His mom used to cut the glob into thin strips and fry it until crispy, but it was nothing like this thick pork chop. Alex decided that he could live with whatever abuse the CDF threw at him as long as they fed him real food like this. He liked the way the meat tasted. It felt good to bite into something of substance, and when he finished eating, he felt satisfied in a way he had never felt before.

"You full, rook?" Purfoy asked.

"Yes," he replied.

"'Yes, Supervisor' is the correct form of address."

"I'm sorry," Alex said earnestly. "I'm full, Supervisor."

"You don't need desert?"

Alex could see other diners filling bowls with ice cream from a self-serve machine, and of course he wanted to try it, but he remembered what she'd told him. The truth was that he was satisfied and didn't feel the need for more.

"Next time, Supervisor."

"Very good," she replied. "Let's get going—there's still plenty to do."

The next stop was the quartermaster, who measured Alex and then gave him a rucksack full of simple, rust-colored fatigues that were just his size: five pairs of pants, five undershirts, five fatigue shirts, five pairs of underwear, five pairs of socks, and lace-up boots.

"When you get a chance tonight," Purfoy told him, "you'll need to stencil your name on all your clothes—that way the laundry department can keep track of things."

"Yes, Supervisor," Alex said.

She took him to a building with large numbers painted on the outside: *22*. She opened the door and they walked up to an automated display. Purfoy scanned her ID card, then pushed the icon for a new room assignment. The display made a chime and displayed a message.

Room J is available. Please assign the occupant.

Purfoy typed in Alex's CDF identification number.

"Evans, your ID number is 8261, just like that lump of space rock you came from," she told him as she typed in the numbers. You'll get a scan card that will link your accounts soon, but until then just remember your number."

"Eight two six one," Alex said. "Got it."

She walked him down the hall to a small room. There were two bunks and two lockers. One bunk was bare—just a mattress on a wooden frame.

"Leave your rucksack on the bed," Purfoy ordered. "Tonight you'll have time to unpack everything and get it hung in your locker."

Alex looked at the other bed. It was made, though not well. There were a few personal items under the bed, and the locker was sealed with a fingerprint reader.

"Whose stuff is that?" Alex asked.

"Your roommate," Purfoy said. "Time to move on."

They left the barracks and went to a building that hosted an array of services. Most were computerized, like the bank kiosk, but a few were actual stores with people working inside. Purfoy took Alex to the barber, who buzzed his hair off with electric trimmers. The haircut took less than a minute. The man dusted him off and they were on their way again.

The next stop was the medical center—an entire building dedicated to a specialized procedure that took Alex by surprise. A man in a long white coat met with Alex in private.

"Hi Alex, I'm Dr. Sibert," the man said, holding out a hand.

Alex shook it, suddenly worried that something was wrong. He had never seen an actual doctor before. The colony on NP8261 only had a medical scanner. Meeting with a doctor made Alex nervous.

"Don't worry, nothing's wrong," Dr. Sibert said. "Do you know what we do here?"

Alex shook his head.

"Good, you're not supposed to. The work we're doing is proprietary information, so you can't talk about it with anyone else—not your family back home, not your sweetheart. Do you understand?"

"Yes, sir," Alex said.

"Eventually you'll talk to your controller about it, but that's it. Now, the reason that Ahzco is so successful with mechanized battle suits and vehicles is because our operators have an INC chip. INC is an acronym that stands for Implanted Neural Controller. It's essentially a microchip that we implant here"—the doctor tapped the back of Alex's head—"that can communicate with your brain and with our technology."

"You're going to put a chip in my head?" Alex asked.

"We are. It's not as invasive as it sounds," the doctor said.

Alex thought it couldn't sound less evasive. He was starting to sweat and couldn't help but look at the door. Could he make a run for it? Could he live with himself if he did something rash that ruined his life and that of his entire family? He didn't think so, but he wasn't sure he could live with a microchip in his head, either.

"The good news is that you have no nerves in your skull or brain," the doctor said. "We'll numb your scalp, make a tiny incision, and drill a hole in the back of your skull the diameter of a standard crayon."

The doctor picked up a small metal device. It was a small cylinder the length of Alex's fingernail, with a flat edge on one end that was larger. The doctor demonstrated with the little device.

"We use a protective casing just like this one," the doctor said, showing Alex the device up close. "The INC goes inside the cylinder, and the flat part adheres to the back of your skull. Essentially, we're replacing what we take away."

"Is that safe?" Alex asked.

"Absolutely," the doctor continued. "We've done this procedure thousands of times. We're very good at it. A surgical robot does it all in a matter of minutes. We stitch up the incision, and you're as good as new. After the procedure you'll stay here for a day or two, depending on how long it takes you to adapt to the INC. It's sort of like having a sixth sense. Your mind will be able to control electronic equipment. Once you've proven that the chip is working correctly, you'll be able to finish your basic training and move on to operator training."

"I don't have a choice?" Alex asked.

"No, I'm afraid not. The INC is necessary for you to control the advanced technology that you'll be deployed in."

"I thought I was going to be in the barracks tonight," Alex said. "Supervisor Purfoy told me I needed to stencil my clothes."

"That's right," Dr. Sibert said. "We won't do the procedure for two more days. This afternoon is just to get you ready. I need to run a brain scan so we can know exactly where to place the INC chip. Tomorrow, Vice President Loman has requested that we run a series of tests to help the administrators understand what makes you so unique. Again, nothing invasive—just scans and some basic tests. Any questions?"

"Has anyone died from the procedure?" Alex asked.

"No," the doctor said with a grin that seemed phony.

Alex didn't know if the doctor was lying or just not telling him the whole truth. But since the procedure wasn't optional, he decided not to push the subject.

"Is there anything I can do to make sure things go smoothly?"

"That's an excellent question," Dr. Sibert said. "You may already know that our minds play a powerful role in the healing process. The best thing you can do, Alex, is make up your mind now that the process is going to work just the way it is supposed to. Come in for your procedure with a good mental attitude, and we won't have any problems."

Alex nodded, but his mouth was dry, and he decided not to talk.

"All right then, let's get started," the doctor said.

He had Alex lie back on the exam table. A round hood on a long, articulated arm was lowered from the ceiling and positioned around Alex's head. It was small enough that the inside of the device was only five millimeters from his eyes. Alex decided it was better to just close his eyes and think of something positive. As the device powered on, he could hear something inside spinning around and around his head. He tried to picture what his family was doing. He didn't even know if they had reached Skandia Seven yet. He supposed he should have paid more attention during Galactic Geography in school. When the time came, he decided he would search a star map for the Skandia system. Knowing where his parents were might make it seem like they weren't so far away.

The scan took over an hour, and when it was finished, the doctor helped Alex up and patted his shoulder.

"The good news is, I saw no abnormalities in your brain," he said with a grin.

Alex got the strange feeling that Dr. Sibert would love nothing more than to cut his head open like a watermelon and poke around in his brain. The thought of it sent a shiver down his back.

"Is that all?" Alex asked.

"That's it for today. I'll see you tomorrow."

He held open the door, and Alex walked out. Supervisor Purfoy was waiting for him.

"Come on," she said. "We're going back to the intake center for more video lessons."

"Yes, Supervisor," Alex said.

"There may just be hope for you yet, rook."

Chapter 13

Creedence Three was the newest planet in the Ahzco portfolio of properties: a level-two world with no indigenous wildlife. The flora was mildly toxic but only grew near open water sources. More importantly, the planet had an excess of Rhodium, a rare mineral used in atmospheric converters. Ahzco had developed terraforming engines, but the need for large amounts of Rhodium made the units inordinately expensive and forced the board of directors to call a halt to production. The discovery of Creedence Three was a game-changer. Unfortunately, word of the planet's rich resources leaked, and efforts to construct a colony on the planet had been thwarted by an act of corporate terrorism. The incident was confirmed to be sabotage—the complete destruction of a colony ship just outside orbit of Caldea Prime—but the party responsible had yet to be determined.

The second attempt to establish a colony on Creedence Three was coming from a different location—one considered more secure. A lunar base in orbit around Helena Five, usually reserved for CDF training exercises, had been converted to a storage and supply station. An old freighter was loaded with colony supplies and passengers and mounted with weapons. The hope was that an old trade ship with no obvious ties to the Ahzco Corporation wouldn't draw undue attention—that perhaps it could slip through the open route, through Ahzco's own space tunnels, and into the Creedence system without anyone from the other big companies knowing.

Loman Haley had turned the project over to Colonel Bixby, a staunch military man who trusted no one. Bixby had assured Loman that everything was on schedule and completely secure. He had even suggested that they watch the launch from Loman's office. It wasn't anything the VP was interested in watching; a ship leaving orbit was about as mundane as things could get. A successful launch would be the ship not blowing up, and Loman knew that if he lost a second ship, the company would order a full audit of the security division. The last thing Loman wanted was outsiders poking their noses into his business. Yet losing two colony ships—full of supplies and employees— would be unheard of.

So Loman consented and found himself pulled away from monitoring the progress with his newest obsession. Alex was back in the hospital getting prepped for his INC procedure and having a battery of tests done to add to Loman's inquiry for recruiting.

"You seem preoccupied," Colonel Bixby growled.

The man's voice was rough and gravelly from screaming at his subordinates. He wasn't accustomed to someone not giving him their full attention, and even though Loman was his boss, he refused to be bullied.

"You've assured me everything is secure," Loman said. "Believe me or not, I'm taking you at your word."

"It's not every day that you get to see a resounding success," the colonel growled.

"We can't count it a success until the colony is established on Creedence Three. With a strong security contingent in place."

"Of course, but what we've done is unprecedented," Colonel Bixby said. "All the work and thousands of man hours, kept completely under wraps. You better watch out, sir, or the company might just give me your job after this."

Loman doubted that. The man was on the verge of being insufferable. No one on the board of directors wanted to deal with a VP of security who thought he was more important than the CEO. There was a certain amount of politics to Loman's job. Flattering the other directors and schmoozing with department heads took a certain amount of humility, and if there was one character trait that Bixby didn't possess even a tiny modicum of, it was humility.

Still, Loman respected Bixby's work ethic. The man was an excellent tactician. It had been his idea to bring the project completely into the security division's dedicated system, as well as to use a commercial freighter to further mislead any spies who might be searching for Ahzco's next attempt to set up a colony on Creedence Three. So Loman put his PIL aside, poured himself a drink, and settled into a tufted leather chair beside the colonel.

"Just a few more minutes," Bixby said. "They're doing their final—"

He was cut off by a sudden outgassing near the freighter's engine bay.

"What's that?" Loman asked, suddenly very interested in the project.

His drink was forgotten, and there was a lump of dread forming in his stomach.

"I don't know," Bixby said. "I'm not a naval man, after all. It could just be a normal function of that ship."

It was obvious there was a problem. The ship was shifting around, the fat stern drifting sideways as a result of the outgassing, which seemed to be getting worse. Clouds of misty gas were shooting out of a breech in the vessel's hull.

Bixby snatched up his PIL and shouted into it. "What the hell is going on with that ship?"

The reply sounded small, weak, and more than a little terrified.

"We're not sure, Colonel. There are alarms sounding. It could be a mechanical issue."

"The hell it is. Someone is sabotaging this mission," Bixby said.

"Considered it sidelined," Loman said. "I want those passengers and crew members off that ship."

"Sir, we can fix this," Bixby said.

"We can and we will, but not until I've had a team of operators search that ship in heavy armor," Loman said. "No one leaves the system. Shut down all vessels preparing to leave. I want a list of names of every person who's been on that ship since we acquired it for this mission."

"Roger that, sir. I'll get right on it."

"We may not have a better chance of finding the saboteur, Colonel. And I don't have to tell you how important it is that we find out who knows about Creedence and how much they know."

"I couldn't agree more, sir," Bixby said. There was just the slightest hint of contrition in the old soldier's voice.

"Make it happen," Loman said. "Your job depends on it. I want results, not excuses. Don't come back to me without solid answers, Colonel. I don't care who is implicated. I'll conduct the interrogations myself."

Bixby stiffened and gave the VP a sharp salute, then hurried from the office. Loman was angry and frustrated, but he also saw the opportunity in the delay. Whoever had tried to sabotage the ship had failed—not completely, but enough that Loman could still salvage the mission, and maybe, if they were lucky, draw the traitor out into the open. It wasn't surprising that their competitors had spies in the company, but it was infuriating to realize that some had even found a way into his division. He would have to increase security. He snatched up his PIL and began making a list of things to do. His constant involvement in Alex Evans' training would have to be set aside. It was fortunate that he was in the system when the disaster struck, otherwise he would have had to trust someone else to oversee things. When it came down to it, Loman preferred to do things himself.

Chapter 14

Alex was nervous. A nurse had taken his clothes and left him in a surgical gown. He was in a small waiting room, cold, bored, and trying not to think about having a computer chip inserted into his brain.

Supervisor Purfoy had escorted him to the medical center that morning but then turned him over to the nursing staff. His sense of loneliness had returned with a vengeance, and it was all he could do not to cry. His mind latched onto anything to keep from thinking of what might happen if the procedure went wrong. Dr. Sibert claimed that no one had died from the procedure, but that didn't mean there weren't cases where things went terribly wrong. He could have permanent brain damage and be lost forever in a vegetative state. There were few things that horrifying to Alex. In fact, he would rather die than be helpless for the rest of his life.

So he thought about how often he'd felt like crying. It wasn't a happy subject, but it was something other than the procedure. His birthday was in just a few days. He would be eighteen years old, and he was alone. Perhaps that was why he felt so emotional. He couldn't remember the last time he had cried, yet since joining the CDF and leaving his family, it seemed as if he were on the verge of tears every day.

He had hoped that having a roommate might help, but Julian Van Zant was in officer training and had no desire to have a roommate. He was gone until late in the night and usually out of bed before Alex woke up. The one time they had talked, Alex discovered that Julian hadn't had a roommate since joining the CDF and didn't like the idea of someone else sharing his room. He was only a few weeks away from graduation and then on to the admin track, so he assumed they could ignore each other for that long. Alex got the distinct impression that Julian didn't like operators. It didn't help Alex's case that he had been brought to Helena Prime by the VP himself, and word had spread that Alex hadn't even passed the entrance exams. If the rest of the recruits were like Julian, Alex already had a target on his back.

"Alex," Dr. Sibert said, sounding like a game show host. "Welcome. We're ready to begin."

Alex stood up. Cold chills ran through his bare arms and legs. The doctor waved him into a room with an upright medical chair.

"Just have a seat. We have a few protocols to deal with before we get started," Dr. Sibert explained. "Nurse Phillips is going to shave the back of your head."

Alex thought his hair was already short enough. He had found himself rubbing the stubbly hairs throughout the day and wondering how long it would take to grow his hair back out. None of the security personnel on NP8261 had shaved heads, but most of the recruits did. He wasn't sure if it was cut as a rite of passage or just to make the INC procedure easier.

He felt cold cream being rubbed on the back of his head as Dr. Sibert looked at a file on a large PIL.

"Just to be sure, you're not allergic to any medications?"

"No," Alex said. "Not to my knowledge."

"Good, that's good," Sibert said, speaking more to himself than to Alex.

The razor on the back of his head felt dull. It pinched and pulled the short, stubbly hairs on the back of his scalp before cutting them. But Alex didn't complain. The discomfort was balanced by the nurse's gloved hands on his neck or head. She was the very definition of clinical, and yet it was the first human contact Alex had felt in several days other than shaking a few hands. He tried to focus on the gloved hand that was perched on top of his head. He could feel the heat from it and imagined it was his mother's.

"He's ready," nurse Phillips said after only a few swipes with her dull razor.

"Excellent," Dr. Sibert said. "All right, Alex. We're going to step out of the room and let the surgical robot take over, but let me tell you what's going to happen."

"Won't I be asleep?" Alex asked.

"No, there's no need. Remember, no nerve endings, so you won't be in pain. The robot will spray a topical anesthetic to numb your scalp. You won't even feel the incision, and it's tiny anyway. You will feel some pressure during the drilling and adhesion process, but don't worry, that's absolutely normal. What you should focus on is keeping your head," he said as he lowered a rack from the ceiling, "perfectly still. Now, put your chin here." He pointed at a curved plastic ledge that was mounted between two stiff, vertical support rods.

"And then lean your forehead against this band," he continued, indicating a thick, curved device that was mounted to the same support rods, only higher up than the chin support. "That's it. Perfect. We can monitor your vitals as well as brain activity all through the procedure. Just do your best not to move. The operation will only take about ten minutes."

The nurse and Dr. Sibert left the room. Alex could hear the servos whirring as the robotic arm came down from the ceiling. Being fully awake, yet not being able to see the medical device, was unnerving.

"I will now administer a local anesthetic," a modulated voice said. "It may feel cool on your skin. Please try not to move."

Alex clenched his teeth. There was a slight puffing sound, and he felt the cold spray on the skin that had just been shaved on the back of his scalp. Nothing about it was jarring, and sixty seconds later the robot spoke again.

"I will now begin the procedure. If you feel any pain, please do not move your head. Instead, press the alarm button on the armrest of your chair."

Alex wanted to say he understood, but he couldn't talk with his chin and face pressed into the plastic molding. He could hear the robotic arm moving, but he didn't feel anything. After a few moments, he heard a drill spinning. When it touched the back of his skull there was no physical sensation, but he could feel pressure. His face was pushed gently into the chin rest. The spinning sound changed. Out of the corner of his eye, Alex could see a monitor that was recording his heart rate and other vitals. The number began to climb, and Alex tried desperately to think about something else—anything but the drill that was cutting a hole in his head.

His mother would have been beside herself if she had known what the CDF was doing to him. He was glad they were busy and starting a new life, surrounded by wonderful possibilities they hadn't even dreamed of. It would keep them occupied instead of worrying about him. Alex's mind kept going back to the drill. After what felt like a long time but was probably only thirty seconds, the drilling stopped. There was one last push from behind, and then whatever the robot did was masked by the anesthetic. Alex didn't feel a thing.

Chapter 15

"Dead?" Loman demanded, his voice sounding loud even in the large office. "You can't be serious."

"I'm sorry, sir," replied the hologram.

"That's outrageous. What the hell happened?"

"Looks like suicide," Colonel Bixby said. "Although I have my doubts."

Loman was pacing, and there were questions in his mind that he couldn't answer. He suddenly felt the urge for a drink, despite the early hour.

Colonel Bixby had gone out to the freighter to inspect the damage. Loman had been waiting for his report, but he wasn't expecting to hear that their saboteur was dead.

"And you're sure it was the person who planted the device?" Loman asked.

The device in question was an explosive. Fortunately, the chemicals had failed to mix together before being triggered, which reduced the explosive's power by almost ninety percent. The result was a hull breech, but the engines—and more importantly, the ship's fuel—weren't impacted.

"They had to come check to ensure there was nothing left of their work," Bixby explained.

"I thought you had the crew removed and held under armed guard," Loman said.

"I did," Bixby said. "They're all being held on the lunar base, so imagine my surprise when we discovered the body."

"How'd he die?"

"She," Bixby said. "It's a woman, although we haven't identified her yet. That section of the ship is compromised. Looks like she, or someone with her, opened her helmet and let hard vacuum do the rest. It's not a pretty sight."

"Nothing changes," Loman insisted. "The system is still on lockdown. We question everyone who had access to that ship. It's not possible that one person did this alone. She had to have help."

"If she did, we'll find them," Bixby said. "But we have to be realistic, sir. She was a passenger on the ship."

"What are you saying?"

"That the level of resolve for these people is as high as it gets," Bixby said. "She planted a bomb on her own ship. She was planning to die all along. It was a suicide mission."

"I refuse to believe that she acted alone."

"No, sir, that's not what I'm saying. She's connected —that's for certain. And the probability that she had help from someone else in this system is very high. But my point is, if they are willing to die to protect their secrets, we may not get much from them, even if we find out who was helping her."

"I refuse to believe there is nothing we can do, Colonel. It's beginning to sound like you're hedging your bets and trying to cover your own ass."

"I'll tender my resignation right now, if that's what you want," Bixby said.

"No," Loman snapped. "What I want is answers. Get me some, or your job will be the least of your worries."

Loman disconnected the call and sat down in his chair. He felt sick to his stomach, and when he reached out to pick up his PIL he noticed his hand was shaking. He just couldn't believe how completely off-guard his people were. They had been infiltrated, and not just by corporate spies looking to steal trade secrets. The vaunted CDF, the best corporate military force in the galaxy, had been infiltrated by a cell of...

That was an even bigger problem. Loman wasn't sure who had wormed their way into his division. Were they corporate infiltrators? The CDF had spies in the employ of dozens of companies. He got regular reports of their business secrets, and they made moves as an organization to weaken or hurt their rivals' business dealings, but the problem he faced within his own ranks was much more dangerous. Were they terrorists of some kind? It seemed unlikely. Creedence Three was a relatively new discovery. They had only filed their claim to the planet within the last eighteen months. There was no indigenous life on the planet, and Rhodium was a naturally occurring mineral that was used to filter and clean harmful gases from the atmosphere. It seemed unlikely that eco-terrorists would want to keep them from getting their hands on Rhodium.

Loman activated his PIL and dictated a quick message to Vesper Sikes, his counter-intelligence chief.

"I want to know who has a reason for hindering our efforts on Creedence Three. Don't bother with the obvious corporate entities; this is something else, something more extreme. Bixby discovered the saboteur, but she was dead before we found her, and we're still trying to discover who she is. What we know for certain is that she was a passenger on the ship, which means she was on a suicide mission. This isn't just about profits or market share, Sikes. I want you here, in-system, giving this your full attention. I'll clear you for entry, but come alone. Take a corporate transport and report to me as soon as you're in the system."

He sent the message and decided he needed to get a drink. He could send someone out for it, but a walk might do his nerves some good. His jacket was hanging by the door, and he pulled it on as he walked out. The admin building in Sparta was not his normal workspace. Unlike the grandiose offices on Arcadia, there was no secretary or even security in the building. He rode the lift down to the ground floor and went outside. Every person in the city, on the planet, and in the system for that matter, worked directly for him. Even the pilots bringing in supplies or carrying out new operators and controllers and techs were company employees. There was no need to worry about unwanted visitors. He strolled down a wide, neat street, knowing that a crew of groundskeepers worked tirelessly to hold back the aggressive flora that would overgrow the city if not constantly pruned back. There were very few places on the planet that would support a human settlement, and the air itself was thin. Loman was breathing hard before he reached the bar he was walking to. It was part of a restaurant, quiet, elegant, and rarely busy. The company owned many such establishments, and this particular one was for the upper echelon of the CDF officers and admins.

"Gin and soda with a twist," Loman told the bartender before sliding his leather-wrapped stainless steel flask across the bar in a discrete manner. "And fill that with gin, too. Top shelf only."

He dropped a thousand-credit note on top of the flask, and the bartender swept them up in one smooth motion.

"That should cover it," Loman continued. "You can keep the rest."

"Absolutely, Mr. Haley," the bartender said. "I'll be right back."

Money could buy him a little privacy. He didn't mind extravagant tipping or paying for a lavish meal. He was the vice president in one of the galaxy's big five corporations. He had more money than he would ever spend in two lifetimes. But Loman didn't care about the money or what it could buy; he was passionate about the work, about protecting the company's employees, and about ensuring the company's success. Someone was trying to take that from him. It wasn't a matter of ego or pride—not to Loman Haley. To him, an attack on the company, using CDF personnel of all people, was personal. They were coming after him with an aggression rarely seen in galactic business, but if they were taking their gloves off, then Loman would, too. He could be as nasty as he needed to be and still sleep soundly at night. Whoever was threatening his company with their terroristic acts of violence should be prepared to reap the whirlwind. Loman would find them. He would find out who they were and what they loved most in the galaxy—and then he would take it from them.

Chapter 16

"You can relax," the robot's modulated voice informed him. "I have administered a light sedative."

Alex felt the effects immediately, as if every muscle in his body had suddenly turned to mush. He sagged in the operating chair, and only the apparatus used to hold his head still kept him from toppling to the floor.

"All right, let's get you someplace more comfortable," a muscular male nurse said.

Alex had no idea where the man came from. He rolled a wheelchair over and then slid his arms under Alex's. He seemed to lift him easily; maybe it was the drugs, but Alex felt as if he were floating. He rose up from the operating chair and glided down into the wheelchair.

The world was a blur—the medical facility was a meld of a thousand voices, lights, and colors. After what seemed to Alex like only a minute, someone lifted him up and helped him slump over onto a bed. He closed his eyes, and it felt good. His legs were lifted up and settled on the bed. A blanket was pulled over him, and he slept.

Sometime later he woke up, his body stiff, the back of his head aching. He was in a room with no windows. A light mounted to the wall above the head of the bed cast a dim glow through the featureless room. Alex was surprised to discover there were no monitors, no medical equipment, no computers, and not even a clock to tell him what time it was. He reached up and felt the back of his head. The incision was held together with some type of flexible adhesive and was only a few millimeters long. Touching it sent pulses of pain through his head, but otherwise he had only a dull ache after having a hole drilled into his skull. It seemed like a bad dream, and Alex was glad it was over.

The bed had controls that adjusted the head and foot up and down. Alex pushed the button that raised the bed up into a sitting position. He rolled over onto his back but was careful not to let his head touch even the pillow. The effects of the sedative were slow to wear off. He felt foggy, and thinking was difficult. For a long time he just sat still, not really thinking about anything—just feeling the air move in and out of his lungs.

The door opened, and light from the hallway spilled into the room. Alex turned his head. It sounded as if there were hundreds of people out in the hallway. Alex was surprised he didn't hear them sooner. Dr. Sibert walked in and immediately checked the incision on the back of Alex's head.

"How are we feeling today?" Dr. Sibert asked.

"Today?" Alex said. "How long did I sleep?"

"Eighteen hours," Sibert said with a chuckle, "but that's good. The longer your sleep, the easier the transition. How do you feel?"

"Groggy," Alex said.

"That will wear off soon. Does your head hurt?"

"Aches a little," Alex said. "It hurts if you touch it."

"All right, it seems all went well. You're probably ready for some food."

Alex's stomach growled. "Starving."

"That's understandable. I want you to drink a lot of fluids today. That will help flush out the sedative. After you've eaten, try to take a nap. Your job today is to heal. So let your body do what it was made to do."

"Okay," Alex said.

Sibert left the room so quickly that Alex didn't get to ask for something to help him pass the time. He wanted his PIL. He could play games, go on the network and watch videos, or read, but Supervisor Purfoy had taken his Personal Information Link when he first arrived. He'd been kept busy since then and hadn't had time to think about leisurely things, but if he was going to be stuck in the medical facility all day, he wanted something to help pass the time—maybe even a holo-film projector.

He looked around the room again, but it was completely empty except for his bed and the light fixture on the wall behind him. A few minutes after Dr. Sibert left, an orderly came in with a tray of food.

"Breakfast," the woman said.

She was short, wore her hair in a ponytail, and carried a large tray. She settled it onto the bed rails, then uncovered the food.

"Pancakes, scrambled eggs, sausage, fruit, orange juice, coffee, and for later, a sports drink," she said happily. "Enjoy."

"Thanks," Alex said, his mouth watering as he looked at the enormous tray of food.

"No problem. You need to drink, drink, drink today," she continued. "Doctor's orders. Which means you'll need one of these."

She held up a red container with a handle and a screw-top lid.

"What's that?"

"Urine container. You're not supposed to leave this room today. So eat up, drink all the fluids, and when you have to relieve your bladder..." she held up the container like it was a prize he had won. She hooked the handle over the rail on his bed.

"Thank you," he said again.

"No problem. If you need us, just hit the call button."

She pointed to a green button next to the bed's adjustable controls.

"Can I stand up? Maybe walk around the room a little?"

"I you feel like it," the orderly said. "But don't push it. There won't be many days in the CDF that are this easy, trust me."

She left the room, and Alex once again heard the muffled sounds coming from the hallway. He made a mental note to ask about the noise but quickly forgot about it as he dug into his breakfast. Everything tasted delicious; the pancakes were sweet, the sausages were spicy, and the orange juice was so tart it made him pucker with every sip. He had grown up eating processed foods that had been shipped to the mining colony from other planets. The fresh vegetables from the hydroponics facility where his mother worked had been the only food item he'd had that wasn't powdered, compressed, canned, or dehydrated. Eggs, for instance, were made by adding water to powder. They tasted relatively similar to the real eggs he now had on his tray, only less flavorful and more like a gelatinous porridge.

He ate everything on the tray and drank the orange juice. He didn't care for coffee—he thought it tasted like water strained through burnt toast. Instead, he opened the sports drink and drank half of it before the orderly returned and took the tray away. The sports drink fit into a cup holder that hung on the bed rails. Alex lowered the bed back down, rolled onto his side, and went back to sleep.

When he woke up it was lunch time: roast beef, mashed potatoes, a mixture of steamed vegetables, and a plump yeast roll. There was even a slice of cake with frosting for dessert. Alex ate the entire meal but was no longer sleepy. He actually felt like getting up and doing something, but there was nothing to do.

When the orderly came in for his tray, the door remained open, and Supervisor Purfoy came in. There was still a lot of noise coming from the hallway, but it wasn't as loud as before.

"How ya feelin', rook?" Purfoy asked.

She smiled, and he couldn't help but smile back.

"Actually, I feel pretty good."

"No headache?"

"Not unless I touch it," Alex said.

"Good, 'cause you've got work to do."

"The doctor said my only job was to heal."

"That's what they all say. Too bad it isn't true," she said. She dropped eight brightly colored brochures into his lap. "These are the promotional materials for the battle suits used by the CDF. We design and build them ourselves —no outside tech. The company is big on that. Each one has its uses. I believe you're familiar with the first one."

Alex picked up the brochure on top. It was larger than a PIL and printed on thick paper with glossy pictures covering everything. Alex knew that long ago books were printed on paper, as were magazines and newspapers, but he'd never actually seen them. The brochure was flexible, and while the pictures were very high quality, there was no video on the glossy pages and he couldn't zoom in. He saw that the first brochure was for the MP Defender.

"Word is you've been in one of those," she said. "That just a rumor?"

Alex shook his head. "The colony was attacked. I saw one of the Defenders get hit with something, some sort of energy blast. It rebooted the battle suit. I had to pull the operator out and give him my rebreather. So I got inside just so I could breathe."

"Well, your job now is to learn all about them. Think of it as homework to prepare you for operator training. That should keep you busy for the rest of the day. I'll see you tomorrow."

"Thank you," Alex said, glad to have something to do.

He found the brochures fascinating. Actual, physical books with real pages were absurdly expensive, and he marveled at the colorful brochures. The battle suits themselves were amazing, and Alex spent the next several hours poring over them. He only stopped long enough to eat his dinner, and then he read late into the night. When he finally went to sleep, he couldn't believe how lucky he was. It was a strange twist of fate that brought him to the CDF training facility in the Helena system. He had been trying to wrap his mind around the fact that in all likelihood he would never have left NP8261—but a window of opportunity had opened in front of him. He shuttered to think what he might be doing if he hadn't climbed inside that MP Defender. That one decision had changed his life. He was getting to do something he had only dreamed of, something he knew deep in his bones that he wanted. He was going to be an operator in the

Corporate Defense Force. He fell asleep with a smile on his face, thankful for the opportunity before him and determined not to let it slip away.

Chapter 17

Alex was just finishing up his breakfast when Dr. Sibert returned to his room with Supervisor Purfoy. They were pushing a large device on wheels into his room.

"How are you feeling today?" Dr. Sibert asked.

"Great," Alex said.

"Outstanding. I have very high hopes for you, young man. Very high."

Alex wasn't sure what the doctor meant, but he felt as if he were some type of experiment, and that made him slightly uncomfortable.

"The Implanted Neural Controller allows you to interact with technology using brainwaves," Dr. Sibert began to explain. "That means you'll hear technology inside your mind. You may have noticed an increase in the noise around you recently."

"You mean there's not something unusual going on in the hallway?" Alex asked.

The noise had actually decreased to a quiet murmur, but he still heard it when anyone opened the door to his room.

"No, Alex, there's nothing unusual going on," Dr. Sibert continued. "What's changed are your senses. Most technology has an effect on the physical world beyond what they were made to do. Electricity creates ionic fields and emits magnetic waves, similar in many respects to the human brain. When a person gets hurt, we can test their brain activity to see if it is still producing electromagnetic pulses called brainwaves. You've heard of this, I'm sure."

"Only in holo-movies," Alex said.

"Well then, the INC chip is like a radio in your head. It picks up the waves made by electronic devices and can amplify and transmit your brainwaves that can be read by devices with the proper interface."

"Like the battle suits?" Alex asked.

"Precisely. The Mechanized Battle Suits are equipped with powerful computer systems that can be interfaced with your INC, allowing you to control the suit with the power of your thoughts. Essentially, the suits become an extension of the operator. But controlling your brainwaves takes time and practice. Unlike a computer, for example, your brain is highly responsive to your feelings."

"Fear," Purfoy said. "If you get scared, your brain gets glitchy."

"Fear, joy, excitement, dread," Dr. Sibert continued, "all affect brain chemistry and the way in which brainwaves are produced. So, the first step is learning to control your mind. This room is insulated. It's what's called a Faraday cage, because it uses insulation to block electromagnetic waves. While you're in here, you aren't hearing the machines being used in the medical center."

"What do you mean when you say 'hear them'?" Alex said.

"Ah, you are astute, young Mr. Evans. No, you don't actually hear a sound. But, just like sound, which strikes the ear drum and is converted to electrical information that your brain recognizes as sound, the EM waves produced by electrical devices create a sound in your brain. If we had let you walk out of the medical center, you might have gone mad. Once the INC begins to interface with your brain, which usually happens within the first twelve hours, the noise is intense."

"So you put me in here..." Alex began.

"To let you slowly acclimate. The brain is an incredible organ and can readily adapt to most anything. If done correctly, you will grow accustomed to the sounds of regular devices, and your brain will tune them out entirely."

"This," Supervisor Purfoy spoke up, "is an INC training system. There are levels of control; for instance, level one will simply power the machine on and off. When I turn it on, you'll hear it, rook. People say it sounds like a rushing river or applause from a large crowd. You'll need to let your mind get used to the sound so that you don't shut it off automatically."

"How's that?" Alex asked.

"When you hear it, you'll want it to stop. Your brain," Purfoy said, "will actually *will* it to stop, which the machine will respond to. You'll have to teach your brain not to turn the device off. You follow?"

Alex nodded. It was a lot to take in, but it all made sense. He was nervous that he wouldn't be able to do what they wanted him to do. What if his brain wasn't strong enough? What if he couldn't adjust to the noise in his head? He wanted to ask if it was possible to withdraw the chip and just go back to being normal, but he was afraid that would send the wrong message. He would have to make it work, one way or another.

"Once you can leave the machine on for a minute," Purfoy continued, "it will automatically move to the next level. Complete that, and you move on. Think of it like a video game. You want to beat the machine. Okay?"

"Okay," Alex said.

"Now," Dr. Sibert said. "Take your time. Don't rush through this process. The point is to adapt to this new sense, not to work through the levels faster than someone else. In fact, it's better if you go slow."

"Take it slow," Alex said. "Okay, I can do that."

"Once you beat the machine," Purfoy said. "We'll open the door. When you're ready, we'll take a stroll through the med center. If that all goes well, we'll go outside for a while. And when you feel up to it, you can return to your barracks for the night."

"You think I'll be ready by then?" Alex said.

"You won't be fully adapted. That process takes several weeks," Dr. Sibert said. "But it's like learning a new language—total immersion is the best practice. We'll ease you into it, but you'll need to be around technology on a constant basis for your brain to start sifting through the different noises and learning to switch off the sounds that have no meaning."

"All right," Alex said. He was warming up to the idea. Perhaps being able to interact with a computer using only his brain would be fun.

"Good luck," Dr. Sibert said, leaving the room.

Purfoy waited until he was gone, then flipped the switch on the machine and walked out. Alex waited. At first, nothing happened. He was starting to fear that his INC was defective, but then he heard a very quiet hum. It was low-pitched—just a steady rumble—and then the screen on the INC-compatibility machine turned on. A much higher-pitched whine suddenly filled Alex's head. It was uncomfortable—not quite as bad as the sound of pieces of metal grinding together, but close. There were words on the screen. Alex focused on them, cringing a little at the annoying sound but determined not to turn the device off: *Think BEGIN to start the countdown.*

Alex thought "BEGIN" without any conscious effort. He just saw the word in his head, and the message on the screen changed to a sixty-second countdown. The hum and the whine were grating on his nerves. It was like he was hearing an audio representation of pain. He forced himself to breathe through it and embrace the pain, willing his mind to adapt.

He made it nearly ten seconds before finally thinking he wished the sounds would stop. And just like that, as if it were magic, the sounds did stop. The screen blinked off, and everything was quiet again.

Alex leaned back in his bed, careful not to let the back of his head touch. He felt tired, but he knew he could do it. The hum started again—low and not too unpleasant on its own—and then the less pleasant whine began once the words appeared on the screen. Once the words disappeared, the countdown timer started. Alex clenched his teeth, letting the sounds reverberate in his head. He stared at the timer, watching it slowly descend. He made it half a minute before his mind shut the machine off again.

"It's a game," he said aloud, just to hear a regular sound. His voice sounded the same. "Okay, I can do this."

He flung back the covers on his bed and stood up, holding onto the rail in case he felt dizzy, but he was fine. He flexed his knees a little, and the low hum started once again.

"I can do this," he said. "I've got this. No problem."

The screen came on along with the high-pitched whine. He thought that perhaps it too would be tolerable by itself, but combined with the low hum it made his brain rattle in his skull. He accepted it, accepted the discomfort, let the noise roll through his body, and began to pace. It's just noise, he thought to himself. I can deal with it.

With only twenty seconds left, a third sound came on: an oscillating noise that rose and fell in pitch. It wasn't high or low, but rather it fluctuated between the pitches of the hum and whine. Alex puffed air through his nose. He felt queasy and grabbed onto the rail of his bed, squeezing it hard.

"I can accept this," he said out loud, but his voice sounded strange. It was as if he were hearing a recording of his voice—just the auditory register without the mental accompany of it. The sounds from the machine were drowning out his ability to hear his own voice. He looked at the screen. There were less than ten seconds left, and the thought went through his mind: *and then it will stop*.

Just that thought caused the machine to stop. He was simultaneously elated and frustrated. He hated the noises. In fact, he feared that if he had to hear them all the time, he would go stark raving mad. Even just the short break when the machine reset was such sweet relief...but then it began to hum again. Panic gripped Alex. He wanted to smash the machine to bits. He thought about digging the INC out of the back of his head with his bare hands. When the high-pitched whine started again, he almost screamed.

And then a new thought broke through the noise. He had heard something out in the hallway. When the orderly brought his meals, when Dr. Sibert made his rounds, or whenever they opened the door, he heard it— and it wasn't the painful, screeching rumble of the INC machine. It had sounded like a lot of people in a confined space. The noise had diminished over time, even though he only heard it fleetingly a few times a day. What could it be?

The oscillating sound again joined the low hum and the high whine, bringing his thoughts back to the INC machine. It was torture, but Alex knew it was temporary. It was the extreme, he told himself. It was what they used to make the normal sounds seem quaint by comparison. He looked at the screen, watched the numbers count down slowly, and thought to himself once again: *I can do this.*

He let his body relax. His mind stopped trying to block out the sound. He let the unpleasant sounds wash over him like a cold shower. When he quit fighting it, his body began to adjust and his mind began to adapt. Before he knew it, the sounds stopped and were replaced by a new noise. It sounded like rushing water over rocks in a wide riverbed. He smiled and looked at the screen. There was a red circle on the left side of the screen. On the right were a black square, triangle, and a circle. He imagined the red circle sliding across the screen to the black circle. And to his delight, it did exactly that. The screen lit with flashing lights and the words "LEVEL THREE" appeared.

That was easy, Alex thought. He could still hear the roar in his ears, but his mind was occupied by the tasks on the screen. Each level was a little more complicated. Some required precise thoughts. For instance, one level showed an equation: a simple addition problem, the number forty-four above a six with a plus sign. The space below the numbers was blank, and Alex thought *fifty* and the answer appeared.

Other levels required multiple thoughts to complete. When three chess pieces appeared on a board, he had to think out three separate moves to reach checkmate. Once he did that, the system went on to the next level. With each level he completed, the sound of the roar receded a little further in his mind.

There were sixty levels. The final level required multiple thoughts all at the same time. He had to shift back and forth between them. The screen showed a marble in a maze. He had to direct the marble with his mind around obstacles, avoiding pitfalls, all while answering questions. Occasionally, distractions would shoot across the screen. It took him several tries to reach the end of the maze, but he did it.

Congratulations, you have completed the INC compatibility challenge.

The machine powered off, and all the sounds ceased. It made Alex feel strangely hollow. Somehow, in the two hours it had taken him to finish, he had actually grown accustomed to the machine's sounds—and he missed them now that they were gone.

The door opened, and the familiar rumble returned. There were different pitches of sound—some constant, some oscillating, but none jarring or irritating. Supervisor Purfoy tossed his clothes onto the bed.

"Get dressed, rook. Let's go for a walk."

Chapter 18

Perrin was an apex planet, perfectly situated close to its dwarf star. There were no other planets in the system —just chunks of crystal that cast rainbows of color all around the small planet. Ahzco bought the level-one planet to create a private resort and exotic animal preserve for their executives. Construction was ongoing, and no guests had yet arrived. The garrison had not been staffed, and there was no commercial value to the planet; it was simply a place for the company to invest their mammoth profits while offering yet another perk to the heads of their various divisions.

The attack was not random. A dozen mechs launched out of fast-attack airships, which then dropped munitions on all of the completed buildings in the resort. Explosions rocked the ground and construction workers ran for cover, but the invasion force was not satisfied with blowing up empty buildings. The mechanized warriors hit the ground in heavy armor with weapons blazing. They blasted anything that moved. Construction workers were vaporized by laser blasts, blown apart by projectiles, or buried in the rubble as the buildings they took cover in collapsed around them.

It was chaos. Animals that were in the process of being released into the park-like settings around the resort were slaughtered in their cages. Dirty bombs were released in the atmosphere, poisoning the air and water, killing the flora, and leaving the planet a desolate wasteland. There was no one to fight back and no weapons that could penetrate the armor of the warriors hidden inside their unmarked battle suits.

In orbit, supply ships were attacked. Some were destroyed completely, while others were left crippled in a decaying orbit with no hope of surviving as gravity slowly pulled them down into the planet's atmosphere. The devastation on the ground was temporarily masked by boiling black smoke and clouds of dust kicked up from fallen buildings. The warriors were picked up by a shuttle that whisked them away back into space—but not before they left a swarm of mines waiting just outside the space tunnel.

It was a completely one-sided attack. One damaged supply ship, on the verge of losing life support, transferred all remaining power to the communication system to send a message back to Ahzco headquarters about the attack and warning them of the dangers still in the system. The crew watched the lights on the ship go dark and held onto each other as they waited to die.

Chapter 19

"Two hours? Are you serious?" Loman asked.

He felt a huge grin building on his face. It felt strange after days of tracking a phantom, trying to discover who was sabotaging their ships. Word had come in of an attack on the Perrin system, and he had been summoned back to the Ahzco world headquarters. The board of directors wanted answers and reassurances, of which Loman had none. But in all the years he had served as VP of security, no one had ever adapted to the INC as quickly as Alex Evans.

"Oversaw the entire process personally," Supervisor Purfoy said. "I've already forwarded the video footage to your private servers. I took him out immediately afterward, and he seemed fine."

Loman felt a sense of intense satisfaction. His pet project was reaping rewards already. There was something about this boy from the backwater planet who had failed the entrance exams; Loman still didn't know what it was. Nothing of interest had come up during the scans and tests the medical teams had performed, but he was responding to the INC procedure better than Loman had dreamed possible. Most recruits took at least a full day to work through the compatibility testing. Some were even bedridden for days trying to adjust. And no one had ever gone outside immediately after testing.

Purfoy had sent Alex to the cafeteria for dinner while she met with Loman. The VP was thrilled to have the news, especially since he had nothing else to give the board of directors.

"Tomorrow you begin the psychological adjustment protocols?" Loman asked.

"That's correct. We'll put him through the gamut and see how he responds," Purfoy said. "We're ahead of schedule, so there should be no problem getting through it, even if he needs extra time."

"I want regular reports," Loman said. "Odds are I'm in for a fight when I get to Arcadia. Someone out there is trying to destroy the company, and there will be members of the board who will try to use this opportunity to push me out of my job. I want him processed as soon as he gets through basic training. We can't afford not to have him in our ranks, and if I'm not here to advocate for him, my replacement might throw him out of the program just to spite me."

"Politics suck," Purfoy said, "if you don't mind my crude appraisal."

"I don't mind," Loman said. "To be honest, I agree, but we're toeing the line between accomplishment and chaos. Without us, the company would break apart from sheer size. There are too many innocent employees who depend on us, Soup. And that boy is the future."

Purfoy nodded. She didn't entirely agree with Loman's assessment of Alex Chester Evans, but she didn't disagree, either. She was a supervisor, and it was her job to oversee, not predict the future. If she were pressed, she would have to admit that she thought the VP was putting too much pressure on the rookie. But that was his job, and hers was to oversee Alex as he made his way through the training programs on Helena Prime.

"I think I've found the perfect controller to pair with him," Loman continued, swiping his PIL to send Supervisor

Purfoy the file. "She's young, bright, and intuitive. I want you to arrange a meeting, off-book. Put them in a room at the same time. See if they click, so to speak. I want complete AV coverage and a report with your honest opinion on whether you think they're a match."

"Yes, sir," Purfoy said.

"Good. I'll be in touch as soon as I can," Loman said. "Remember: keep your eye out for anything strange around here. I don't know who we can trust anymore."

"Trust is overrated," Purfoy said.

"You'll make a great VP one day," Loman said.

She left his office, and Loman gathered the rest of his things. His flask was nearly empty, which was good. He would have to go through customs when he reached Arcadia, and they would never allow an open container through their tight security. He would drink it on the flight, and maybe he'd find the answers that the board needed to keep his job. The trip would take several hours, and his sources still had time to make a breakthrough.

He powered down the lights and the computer, then headed for the door. There was something nice about the slower pace on Helena Prime. Without having a hundred requests for his time each day, he could actually get some work done. But he was only a VP, and he still answered to the CEO—and more importantly, to the board of directors. It was time to face the music, whether he was ready or not.

Chapter 20

Private Nyx West was nervous; she couldn't imagine why she had been recalled from her training program and sent back down to the surface of the planet. It was embarrassing, really. Controllers preferred to stay at a distance—not that Sparta was as wild and dirty as the rest of Helena Prime, but she preferred the controlled environment of a spaceship. Perhaps it came from growing up on a scientific outpost. Her parents were researchers who studied the decay of stars. In space, there were rules. While some people hated life inside a space-faring vessel, longing for wide open spaces and fresh air, Nyx felt secure. On the surface of a planet, even in a city, she felt exposed. Danger could come from anywhere, and it was impossible to retain the map of an entire planet in one's mind. Nyx liked that fact that on a spaceship or space station she could know the entire layout—she could visualize the structure down to each nook and cranny.

But orders were orders. She had been recalled, and the only explanation was that there were administrative records that needed to be clarified. Nyx had filled out all the electronic forms when she joined CDF. She wasn't hiding anything, and she certainly hadn't skipped any steps. She was, if anything, a rule-follower. Rules, in her mind, kept one safe. Perhaps it was ironic that someone obsessed with safety had joined the CDF, but the controller program was a perfect fit for her. She preferred observing from a distance, had a knack for computers, and wanted to make a difference. Her only drawback was her social skills. Growing up as an only child of researchers on a space station with no other children had left her a little awkward around others and absolutely paralyzed in large groups.

She reported to the admin office on her own. Getting from one place to another wasn't a problem. She always did what she could to hide the fear she felt on-planet and moving through groups of people. Fortunately, the waiting room wasn't large: just two chairs separated by a narrow side table. And she was alone, at least for the moment. The clerical worker who had shown her in had assured her that Supervisor Ewing would be with her shortly. All Nyx wanted was to correct whatever error had appeared in her file and return to the training facility in orbit.

The door opened,and Nyx expected it to be the administrator or at least the clerical worker to escort her to Supervisor Ewing's office. Instead, it was a boy: a tall, almost painfully thin boy. He came in, glanced around, and realized he only had one option.

"Hi," he said as he lowered himself into the chair beside her.

"Hello."

An awkward silence followed. Nyx resented the fact that simply because two people were in a room together there was a social implication that they should converse. She preferred the silence.

"My name's Alex," the boy said.

"Nice to meet you, Alex," Nyx said, remembering when her mother had taught her how to respond to a stranger. "I'm Private West."

"Oh," Alex said. "You're already in training?"

"Yes," she replied, knowing that he was going to tell her all about his own place in the CDF. Boys, it seemed, loved to talk about themselves.

"What division?"

Nyx was surprised, but only by a minor miscalculation on her part. She had assumed Alex was like most males in the CDF. He had taken the opportunity to ask about her, but she suspected it was a ploy to get her to lower her guard—not that she had any reason to fear Alex, but he was a stranger, and strangers made Nyx nervous. She preferred to know what a person wanted from her, and then she could either give it to them or refuse. She couldn't control other people, but she could make her own choices. Unfortunately, her experience in life was that many people enjoyed manipulating others. She didn't want anyone trying to manipulate her.

"Controller," she said, without adding any details.

"Cool. Do you like it?"

"Yes," Nyx replied, still not sure what Alex was up to.

To her surprise, he didn't continue pestering her with questions. She tried not to look at him, but there wasn't really anything else to focus on in the small room. They were both watching the door, but as long as it remained closed there was nothing to see. When Alex leaned forward, propping his elbows on his knees, Nyx risked a glance over at him. There was a scar on the back of his scalp, still red. There were no stripes on the sleeves of his fatigues. Alex was an operator and still a recruit. Perhaps he was struggling with basic training. She couldn't help but worry that they had both been sent to the tiny waiting room because they were being dismissed from the CDF. Her fears prompted her to action.

"You're an operator?" she asked, even though she knew full well that he was.

The hypocrisy of manipulating him into sharing why he was there wasn't lost on Nyx, yet she didn't want to come right out and ask him. She was too afraid of the answer.

"Yeah, still in basic," Alex said.

"How's that going?" Nyx said. "I hear it can be difficult."

"So far, so good," Alex replied, glancing over at her. "I really have no complaints."

Nyx nodded as if she completely understood, but in truth his answer only made things more convoluted. She decided to bite the bullet.

"Any idea what's going on?"

"What do you mean?" Alex asked.

She looked at him, studying his face. Her experience in the CDF had been constant training. Even when she thought something was happening spontaneously, it was often staged as a training exercise. Perhaps this was just another one of those staged encounters, but if so, Alex was an excellent actor. He seemed completely genuine.

"Why are we here?" she said, pointing at the floor.

"This isn't normal?" Alex asked.

Again, she worried that she was missing something, but Alex didn't appear to be hiding anything.

"Maybe, I don't know," she said. "I just got pulled from training with no explanation."

"I just go where they tell me," Alex said. "My supervisor brought me and told me to wait in this room. She never gives me a reason for anything."

Nyx sat back, her mind working the problem. Perhaps she was making something out of nothing, but it seemed strange. None of the other controllers in her training class had been called to Sparta, but perhaps she was the first. She was good at her job—and maybe that was why she had been called in first.

"I guess we'll have to wait and see," she replied.

"What's controller training like?" Alex asked.

Nyx shrugged her shoulders and looked at Alex. She was trying not to be paranoid, but his question was exactly the sort of inquiry a spy might make. Perhaps Alex was a ringer, trying to get her to talk about things she shouldn't. But he looked so earnest that it was hard to know. Nyx found herself wanting to talk to him. There was something about him—perhaps it was the way he looked at her—but she felt safe with him. He was guileless, and Nyx appreciated that.

"School," she said, although she had never been to an actual school. Nyx was a product of homeschooling and online academic work.

"Oh," he said. "I'm sorry then."

"No, I love it," she said. "It's like studying something you really want to know."

Alex nodded encouragingly but didn't interrupt.

"What about you? Do you like being an operator?"

"I think I will," Alex said. "To be honest, I'm just happy I'm here."

"You make it sound like it was a mistake."

"I guess I think of it that way sometimes," he replied. "Everything's happening really fast, and everything is different."

"Different how?"

"Well, the food, for one thing," Alex said. "Being outside without a re-breather, the colors, the attitudes of the people—it's all different from where I came from."

"Where did you come from?" Nyx asked.

"NP8261. My dad was a mechanic there for most of my life."

"NP8261 is a mining world," Nyx said. "Level-three planet, right? There's not much information about it. Ahzco property somewhere in the Lima Section, right?"

"You know more about it than me," Alex said with a grin. "There's really not much to know. There's only one colony. It's a dull place. Like I said, this is such an improvement—I'm just glad to be here."

The door opened, and an older man with black skin, white hair, and a sour expression stood there. He glanced at his PIL before he spoke.

"Private West," he said.

"That's me," Nyx replied.

She started forward but then stopped and turned back. Most people made very little of an impression on Nyx. She was a guarded, introspective person. Yet there was part of her that didn't want to leave Alex. He made her feel like he actually cared, and it was rare that she actually felt like she could be friends with someone.

"It really was nice meeting you," she said. "My first name is Nyx. I hope we see each other around sometime."

Alex smiled. It was pleasant smile—certainly not predatory or superior, as if he had gotten something from her. It was just one more thing that made him seem genuine. Controller training was highly competitive, and everyone seemed to be looking for anything that would give them an edge. But Alex wasn't like that—at least Nyx didn't think he was.

"I would like that," he said.

She turned and followed the supervisor from the room, feeling a little bit lighter somehow.

Chapter 21

Alex was still thinking about Private Nyx West when he followed Supervisor Purfoy to a large warehouse-like structure. He couldn't get the girl's eyes out of his mind. She had large, teardrop-shaped eyes that made him feel nervous, but in a good way. She was definitely the prettiest girl he had ever met. He kept playing their encounter over and over in his head, especially when she'd told him her first name. Nyx: it was exotic sounding. But then, she was exotic. He was pale and awkward, but she had darker, dusky brown skin and moved with precision. She had risen from her chair in a fluid motion and walked so gracefully it was like she was floating.

"Get your head in the game," Purfoy said as they approached the entrance to the building. "There are a lot of electronics in this building. It may be overwhelming at first."

"Okay," Alex said, grateful for the warning.

He was still adjusting to his new ability to hear EM waves, and occasionally the more powerful ones startled him. It was like someone unexpectedly screaming right behind him. Once he had a moment to get used to it, the sounds diminished, but he didn't like being surprised.

"And some of the devices in here respond to your INC," Purfoy continued. "They're going to sound different. The good news is that once a device syncs with an INC, it won't respond to someone else. When we first developed the technology, the computers kept responding to multiple commands. We've fixed that, but you need to let your mind adjust at its own pace."

"Yes, ma'am," Alex said.

Purfoy nodded, then pulled open the door. To Alex it seemed like they were walking into a preschool. The sounds were much louder in the warehouse building, and there was a wide variety of pitches. Many were oscillating, almost like a child wailing or trying to sing. Alex's face twitched, but he stepped inside. Purfoy didn't rush him. She stood patiently waiting until he nodded that he was okay.

The cacophony took some getting used to, but he managed it. The raucous sound died down to a manageable roar. Amidst the noise, Alex noticed notes of what sounded like music.

"What?" Purfoy asked as he grinned.

"There's some type of music," he said. "It's different."

"What you're hearing is a device that has synced to a person's INC," Purfoy explained. "Once the two systems begin to work together, it sounds different. Some people do claim it sounds like music."

"It does—it's sort of a strange, breathy, quavering sound. Like a bamboo flute or something."

"Okay," Purfoy said. "Let's go. We're going to hook you up to an INC-compatible system today and let you play for a while."

"Sounds like fun," Alex said.

"That's what they tell me."

The warehouse was filled with stalls, each one housing different kinds of simulators. Alex looked into the ones that were open. He was reminded of an arcade. He'd never been to one personally, but he'd seen them in holo-films. Some of the stalls had simple interactive devices with a single screen, not unlike the INC-compatibility machine. Others were more immersive, with screens all around the stall and even on the drop ceiling.

"All right," Purfoy said, stopping outside an empty stall. "Here is where things get real, as they say. Go in and follow the instructions. If you have problems, just step outside and take a breather. There's no shame in that. You're learning to use an entirely new set of skills, and it takes time. I'll be back to get you in time for dinner."

"Okay," Alex said.

He went into the stall, and Purfoy closed it behind him. There was only one screen, but it was as large as a full-length mirror. Inside the stall, the sounds of the other devices diminished, and he could hear a strong, solid hum. The sound reminded Alex of the fans used to circulate air down in the mines on NP8261. Oftentimes at night, when everything was quiet, he could hear them humming away in the distance.

The screen was a calm, blue color with the word "Welcome" in gray letters. He stepped forward and felt a nudge in the back of his mind. It wasn't physical, yet a nudge was the only way he could describe it. It was as if something solid was touching the back of his head. He reached up and stroked the bristly hair where his INC had been covered over with the skin of his scalp.

The nudge began to change. He wanted to push into it, as if his thoughts were outside of something soft and inviting. It felt strange but natural at the same time. He didn't have to think about if he wanted to do it or not; the desire was there, the way a person coming upon a piano keyboard yearns to press the keys.

He let his mind respond to the nudge, and suddenly he felt a connection—like two magnets coming together with a solid snap. The image on the screen dissolved, and a series of options came up. They were game titles. Alex stood with his hands at his sides and read the options: Racer, Flier, Dodge, Explore, Combat, and Build. He decided in his mind to try "Racer," and immediately the program loaded.

The speed of the decision happened so fast that it took Alex by surprise. It was almost as if he hadn't decided until after the title appeared. But he knew he had made the selection. There was a sense of accomplishment in the back of his mind that reminded him of the way it felt to move after sitting for a long time. He often enjoyed stretching his legs after a long day in school. The act of engaging those muscles felt like strength, and on some level, pleasure. Selecting the game felt the same way. He was using his mind in a new way, but it felt good.

The screen showed the interior of a racing car. The steering wheel was familiar, but on the dash were dozens of gauges and push-button controls. Through the windshield, Alex could see the track and other cars. A large light flashed red as Alex prepared for the race to begin. Suddenly the light turned green, and the other cars raced forward. Alex joined them, accelerating simply by thinking it. Steering was an act of his will. Occasionally, as the race called for it, he thought of pressing one of the buttons. Some gave his vehicle more traction, others increased his speed or the precision of his steering control. After a few laps, he heard a voice in his mind.

Time to make a pit stop, driver.

It sounded like his own voice—like he was simply thinking the thought—but Alex knew very little about racing. He wasn't a fan of the various race leagues. Ground racers were old-fashioned, but the sport was still big on some worlds. It was his own lack of knowledge that confirmed the voice he'd heard wasn't his own—he didn't even know what a pit stop was.

An arrow showed Alex where to go, and he steered his car where it indicated. A crew of technicians ran around the car, making adjustments. A woman with crude features (the game clearly wasn't well-designed and certainly wasn't as graphically artistic as the games on his PIL) leaned in the door window.

You're doing well, but you have to be more aggressive if you're going to win.

Alex saw the woman's mouth moving as she spoke the words, but he heard her in his own voice. She stepped away, and the crew fled back so that Alex could drive away.

Go! His own voice boomed in his head.

He continued racing. It was amusing enough, but mostly because he had no physical controllers. The entire game was controlled using only his mind.

When he finished the game, coming in third place in the race, the program went automatically back to the game selection window. He noticed that the only sounds he was hearing were the pleasant, musical tones of his INC connected to the game.

He stepped backward, willing his mind to disconnect from the device. The result was like removing noise-canceling headphones. His mind felt lighter, and all the noises of the other devices became noticeable again.

After a few seconds, he stepped forward and reconnected with the computer. The game selection screen reappeared, and he chose another game. He realized exactly what the device was for. There were many subtleties that he needed to learn to differentiate, such as hearing everything in his own voice or the ability to monitor multiple things at once. He could do it, but he was clumsy. He still thought of the entire game as if it were on his PIL, and when he made a decision, like flipping a switch, he imagined it as if his hand was physically doing the task. It didn't take a genius to realize that once he let go of his perceived limitations, he would be able to do things much more quickly.

Alex couldn't remember if it was Supervisor Purfoy or Dr. Sibert who had mentioned the ability of the INC to make the operator feel as if the battle suit were merely an extension of their existing body, but it was starting to really make sense. There was so much the INC enabled him to do, and all he needed was time and practice to make it all second nature to him. His mind wasn't clumsy or slow. The more he played the games, learning the rules and the built-in tools provided to him as part of the gameplay, the more he was able to focus on letting go and being completely responsive. His mind was slowly becoming more accepting of the fact that he could do more with the INC than ever before. He couldn't wait to connect with a suit of actual Mechanized Battle Armor and see what he was truly capable of.

Chapter 22

Loman sat outside the CEO's office, feeling like a child waiting to see the principal at school. He hadn't done anything wrong, but the security of the company's employees and assets was his responsibility. Somewhere there was a leak feeding a very dangerous enemy vital information about Ahzco. Fortunately, some things were starting to take shape. Loman had spent the entire trip going over what the investigators knew about the attacks on Ahzco's planets. First, the attacks on the colony ships and on the apex planet Perrin had been attacks aimed at building projects. The attack on NP8261 was different; it seemed like more of a probing mission. It felt to Loman more like a distraction than an attack meant to accomplish something. That, of course, brought up two more questions: Was the attack meant to throw the company off the scent of whoever was behind the more deadly attacks? Or did the disruptor drones accomplish something on NP8261 that Loman's people had overlooked? In big business, information was priceless. Loman feared that the drones had transmitted something to their enemies that was worth losing millions of credits in drone technology for.

Unfortunately, none of that was going to be enough to satisfy Loman's boss. Ian Gentry was a hands-off CEO who gave his people plenty of space to do their jobs. If they failed, he preferred replacement over training. Loman had risen up through the ranks of the CDF and knew the division better than anyone else in the company, but that didn't necessarily guarantee job security. If he didn't find who was behind the attacks and stop them, he would be fired. It was a race against time, and he was about to find out how far behind he really was.

"Mr. Gentry will see you now," a beautiful young woman said as she stood up from behind her desk. Secretaries were obsolete, yet the wealthiest companies still used them to give visitors a sense of a businessperson's power and prestige before they even met. Ahzco's CEO always had a female secretary. The woman was stunningly beautiful, so much so that Loman had no doubt that she had been artificially enhanced. She wore a skin-tight dress to accentuate the curves of her body, and she moved with the ease of a professional dancer. She stepped to the large double doors and pulled one open for Loman.

Knowing the reason behind the facade didn't lessen the effect. Loman's mouth was dry, and he felt tired and soiled from his long flight from the Helena system. He walked past the woman, forcing himself not to look at her, and into the CEO's office. The room was huge, taking up half of the entire top floor, with multiple sitting and lounge areas. Some lounge areas were carefully arranged near items that showed off Ian Gentry's accomplishments and wealth. Loman found his boss behind a small desk. It was little more than a narrow platform with a charging dock for his PIL. The boss did not look happy.

"What is happening, Loman?" Gentry growled. "Are your people all on vacation or something?"

"No sir, we're working around the clock—"

"And?"

Loman hesitated. He could sense the animosity Gentry was directing at him, and he needed to turn the tide. Gentry could focus his anger on something other than the VP of security, but only if Loman gave him a better target.

"We're in the midst of taking steps to better secure all our properties and assets," Loman said. "But we're also on the trail of whoever is behind these attacks."

"You don't know who's doing it?"

"I could venture a guess, but we're not talking about the usual suspects."

"What does that mean?" Gentry almost shouted.

"Sir, we've been at this for a long time. Security, as you well know, is a huge expense to any business. There are certain rules that are the unwritten code of conduct in matters like these."

"Loman, what the hell are you talking about?"

"I'm talking about profit and loss, sir. About the very things every business cares about more than anything else. Take the attack on NP8261, for example—six disruptor drones dropped on our colony there."

"Tell me something I don't know," Gentry growled.

"Do you know how much a disruptor drone costs?" Loman asked. "They're made by Hanoi Enterprises and sold on the open market for eighty-two million credits each. The control software is another thirty-seven million credits, although it can be synced to different drones."

"Get to the point," Gentry ordered.

"The point is, none of our competitors are foolish enough to waste half a billion credits to knock holes in some buildings on NP8261," Loman said. "You've read my report from the Helena system."

Gentry nodded.

"Then you know whoever tried to blow up the colony ship was on board. It was a suicide mission. We have the most dedicated CDF in the galaxy, sir—men and women willing to give their lives to protect company employees and assets. But if we started talking about suicide missions, we'd have a riot on our hands. No company commands that kind of selfless loyalty."

"You're talking about zealots," Ian Gentry said, his hand stroking the stubble on his unshaven jaw.

"Of some kind or another," Loman said. "Whoever they are, we know they're dedicated, well-funded, and damn good at their jobs. We still haven't identified the woman who tried to blow up the freighter. I would have said it was impossible for a person to get on one of our ships without being an employee in good standing, but that woman did, and I'm guessing the same thing happened with the first colony ship, too. That's total dedication."

"It has to stop," Gentry said. "We're bleeding money."

"I understand that, sir," Loman said. "Believe me, this problem has my full and undivided attention."

"Good," Gentry continued. "Because it's got the BOD up in arms. They're talking about replacing everyone. I don't think they'll go that far, but suffice it to say that your name is at the top of their list. You better come to the board meeting tomorrow with more than hunches. They want names, Loman. If you can't give them one, they'll find someone who can."

Loman knew no one could do his job better, but the board of directors didn't know that. The head of every division, including Loman, sat on the board, but the real power lay in the two men and four women who were shareholders but not employed by the company, including chairwoman Lynn Faulk. They alone held the right to fire anyone in the company, including the CEO, if they saw fit. They were known within the company as the "scary six." The other directors would never cross them for fear of losing their jobs.

"I understand, sir," Loman said. "I'll be working on that through the night, rest assured. We'll have answers for the meeting tomorrow."

"Good, but I want to know when you know," Gentry said. "I don't want any surprises at that board meeting. Everything else can wait. We need a target and a solid, measurable plan of action. Anything less won't satisfy the scary six."

"Roger that," Loman said. "I'll get right on it."

He didn't wait for a dismissal. Loman and the CEO both knew that the meeting was nothing more than a fishing expedition. Loman's neck was on the line, but if he failed, the CEO would also be in danger. Ian Gentry was probably more concerned about finding a way to spin the news that would keep him out of hot water than anything else. When Loman found out who was behind the attacks, he would forward that information to Ian Gentry on the way to the board meeting. There was no reason to give the man ammunition before a meeting that might turn into a battle.

He took the executive lift down a few floors to his own office, which was only a quarter of the size of the CEO's. The floor was shared by three other VPs. They all shared a posh waiting room, and their secretary was actually a former trainer for Loman's operators on Helena Prime. The man had been a wrestling champion before joining CDF to help train operators and infiltrators in hand-to-hand combat. After he had taught for nearly twenty years, Loman had rewarded him with an easy job greeting visitors, where his hulking physique sent a message just as potent as the CEO's beauty queen. It was just an entirely different type of message.

"Hello, Mr. Haley. Good to have you back, sir," Raz Goreman said. "How are things in Sparta?"

"Good," Loman said. "Thank you."

He didn't have time to shoot the breeze. He had less than twenty-four hours to get answers, and his job depended on it. He hurried into his office, closed the door, hung up his coat, and collapsed into the chair behind his desk. There were half a dozen messages on his PIL listed as urgent, but he opened a different one first. It was the report from Supervisor Purfoy on the meeting between Alex and Nyx. He didn't have time to watch the video footage and had to settle for reading Purfoy's report. The big desk drawer slid open easily, and he separated some files to get to the flask hidden there. He poured himself a drink from the flask into a coffee mug, which he set on the table until he could get the flask closed. He dropped the metal container back between the files and sipped a mouthful of the lukewarm gin. It burned across his tongue like liquid fire, then dropped down his throat and into his empty stomach, spreading heat that drove away the tension from his body.

Loman skipped the salutations and jumped right to the meat of the report.

Both parties quickly bonded. I would estimate that Private West and Recruit Evans would make a remarkable team. My only cause for hesitation would be the possibility that they might cross the line between a professional and personal relationship. One thing seemed clear: both

*seemed reassured after only a short time together. One
would naturally assume that they could continue to build
upon that bond as they navigate the rigors of their mutual
CDF assignments in the future.*

Loman had been right—but maybe too right. He
took another drink, wondering if he should make other
arrangements. Controllers were meant to be close to the
operators they partnered with, but crossing the line from
cohorts to lovers was dangerous. Love could make people
do irresponsible things. A man in love might throw away
his career for the woman he loved. A woman in love might
sabotage a mission or ruin months of planning to save the
man she loves. He would have to give it all more thought,
but he couldn't afford to spend time on it when his own
career was in jeopardy. He needed answers, or at the very
least he needed a scapegoat. Colonel Bixby came to mind,
but Loman didn't think the board would be satisfied with a
colonel. If he couldn't satisfy their anger, they would
demand his job, and he had too much left to do to let that
happen.

Chapter 23

Nyx was back where she belonged. She wore a simple headset that allowed her to speak to her virtual operator. The AI could engage in dialogue, but a good controller knew better than to distract them with needless banter. Her job was to assess the greater situation.

Not every operator had a controller. MP models didn't require a controller, and most that were garrisoned didn't have the advantage of an eye in the sky. Sometimes drones were used to give land-based controllers a more direct overhead assessment, but in most cases, controllers were only used with the elite units that were dropped into hotspots or planets owned by rival corporations.

Her current operator was controlled by an AI computer. It was fighting its way out of a city overrun by hostile, indigenous life forms. It had been decades since hostile life forms had been an issue, but it was still part of her training. She had to direct the operator out of the city and to the evac zone.

"Hostiles closing in from the northeastern section of the city," Nyx said. "I'm boosting power to your thrusters. Navigation will be offline."

"Roger that," crackled a human voice that sounded far away and desperate. It would have sounded realistic if she hadn't heard the same response multiple times. Still, she felt a little like a child watching another child play a video game and shouting instructions over their shoulder.

The aliens in the training simulation looked like canines, only smaller, faster, and much more savage. The operator turned back and fired at the building, sending a deadly rain of debris down on the creatures chasing it. The sim was run with her operator in an AT Destroyer, the heaviest and slowest of the mechanized battle suits. Instead of legs, it rolled on treads that could easily take the operator through almost any environment. Unfortunately, it had no repulsor or flight capabilities, making it extremely vulnerable to the canine lifeforms.

Strictly speaking, firing on structures was frowned upon—even as a means of escaping deadly hostiles—but the sim was being run on a foreign-owned planet, so she had given the order to use the structures to her operator's advantage. So far, she had managed to keep her operator away from the aliens, but it was her third attempt at the sim and the hostiles were closing in.

"Switching to laser blasters," Nyx said. "You've got a wall ahead of you. Hit it with concentrated laser-fire and burst through."

"Roger that," crackled the human recording.

There was nothing left for her to do. The MBS was at full speed. Its only chance to escape lay in getting through the wall quickly. It was a stone edifice, built to keep the canine aliens out. Nyx's operator didn't have time to reach one of the many gates in the wall. He needed to break through the wall with enough of a lead that he could continue running while he fired his concussion grenades through the opening. If everything worked perfectly, he might build up just enough of a lead to make it to the evac zone, which would give her a win.

The operator started firing. She saw from her elevated position—her screen mimicking the view from a geosynchronous orbit that was zoomed in to street level—the laser blasts burning through the wall and streaking out the far side. She hoped it was enough. A concussion grenade wasn't strong enough to break it down and would slow the operator's approach.

"Good luck," she couldn't help but say.

"Roger that," crackled the overused response.

The impact was too jarring. Dust and rubble clouded the wall and blocked her view. She wasn't even certain the operator had gotten through, but there was no time to waste.

"Switching weapons to concussion grenades," she said. "Fire straight back through the wall."

"Roger that," the sim response crackled through her headset, making Nyx want to scream.

She saw the operator come out of the cloud, but it wasn't moving fast enough. Four concussion grenades were fired through the hole in the wall. They went off with echoing booms. Dozens of hostile aliens died, but not all of them. She saw a thick pack race through the hole before the first grenade detonated.

"You've got hostiles on your six," Nyx warned.

"I can't outrun them," the virtual operator replied.

"Escape and evade," Nyx ordered.

A glance at her monitor showed almost no depleted uranium rounds remaining. Laser power was down just below half. The AT Destroyer was out of grenades, and the aliens were closing in. She needed something—anything— that would stop the alien hounds, even if only for a few seconds.

Suddenly, inspiration struck. She hit the keys on her command board in a flurry. Out of the back of the virtual mechanized battle suit, just above the triangular, off-road treads, a liquid sprayed out in a wide pattern.

"Zigzag back and forth," Nyx ordered.

"Roger that," the voice crackled.

The MBS altered course, which only slowed the operator down. The canines seemed to pick up on the virtual operator's fear and charged ahead even faster. A warning light began flashing on Nyx's control board. The MBS was nearly out of oil. She shut off the spray and switched the weapon back to laser-fire.

"You've got lasers. Fire at the ground in front of the aliens," Nyx ordered.

"I don't understand," the virtual operator said.

"Shoot the oil on the ground," Nyx said, suddenly worried that the sim wouldn't do what she envisioned and the aliens would race past the oil before her plan had a chance to work.

But the operator swiveled its body and fired. A single laser flashed, then flames jumped up around the aliens. Some caught on fire, but most simply turned away. They weren't gravely injured, but they lost the will to continue chasing her operator. Nyx wanted to shout for joy, but another warning light came on. It was the high-temperature warning light. There was nothing Nyx could do about that. There were too many aliens in the simulated city. If she didn't get her operator to the evac zone, more would pick up the chase. She thought about telling him to slow down, but a quick mental calculation told her that slowing wouldn't reduce the heat enough to offset the danger to the MBS. Better to get to the finish line as quickly as possible, she thought.

She watched as the operator continued running. More warning lights came on. The heat was burning out the suit's cooling system. The weapons, dependent on wiring and the movement of ammo through the suits armor, went offline. Smoke began to waft from the operator, but he was almost to the end of his run.

A warning alarm sounded while he was just meters from the evac zone. The system had suffered a catastrophic failure and was shutting down. Nyx typed a quick order that kept the emergency brakes from engaging, and the ruined AT Destroyer coasted into the evac zone.

The program began scoring the simulation and producing a full report. Nyx knew she would hear criticism, but the first and greatest rule among controllers was to get the operator back safely. She had done that. Had the simulation been real, the operator might have burned to death in the MBS. They might have suffered any number of problems, and her job was to overcome them. As a controller, she could operate the suit's systems, bypass problems, and if needed, create solutions that were non-traditional. Maybe she would get some bonus points for her oil-slick fire. It had worked, mostly.

"Good job, West," her training officer said. "Take a break and then report for mission briefing."

"Thank you," Nyx said.

She walked away from her station, which was set up in a row to mimic conditions on a carrier ship. Being a controller didn't call for the strongest candidates. They didn't run for miles or lift heavy weights. They weren't on the front lines in mechanized battle suits. Rather, they faced soul-crushing stress. Their job was to keep operators alive, and sometimes they failed. When that happened, they were the last ones an operator called to for help. There was nothing as devastating as watching someone who was following your express orders die—and having to live with the knowledge that at best you couldn't help them, and at worst, that you were the reason they died. Nyx didn't like second-guessing herself, but she couldn't help but wonder what it would be like if the operator she was working with was a real, live person and not just a poorly created virtual soldier.

Protocol called for a mandatory de-stress period after every mission. Nyx walked into a quiet room and sat in a comfortable captain's chair. A pod came down over her, offering privacy and a variety of soothing sounds, colored lights, and even aromas to help her deal with the stress. Nyx really didn't feel worried. She was good at her job, but she was still learning. The AI didn't fool her into thinking her decisions were life-or-death to a real person on the ground. Still, she enjoyed the half hour in the dimly lit stress pod. Her favorite setting was "thunderstorm." Since she grew up on a space station, her only exposure to weather had been from network videos and holo-films. She liked the gentle roll of thunder and the sound of the rain pelting down on a metal rooftop above her. She kept the light dim so that it felt like the shadows of night, and closed her eyes.

As had happened frequently since being sent down to the admin offices in Sparta, Nyx found herself thinking about Alex. He was an operator; perhaps she would feel different about everything if he were her partner. She tried to push the thoughts away, but she couldn't help it. Her normally analytical mind was fascinated by the boy she had met. Her mother would not approve, but Nyx couldn't deny the fact that thinking of him filled her with a kind of giddy excitement she had never believed was real before. She hoped that she might get the chance to meet him again, if for no other reason than to have her unrealistic fantasies about him dashed. Just as she preferred to keep her distance from the planets, she preferred to stay above her own emotions, as well. She always wanted to make sure she could see what was coming and keep herself safe.

Chapter 24

"Fear is your biggest enemy," Master Sergeant Grossman said.

He was a small man who looked like he'd gotten caught in a meat grinder. There were burn scars up the right side of his neck. His face was pulled to that side by burns that had consumed his ear and a third of his hair. The right eye was milky white and watered constantly. He wore standard fatigues but with one sleeve pinned up on his right side where his arm should have been, and Alex had noticed the master sergeant's prosthetic leg on his right side as well.

"Fear is a disease of the brain," the NCO continued, "because fear isn't real. It isn't a tangible thing. It isn't something you can avoid. It has to be mastered. Fear will turn your mind inside out, and that's dangerous in an MBS when you're synced with some of the most destructive weapons at your disposal."

Alex understood the concept, but he had no idea how to master his fear. As a child he had struggled with fear of the dark, thoughts of dying, and even the epic size of the universe. Over time, he'd learned to think rationally about his thoughts and reason out the probabilities that gave him comfort, but occasionally fear still ran rampant. He had been afraid of what basic training would be like. He had been afraid to say goodbye to his parents. He had been afraid that he had made a mistake by joining the CDF, and he'd been terrified of the INC surgery. It seemed to Alex that he was far from being able to conquer his fear.

"You are all lethal weapons," Master Sergeant Grossman continued. "Your thoughts and your will can result in deadly force greater than you can imagine at this stage of your training. That is why we will begin mastering your mind."

Alex sat with two other recruits. It was the first time he'd met anyone in basic training. One was a girl who was perhaps a year older than Alex. With her head shaved and wearing fatigues, it was difficult to tell for certain. Her name, stenciled on her fatigues, was "Everett, S," but she introduced herself to Alex as "Sev." The other recruit was a boy. He looked to be about Alex's age, but there was something about him that seemed different. He was shorter than Alex and solid muscle. He had just the hint of a mustache at the corners of his upper lip. His name was Tito Barnes.

All three recruits sat in chairs in a small classroom inside the intake building. Neither of the other two recruits seemed as uncertain as Alex, but he did his best to hide his insecurity. Tito seemed almost arrogant, like he'd heard Master Sergeant Grossman's lecture a hundred times. Sev was cool, calm, attentive, and unfazed, as if the subject matter were beneath her.

"Let me begin with an example," Grossman continued. "How many of you have watched a scary holo-film and then lain in bed at night fearful?" He didn't wait for an answer, even though Alex was halfway through the process of raising his hand. "You know it's a movie—that it isn't real—but fear has convinced your brain that at any moment, that story will come to life and you'll be killed. We've all had nightmares that woke us in the night. Lying there, in the darkness, we feel the effects of a dream."

The lecture continued, but Alex was lost in thought. How often had he felt the chains of fear trying to hold him back? He couldn't say for certain, but it was more often than he wanted to admit.

"Our thoughts create our feelings," Master Sergeant Grossman announced. "To be an effective operator, you need to maintain a neutral mindset."

They went through several mental exercises. Some were difficult to think about, even though they were merely hypotheticals. At one point, imagining he had just gotten the news that his mother had died, Alex felt tears stinging his eyes. The last thing he wanted was to cry in front of the other recruits. To his surprise, the mental exercises to return his mind to a place of neutrality actually helped.

The lessons went on all morning long. At one point, Grossman started screaming at Alex. The sudden hostility caught him off-guard.

"Why are you even here, rook?" Grossman screamed. The master sergeant was so close to Alex that little flecks of spit sprayed across Alex's face. "You're a failure—a lying, conniving scrap from the dung heap. You didn't even pass the entrance exam. You don't belong here. You'll never make it. You're a pathetic, fearful bucket of slime and piss."

The mental assault was so shocking that Alex didn't move. He could feel the looks of awe from Sev and Tito. His greatest fear had been that people would find out he didn't belong. Alex's insides were turning to ice, but instead of running out of the room or breaking down in tears, he thought to himself, *Master Sergeant Grossman's opinions about me don't define me or my circumstances.*

"Do you want to hit me, rook?" Grossman bellowed only a few millimeters from Alex's face.

"No, Master Sergeant," Alex said, more calmly than he thought possible.

"You want to cry?"

"No, Master Sergeant."

"Are you going to quit, rook? I'll send you back home on the next transport as long as I never have to see your ugly face again."

Alex heard snickering. He wasn't sure, but he guessed it was coming from Tito. He didn't bother to look around. Instead, he stared straight ahead, feeling a sense of mental strength he didn't know that he had.

"No, Master Sergeant."

"We'll see," Grossman said, straightening back up and pacing over to where Sev sat.

"What about you, rookie? You're not strong enough to compete in this job. You're a pathetic, weak, scared little girl. I wouldn't trust you with a PIL, much less a battle suit. You're a quitter—I can see it in your eyes."

"No, Master Sergeant," she replied.

Alex didn't want to stare, but he couldn't help it. Sev's face was stony, revealing no emotions, but her voice shook when she answered.

"You should go home, rookie. No one wants your kind here. Just get up right now and leave!"

"No, Master Sergeant," she said, her voice barely even a whisper.

"You feel upset, Everett?"

She nodded.

"Good, that's the point of this. I want you to feel upset. But I also want you to control your thoughts and change your feelings."

The master sergeant's voice had changed. He was no longer the gruff, profane drill instructor, but the calm, rational teacher. Sev nodded. Alex thought he saw tears welling in her eyes.

"You have to control your thoughts," Master Sergeant Grossman said. "You grew up with no mental discipline. What I mean is, you never had to filter what you thought. It was always personal and private. Your thoughts had no impact on the real world apart from your actions—but in an MBS, your thoughts could kill someone. An undisciplined mind can cause a weapon to fire or a hydraulic pincer to crush or a hundred-million-credit battle suit to run straight off a cliff. You can't let what you see or hear influence how you think."

The man was small, scarred, and some might even consider him crippled, yet he moved so fast it caught everyone off-guard. He jumped toward Tito's spot at the table and slammed his hand down so hard that it sounded like the crack of a lightning bolt splitting the air. Tito jumped back, his chair tilting on its hind legs. For a second he was suspended—a look of terror on his face, his arms and legs stiffly protruding as if he expected them to support him on thin air—then he fell back with a crash. He managed to turn his head just in time to keep it from slapping back on the fresh incision from his INC.

"What the hell, man?" Tito bellowed.

"You have to control your mind," Master Sergeant Grossman said calmly.

Alex caught Sev's eye. There was the tiniest hint of a smile on her lips. Tito got to his feet and swiped a finger under his nose. He was breathing hard, a look of fury on his face. Alex understood the recruit's anger, but he was starting to understand Master Sergeant Grossman's lesson, too. He could hear the rumblings of nearby electric devices. They reminded him that his mind worked differently now. It was, in many respects, much more powerful. And he had to learn to control that power so that it didn't hurt people.

When they finally got to lunch, the three recruits sat together and talked. It was the first time since he had arrived on Helena Prime that Alex felt like he wasn't alone. There had always been people around, but it had felt to Alex like they all knew more than he did. But considering his lessons on mental discipline, he realized that his feelings of loneliness and inadequacy were merely thoughts he had allowed to fill him with anxiety and fear. His perspective had changed with the inclusion of Sev and Tito in his basic training. They, like him, didn't know anything. They were learning what he was learning. He wasn't alone, and he wasn't hopelessly behind, destined to never catch up with the people who filled the city around him.

"Man, what a load of crap," Tito said, his mouth full of spaghetti.

"How's that?" Alex asked.

"Don't tell me you're buying all that mental mumbo-jumbo," Tito said. "I mean, I get it. You can't let your thoughts run wild in a battle suit, but damn, man. Someone screams in my face, they're gonna feel my wrath. You know what I mean?"

Alex nodded but looked at Sev. She hadn't said a word. It seemed odd to him. They were peers, and he was certainly more than happy to have friends to talk to, but she was completely reserved.

After lunch, they were taken to the airfield. Master Sergeant Grossman handed each of the recruits parachutes.

"Any of you ever skydived before?"

"No, Master Sergeant," they all said in unison.

"Well then, this ought to be fun," he said. "Load up."

He ushered them into a small transport. Alex felt tense as the transport took off. The ship was small, and they felt the pull of gravity as it climbed into the air. Alex's hands began to tremble, so he crossed his arms over his chest and stuck them under his arms so that no one would notice. Master Sergeant Grossman sat across from them, watching each one of the recruits closely. It made no sense that they were being taken up in the transports without training of any kind. They couldn't really be expected to jump, Alex thought. The idea was absurd. He could feel his fear building like a monstrous wave in his chest.

"Three thousand meters, Master Sergeant," a voice boomed through the cabin speakers. "You are cleared to jump."

"You three ready?" Grossman barked.

"Master Sergeant," Alex said. "I haven't been trained for this. I have no idea what I'm doing."

"Me neither," Sev said.

"I was wondering when someone was going to speak up," Grossman said. "Don't worry about anything. The chute is completely automated. All you need to do is practice what I taught you."

"You mean overcoming fear by controlling what we think?" Alex said. The truth was, he thought the master sergeant had gone mad.

"Trust me, there's no way the chute fails," Grossman continued. "You have to change your perceptions. Once you're in a battle suit, what you can and can't do are different. What can harm you and what can't are different. So you have to get your mind to that neutral place. On this jump, just focus on staying calm and trusting your gear. Tito, you're up first."

"You're insane," Tito said, trying to sound tough and failing.

"You can jump, or I can throw you out," Grossman growled. "Makes no difference to me."

"You're crazy," Tito said, but he moved to the open door and looked out for a second. "No way. I'm not doing it. Take me back down, you one-eyed freak."

"Listen, you can call me a freak. You can make fun of the way I look or sound. But don't start giving me orders. I earned these stripes, you little pansy. You haven't."

He grabbed Tito's shoulder and shoved him so hard that Tito went tumbling out of the transport. Alex heard him scream for a split second, and then he was gone. Alex and Sev both leaned toward the door without actually getting any closer to it, trying to catch sight of Tito. The transport was in a slow turn, just circling at three thousand meters so that the jumpers would come down in roughly the same area.

"Who's next?" Grossman asked.

Chapter 25

Alex saw Tito's chute open and felt a sense of relief, but he was still terrified of jumping out of the transport.

"I can't do it," Sev said.

"You can and you will," Grossman declared. "An operator has to be willing to step into dangerous situations. Maybe it's a firefight, or maybe it's a volatile accident scene. You'll be outside spaceships in orbit, rescuing company employees with no other hope. You can't hesitate because you're scared. Change your thoughts. Jumping from this transport with that auto-chute is just as safe as taking a walk down the street."

"Okay," Alex said. "I'll go."

He was still terrified, but he knew what was coming. He could either jump or be pushed out—and being thrown out was more frightening to him than jumping alone. What frightened him most, though, was failing. When he was in the battle suit on NP8261, he had reacted on instinct, but there was plenty of fear. The fear had been almost tangible: fear of getting hurt, fear of getting in trouble for getting into the battle suit, fear that he might be too late to help someone. He had thought that he was able to set that fear aside and do what needed to be done, but after his interactions with the INC-compatible devices, he knew that he would have to master his fear in a way he'd never imagined before. If jumping from the transport would help, he would do it.

"Good man," Grossman said. There was a look on his face that would almost pass for surprise, but Alex couldn't be sure—the master sergeant's scars made it impossible.

"What do I need to know?" Alex asked.

"Nothing," Grossman said. "The chute will do everything."

"No buttons or controls?"

"Not a thing," Grossman said. "Just jump and try to control your mind."

Alex looked out the door. His heart was crashing so hard in his chest that he thought he might have a heart attack and die. Below, the red desert of Helena Prime awaited. Alex closed his eyes and then flung himself forward.

Wind screamed around him. He could feel his body flipping and turning. In his mind, his voice was screaming that he had made a mistake and that he was going to die. But Alex kept his eyes and mouth closed. Breathing in was easy, breathing out was hard. He focused on that one thing: breathing. The air began to pass through the harness he was wearing, and somehow he stopped tumbling. He was still falling, but the auto-chute was designed to control the fall. He opened his eyes and saw the ground far below. There was nothing but ground in every direction—so much hard, unforgiving ground, just waiting to pulverize him.

Alex needed to pee so badly that it took all his strength to hold it in. His stomach was in knots, his arms and legs were shaking uncontrollably, and he felt woozy, as if he might faint. But he also remembered Tito's chute opening. It gave him hope. He told himself that the auto-chute had corrected his tumble and was keeping him in the right position, but the ground seemed to be rushing up toward him too fast, and he felt like he had been falling for too long. Something was wrong—he was sure of it. He was going to die, and he didn't want to die. He wanted to live. He wanted to leave Helena Prime and go back to NP8261. He missed the dingy little apartment he had lived in with his parents. Tears stung his eyes, but the wind wiped them away so fast they felt like cotton balls. He shut his eyes and tried to breathe.

A pop sounded behind him. Alex turned his head, instinctively looking to see what had made the noise, but he couldn't see anything. A ruffling sound followed the pop, and then suddenly a pressure squeezed Alex so hard he thought he was dying. But after a second the pressure disappeared, the howling wind stopped, and Alex could feel his body weight pressing into the harness of the auto-chute. He looked down and discovered that he was still incredibly high, and then he looked up and saw a white parachute against a cobalt-blue sky. He felt a sudden surge of relief; he was still alive. The chute had worked, just as Master Grossman said it would.

It took a few minutes to reach the ground. Just before he landed, the auto-chute flared and he landed on his feet, took a few shaky steps, then fell to his knees. He was on the ground, on the red dirt of the planet, and he'd never been so thankful before in his life. He rolled over and looked up, but he couldn't see Sev. The transport was still there, still circling. It seemed as if hours of unrelenting terror had passed while Alex fell, and it didn't make sense that she hadn't followed.

"Man, that was a trip," Tito said.

He came walking over and looked down at Alex. "The old freak tossed you out too, huh?"

"No," Alex said. "I jumped."

"Liar," Tito said.

There was a look on his face—an expression somewhere between disbelief and anger. Alex sat up and got to his feet. His legs were still trembling and his hands were shaking, but every second on the ground felt good, and he was regaining his confidence.

"I'm not lying."

"Whatever," Tito said.

He turned away, and Alex didn't pursue it. Instead, he looked up. A figure was falling, but it was nothing more than a speck of darkness against the blue sky. There was nothing to do but wait. After a few seconds, Alex saw the chute open. His own fall had seemed much longer, but he knew if the chutes were automated, then surely they all opened at around the same altitude. Was it possible that his own experience was colored by his mind? Had fear influenced his thoughts, even his perceptions of the fall?

Alex looked up again. There was something wrong with Sev. It wasn't her chute, thankfully, but her body looked wrong. Alex shaded his eyes and watched. It quickly became clear that it wasn't Sev dropping through the air toward them. It was Master Sergeant Grossman. He was coming down toward Alex and Tito.

Alex watched as the chute flared and Master Sergeant Grossman landed. Despite only having one leg, he stayed on his feet.

"Take those auto-chutes off," he grumbled. "We've got a long hike ahead of us."

"Where's Sev?" Alex asked.

"She refused to jump this time," Grossman said. "Gather up the parachutes too—just fold them however you can. We'll carry them back to Sparta."

"What do you mean she refused?" Tito said angrily. "Why didn't you throw her out?"

"She wasn't ready," Grossman said.

"None of us were ready, you old—"

Grossman moved with speed and purpose, getting right in Tito's face.

"Go ahead, say it," Grossman said. "Tell me I'm a freak, a cripple, a one-armed bastard if you want to. But know this, rookie: I may only be half a man, but I can still turn you into a pretzel and not even break a sweat. You hear me?"

Tito's face was as white as it had been on the transport.

"Yeah, sure," he muttered.

Grossman grabbed Tito's fatigues and shoved him backward. Tito nearly fell, but Alex grabbed hold of his arm. Tito looked at him, grimaced, then pulled away in a huff.

"The correct response is, 'yes, Master Sergeant,'" Grossman said. "Just keep in mind: the harder you resist, the more difficult your life is going to become. Let's move."

Grossman pulled his chute up, bunching it together. Alex did the same. Tito kept his distance from both of them. Once they had their parachutes gathered together, they started walking. Sparta was visible in the distance—a shimmering green smudge with sunlight reflecting off the windows of the taller buildings. Alex had expected it to be hotter in the desert, but it was chilly. The sun felt good on his shoulders as they walk across the barren landscape, each step sending up puffs of red dust that clung to their fatigues and boots.

After a while, Alex drew closer to Master Sergeant Grossman. The man had a prosthetic leg, yet he walked faster than Alex did. For several minutes Alex debated asking the question that was on his mind, but eventually he decided that it was just a question and there was nothing right or wrong about it. How Grossman perceived it was completely out of Alex's control. He didn't want to get barked at by asking an annoying question, but Alex figured that he was in training for a reason. Master Sergeant Grossman was a teacher of sorts, and Alex needed to know what happened to Sev.

"Master Sergeant?" Alex asked.

"She quit, Evans," Grossman said, matter-of-factly. "I was wondering if you were ever going to ask."

"I don't understand," Alex replied.

"Look, the CDF can't use people who don't want to be here," Grossman said. "They're not going to put a reluctant operator into a million-credit battle suit and hope for the best."

"What'll happen to her?"

"She's contracted for six years, just like you and every other recruit that comes through. Those that don't pass basic get assigned to jobs that no one else wants, like janitorial services or orderly duties in the med clinic."

"She just quit?" Alex said, a sense of horror at the very thought of it welling up inside.

"Just like that," Grossman said. "Gave up her career and walked away."

"How?" Alex asked. "How could she?"

"Not everyone's cut out for this life," Grossman explained. "She couldn't face her fears. The question you ought to be asking yourself is, how come you can? There's strength in being able to do something when other people turn away. Controlling your mind is the first step, Evans. You keep it up and you'll make a good operator one of these days."

"What about Tito?"

"What about him?" Grossman said.

"Will he make it?"

"If he changes his attitude, maybe," the master sergeant said thoughtfully. "But you can't hang on to these other recruits, Evans. They may be your friends, but they have to be able to do the work—otherwise we're putting one another in danger. When you're in battle, you'll lose people, maybe even right in front of you. And you have to be able to step over their broken, twisted bodies, and continue on."

Alex fell silent. It was a difficult reality to face—in some ways even worse than jumping from the transport. Alex had always been a team player, and the idea of leaving people behind was difficult to think about. He hadn't considered what it would be like to lose someone in action. Even realizing that Sev was no longer in the program, that she had willingly walked away, bothered him. He wanted to go and convince her that she could do it, but that wasn't his place. Not to mention he had no idea where she was.

They walked in silence for a long time before a ground transport finally came and picked them up just before dark. By the time Alex got back to the campus, he was tired, hungry, and thinking completely differently about what it meant to be an operator in the CDF. Growing up, all he had ever thought about was the adventure. Even up until that day, he had still considered it some type of game, even though he had pulled an operator from a downed battle suit on NP8261 and knew that his actions had saved the man's life.

He was quiet through dinner, which suited Tito. Alex could feel the anger coming off the man in waves. Alex barely tasted his food. It fueled him, and nothing more. He even left without getting dessert and returned to his room. It was empty, fortunately for Alex. He didn't want to be around people. Everything in his life suddenly felt temporary and unstable. He did his best to control his thinking and change his thoughts, but the lessons of the day had left their mark. He had stepped out of his childhood and into a frightening world with very real consequences. The only thing he could do was continue pushing himself to succeed and hope that when the time came, he would do something to help those around him. He fell asleep that night pondering his own mortality. He knew that he wouldn't live forever and that his work in the CDF might take a toll that was greater than he wanted to pay. But he also knew that it was important work that impacted the lives of others, so he was determined to make each day count.

Chapter 26

"You're sure?" Loman asked.

The hologram he was speaking to showed a man half in shadows. It was an intimidating image. Only his eyes were clear, like stars peeping through a bank of clouds.

"There is a money trail," the man said.

"Anything else?" Loman asked.

"They covered their tracks well. We had to tap into the municipal security feeds to get evidence of them meeting. Someone is funding them—someone with deep pockets."

"How deep?"

"Changing a person's identity in the galactic database is outrageously expensive," the shadowy figure said, "but it can be done. I've sent you proof, what little there is. And we will keep digging. If you're right and the sabotage is linked to the attacks on company property, odds are good that the money will show us who's behind it all."

"All right, keep digging. This should be enough to buy us some time, at any rate."

"I'll be in touch."

The hologram vanished, and Loman sat back in his chair. The meeting with the board of directors was in less than five minutes, but he had to give the information he'd just received from his chief investigator time to upload to his PIL.

He looked at the information on the People for Reclamation of Planetary Rights. There wasn't a lot known about the group, other than that it was listed as a terrorist organization because they had taken credit for instigating civil unrest on some of the old worlds. According to Loman's investigator, the group had upped their game from protests to criminal destruction of property. There had been no charges filed yet, but the group, which was scattered across a dozen worlds, was being closely watched.

Loman knew there were people who felt that corporations had too much power. It was liberal propaganda, but in every large organization there was bound to be some corruption. Some people protested Ahzco's use of company stores on their privately owned planets. But business demanded some sacrifices. If Ahzco couldn't keep labor costs down on level-three planets, the workers wouldn't have what they needed to live, and the company wouldn't be able to produce affordable products. Most of the planets on which the company controlled everything were closely guarded secrets. Opening the planets to free trade would also open them up to attacks by rival businesses—not to mention that many of the planets had only a single colony. It wasn't feasible for other commercial enterprises to ship goods all the way to a planet with just a single town.

Of course, business ethics wasn't really Loman's concern. His task was keeping company employees and assets safe. Lately, that job was becoming increasingly difficult, perhaps because whoever was behind the attacks was willing to bring such vast resources to bear. Loman could only hope they could uncover the source of the funds and do something to cut off the supply. Business rivals were one thing, but political zealots were another thing entirely.

His PIL beeped, indicating the file download was complete. Loman snatched the device from the dock on his desk and headed out of his office. He hadn't slept in over twenty-four hours. His focus was entirely on finding answers for the board, and they had managed to get a few. It would be enough to keep his job a little longer, he hoped.

The BOD met in a private room, deep underground. The executive lift was the only way down to the secret level, which wasn't marked on the other lifts or on the building directory. It was a lavishly decorated meeting space. The lift doors opened to a large gathering room with a full bar and dark, paneled walls of exotic wood. Leather, brass, chrome, and ivory covered every surface. It was spotlessly clean, although the janitors were only allowed in under armed guard. The rooms were swept for listening devices and hidden cameras before every meeting. Every member of the board was already present when Loman stepped in from the elevator. He immediately handed his PIL over to one of the security technicians to have it scanned.

"About time," Walt Grummons said from a wingback chair covered in calfskin. The dark-complexioned man in a dark business suit was hard to make out in the dim lighting.

"But worth the wait," Loman shot back at his rival.

Grummons was the VP in charge of logistics. His division moved company products, including employees, from planet to planet as needed. He was a stickler for punctuality and delighted in pointing out anyone who showed up late for any meeting he was involved in.

"If we're ready then," Ian Gentry said, with a nervous tremor in his voice.

Loman gave his boss a reassuring nod and picked up his PIL from the security tech. Everyone moved from the opulent lounge to the board room. It was a rectangular room with a long table in the center. A holographic projector hung from the ceiling at one end. The walls were thick and covered with acoustic tiles. The door sealed so tight that a person standing right outside wouldn't be able to hear someone inside even if they were shouting through a bullhorn.

The group settled quickly, and Loman glanced at the chairwoman. Lynn Faulk was thin with a hooked nose and small eyes. She wore no makeup yet had flawless skin without a single wrinkle, despite the fact that she was nearly seventy years old.

"There is only one topic we need to discuss," she said. "I assume you have something for us, Mr. Haley."

"I do," Loman said, standing up and pressing a button on his PIL. The holographic projector powered on and a woman's face appeared. "This is, or was, Gloria Ullory. She was a member of the PRPR movement."

"The what?" Ian Gentry asked.

"People for the Reclamation of Planetary Rights," Loman continued.

"What's that, some kind of cult?" asked one of the scary six.

"A political group with a presence on several of the old worlds," Loman continued. "They're classified as a terrorist organization, but until recently they had no direct ties to violence."

"And now?" Lynn Faulk asked.

"She was found dead on the freighter with supplies and passengers going to our new property in the Creedence system," Loman explained. "The bomb she placed on board malfunctioned, fortunately for us. She got rid of most of the evidence, then removed her helmet in hard vacuum. I have holo-video, if anyone would like to see it."

"That won't be necessary," Faulk said. "Can you tell us why this group has targeted our company?"

"The easy answer is because they believe that all worlds should be free property and available to settlers," Loman said. "But ultimately, I believe they were paid to target our ships."

"Paid by who?" Faulk asked.

"We're still running that down," Loman admitted. "Just finding out who Ms. Ullman was has been difficult. Her information in the network was forged."

"That's impossible," Ashley Van Zant, VP of Ahzco's network technology division, insisted.

"Nothing is impossible," Loman shot back. "Not if you have enough money."

"And this terrorist group has that kind of money?" Lynn Faulk asked.

"We know they paid to have her identity changed in the Galactic Network," Loman said. "It was good enough to pass our security checks. They also managed to get her name on the manifest until she got on board, and then it was erased. We're looking into whoever did the hacking, but so far they've left no traces."

"Don't go pointing fingers," Ashley Van Zant said angrily. "Our job is to maintain the network. Your people are supposed to make certain it's secure."

"I'm not blaming anyone," Loman said. "I take full responsibility for the breech."

Ashley looked relieved, but Lynn Faulk did not.

"A breech is unacceptable," she said.

"I agree," Loman said. "Which is why we're doing a thorough search for the culprit. We will find them. I have my best team of infiltrators working on it as we speak. We're also looking to find where the money came from. The PRPR isn't a popular group. They don't rub elbows with the rich and famous. In fact, they keep a very low profile. The only information about them online comes from news reports about investigations into their activities."

"So who is funding them?" Faulk said.

"I can only speculate at this point, although I'm hopeful that we'll get hard evidence soon. My best guess is going to be a rival—someone with resources they don't mind wasting."

"Wasting?" Faulk asked.

"They're spending big on the attacks," Loman said. "But they're all on low-value targets. It's not a sound business strategy."

"But effective nonetheless," Faulk said. "The company can't continue to cover the losses that should have been avoided had the security division been doing their job. Perhaps it's time for a change in leadership."

"You could do that, but while a new VP is getting up to speed, whoever is behind this will have the perfect opportunity to hit us again. Give me time to solve this puzzle, then if you want my job I'll give it to you, no questions asked."

"How much time?" Faulk said.

"A week," Loman said, as sweat ran down his back. He had no idea if a week was enough time, but he didn't want to look weak. Any longer than a week might send the message that he really didn't have any idea who was attacking them. It might be true, but he wanted to make the board believe he was close to a breakthrough. He could always point the finger at someone else the next time the board gathered, whether it was true or not.

Lynn Faulk studied him. Her small eyes were dark and penetrating. They made him feel like a child who'd been caught cheating on a test. But Loman kept a straight face. He didn't fidget or squirm, and fortunately he wasn't sweating too much yet.

"All right," Faulk said. "A week. But this board needs answers, Mr. Haley, not conjecture. Hard evidence and a plan of action. We won't sit idly by while someone tries to hurt us."

"I understand," Loman replied. "Thank you, madam chairwoman. I won't let you down."

"In the meantime, we continue working, but I want all shipments held until further notice," Faulk continued. "Security on every planet and station should be on high alert. And I want a full, independent audit of the company network."

"Is that really necessary?" Ashley Van Zant asked.

"Holding shipments could be costly," Walt Grummons added.

"Better a late shipment than no shipment at all," Faulk replied. "I want every vessel searched for explosives, and yes, Ms. Van Zant, an independent audit is absolutely necessary. I'll send along a representative I trust to handle the job. In the meantime, let's all check our employee records. If someone inside the company is taking part in these heinous acts, we need to know. Failure is not an option, people. Am I making myself clear?"

"Yes, Ms. Faulk," Ian Gentry said. "Abundantly clear."

"Excellent," she said, with just the hint of a smile.

Loman thought the smile made her face look more skeletal than ever.

Chapter 27

For three days, Master Sergeant Grossman had put Alex through harrowing ordeals. In each instance, he'd insisted that Alex and Tito were safe, but on the fourth day, things went wrong. Alex and Tito were placed in a water tank, each with a bucket. Their instructions were simple: once the tank filled with water, they could hold the buckets over their head with enough air to breathe until the tank drained. They were strapped with monitors to show their heart rate and oxygen levels in their blood. Each of them had the INC synced to a device that would record the desire to ring a bell that would immediately evacuate the water.

It was a simple exercise until the tank began to fill with water. The water come gushing in, frigidly cold. Alex had never swum—in fact he'd never been in so much water before in his entire life. NP8261 had no liquid water on the surface. It had to be pumped in from underground and then put through a rigorous purifying process to ensure that the mining operations didn't pollute the aquifer. The colonists were limited to only a small volume of water for bathing, so when the cold water gushed into the tank it took Alex's breath away.

But it wasn't the temperature of the water or his fear that most troubled Alex; it was Tito's attitude. The cocky recruit had begun to lose control of his grasp on reality. For two days, he'd been hinting that Master Sergeant Grossman was trying to kill him. The steady degradation of his only friend's mental state wore on Alex. It was impossible not to worry about Tito, and the young man's ranting fed Alex's own doubts. The only thing that kept him sane was practicing the mental discipline that Master Sergeant Grossman had taught them. Alex forced himself to think about the other activities that had seemed dangerous but had been proven safe. There was no rational reason to believe that the water tank would be any different, but Tito was convinced they were both going to drown.

Alex was reeling from the cold and the surging motion of the water. When he pulled the bucket over his head, he was in almost complete darkness. The bucket seemed small, and his breath was loud, but he forced himself to work through his mental process.

I'm safe, he thought over and over. *This is just a test.*

Time always seemed to slow down when Alex was exposed to danger. He had been wrapped in protective gear and set on fire. He'd had vicious animals set on him, only to have them called off at the last possible second when Alex was certain they were going to rip his throat out. He had even been hung upside-down by his ankles and over a bed of spikes. Each time, despite feeling like he had endured for hours, he learned afterward that it had only been a few minutes at most.

Every time Alex breathed in, the water level rose up to his chin. With each exhale, the water level went down, but the bucket became harder to hold onto.

Suddenly there was a thrashing near him, and Alex feared that some carnivorous fish had been set loose in the tank. He held onto the bucket and forced himself to believe he was safe. A loud squelching sound heralded the water's unexpected evacuation from the tank, but even before it had drained, rough hands grabbed Alex and heaved him out. The bucket fell away, and Alex saw people jumping into the tank.

Master Sergeant Grossman grabbed Alex and pulled him away, but not before Alex saw Tito lying on the bottom of the tank, his face and lips looking strangely blue.

"What's going on?" Alex asked.

"Just keep walking," Grossman said.

They went into a garage-type building and into a small room. Grossman gave Alex a towel.

"You want to tell me what the hell happened down there?"

"What?" Alex asked.

"In the tank, Evans. What happened?"

"I don't know," Alex said. "The water came in, and I put the bucket on my head like you told us."

"We have your brain response, so stop lying," Grossman snarled. "You and Barnes haven't gotten along since day one."

"What?"

"You had homicidal brain responses, and Barnes was fighting for his life."

"He was scared," Alex said, "but I didn't do anything to him."

"You didn't knock his bucket down and drown him?"

"What? No!" Alex shouted.

Before he could say more, the door burst open and two operators in MP patroller suits came in. Alex tried to move away, but there was nowhere to go. One of the operators stuck out a stun rod, and Alex felt the energy charge race through his body. Every muscle tensed, and then the world went dark.

When Alex woke up, his body was aching, his head was pounding, and his mouth tasted salty. His tongue was swollen and sore. He opened his eyes and found himself in a small detention cell lying on a metal bench. The dull gray, metal door to the cell had a small window with wire mesh.

"Hello?" he croaked.

There was no answer, though he could hear people outside the cell. Alex sat up, waited until the dizzy spell passed, and then got slowly to his feet. He was still wearing only his underwear, which was wet from the water tank. His skin felt raw and cold. Shivers made his body tremble as he looked out the small window.

"Hello?"

After a few seconds, a face appeared.

"Just sit on the bench and wait," the person said.

"What? Why? Why am I here? What's going on?"

Alex tried to see where the man had gone, but he couldn't get the angle right. He called for help several more times, but no one answered. He finally collapsed back on the bench. It was impossible to tell how much time had passed. Alex felt sick. He was freezing cold, scared, and had bitten his tongue when the operator shocked him with the stun rod.

It was obvious that he was in a jail cell of some sort. He guessed the absence of toilet facilities made it a temporary holding room, but the feeling of helplessness was so strong it took all of his mental strength to release it and focus on what little truth he knew.

First, he hadn't done anything to Tito. He wasn't close to his fellow recruit, but they had spent considerable time together. There was no evidence that Alex had ill intent toward Tito, which made Alex wonder if the entire episode wasn't some sort of strange test. It made him angry to think that it might just be a test, but he could see the reason for it. Thinking about it as such didn't make him feel better, but it certainly kept him from spinning out in fear. He forced himself to sit—he was exhausted, but being in the detention cell made him restless. He calmed his mind and focused on the tiny spark of truth he knew with absolute certainty—that he didn't harm Tito—and waited to see what surprises lay ahead.

Chapter 28

"Would you look at that," Master Sergeant Grossman said. "I'll be honest. I've never had a recruit adapt as quickly as Evans. He's practicing the techniques right now. Give him six months and you can put him in any assignment you want—he'll be able to handle it."

Supervisor Cindy Purfoy looked at the computer that was still synced to Alex's INC. The program showed his brain activity and mapped his mental state. She expected him to be frantic, or at the very least angry. He had been falsely accused and stunned without cause, yet he was sitting calmly, waiting for answers.

"The VP will be happy," Purfoy said. "What's next?"

"Nothing," Grossman said. "The kid's good to go. I'd be proud to go to battle with him if they'd let me."

"So, you're recommending graduation?" Purfoy said. "He's only been here a week."

"You ever hear of anyone adapting to the INC that fast?"

"No," the supervisor admitted.

"Me either. I don't know, Soup, he just gets it. It's like he's anxious to learn, whereas most of the recruits that come through are just looking to prove themselves or earn a reward. They hear what we teach and repeat it, but it doesn't get past the knowledge stage and into experience —not this fast. We have to put them through the danger scenarios over and over."

"You're sure?"

"Absolutely," Master Sergeant Grossman said.

"Finish the scenario, and I'll process his file. I've got to send a report to Vice President Haley."

Purfoy got up and walked out of the room. She was glad Alex was doing well. Processing him through made her job easier, but she worried that she could be somehow letting the VP down. She didn't want to miss something about the rookie that would make him a liability.

She pulled up the reports and was struck once again by how perfect he seemed to be. She was a firm believer that when things seem too good to be true, they usually are. She couldn't help but wonder, with the recent attacks against the Ahzco corporation, that perhaps he was a spy. Was it possible, she wondered, that the attack on NP8261 was staged? If so, the VP had completely fallen for it. The question in her mind was whether she should share her concerns or not.

The process of moving him from recruit to private was not hard, but after punching in all the relevant data, she couldn't press the button to complete the work on his file. She needed to speak with him one more time.

She walked over to a monitor that was recording the interview room where Master Sergeant Grossman was completing the scenario. She pressed a button that activated the speaker on the small wall monitor. Alex was sagging in his seat and seemed emotional.

"I've been doing this a long time, Evans," Grossman said. "Tell me what you were thinking in that cell."

"Honestly?"

"You lie and I'll know it, rookie."

Purfoy scoffed. In her opinion, Grossman was such a typical military NCO. He was completely dependent on threats and bluster to make his recruits come clean. If Alex was lying, he was much more subtle than Grossman understood.

"I was focusing on the fact that I didn't hurt Tito," Alex said. "That's the truth, so I held onto it."

"How do I know you're not just telling me what I want to hear?" Grossman growled.

"You don't," Alex said. "But I'm guessing you still had me connected to the INC monitor."

Grossman nodded.

"So you saw what I was thinking," Alex said.

"Well, the technology is good, kid, but it can't read your mind."

Alex shrugged. "I did what you taught me. It helps. And I realized pretty quickly that I couldn't do anything else."

"Keep that in mind, rookie, and you'll go places," Grossman said. "Let me be the first to shake your hand and say welcome to the CDF."

He extended his hand to Alex, who looked skeptical at first. He glanced around, expecting the other shoe to drop. Grossman chuckled.

"No more tricks, kid. Supervisor Purfoy is processing you through basic right now."

Alex shook the master sergeant's hand. A bright smile lit his face. Purfoy stared hard, but she couldn't deny that it looked genuine.

"Really?" Alex said.

"You are officially Private Alex Evans," Grossman said.

Supervisor Cindy Purfoy looked at her PIL again. Alex's file was still up. She decided that she would process the promotion but keep herself on his case. Vice President

Haley might not approve, but she felt it was the prudent thing. She couldn't deny that she had her doubts regarding his loyalty. Listening to her gut was part of her job, and she was good at it.

She pressed the button, and the file was accepted. Opening the door, she found Grossman and Alex heading toward her down the hall.

"He's all yours, Soup," Grossman declared.

"Thank you, Master Sergeant."

"Good luck, Evans. I'll see you around."

"Yes, Master Sergeant," Alex said. "I'd like that."

Purfoy saw the hardened veteran stiffen a little. It was a tiny gesture, and she had no idea if Alex noticed it, but she was certain that Master Sergeant Grossman didn't have many people who enjoyed seeing him. The man was hideous to look at and a walking, talking reminder of just how dangerous being an operator was. She knew the story of his injuries, but it was his alone to tell. If Alex followed through, perhaps Grossman would choose to open up. The master sergeant walked from the room in his uneven gait without looking back.

"Congratulations," Purfoy said. "You're officially a private in the CDF. I just processed your file."

"Awesome," Alex said.

"There's a bonus for completing basic. A full month's pay will be added to your banking account by 0900 tomorrow morning."

"Really?" Alex asked.

"Of course. The company takes care of its own. Normally, we also give operators liberty for the weekend after they complete basic, but you're scheduled to begin training the day after tomorrow. So why don't we go get your new Personal Information Link, and you can have a night out on the town."

There was a look on Alex's face that seemed so genuine and earnest that she felt a little better about her decision to send him through to operator training.

"A new PIL?" Alex asked. "Can I write my parents?"

"Yes," Purfoy said, not bothering to tell him that all incoming and outgoing messages from the Helena system were being monitored. Perhaps, if he wasn't being honest, he might slip up and send whoever he was working for a message.

They made their way back to the intake center. She opened a drawer at her desk and pulled out a new, state-of-the-art PIL. Ahzco manufactured their own line of personal data devices, including a military-grade Flex PIL. It was still in the box, and Alex took it eagerly. She remembered the secondhand clothes he'd arrived in. Threadbare in places, too small, and woefully outdated. His PIL had been on the verge of obsolete. She could only imagine what he must think of the new one.

"Do you need help setting it up?" Purfoy asked.

"No, I'll do it," he said, grinning like a child at Christmas.

She picked up his ID badge and scanned it to make sure his promotion had gone through. It was up to date and even showed his liberty the following day.

"You'll need this to get back onto campus," she told him, holding out the ID card with his picture on it. "It's also your link to your bank account, so don't lose it."

"If I want to buy something, I can use this?"

"Yes, although I don't recommend that you make a lot of purchases," Purfoy said. "That money in your account has to last you all month. And you sent some of it your family, didn't you?"

Alex nodded, his eyes flashing with pride. She had to admit if he was a spy, he was a world-class thespian.

"You know there's not much room in your quarters, so be careful."

"Yes, ma'am," he said.

"I'll send instructions to your account for your training," she said. "And if you have trouble getting your PIL set up, come and see me. I'll be here tomorrow most of the day."

"Thank you," Alex said.

"Just doing my job, roo...I mean Private Evans."

The look on his face was pure joy. She hoped that he was as sincere as he seemed—otherwise they were all in trouble.

Chapter 29

Alex could hardly believe his good fortune. Things were going better than he could have dreamed. His basic training was over, his parents would actually get some money from him the following day, and he had a brand-new PIL. He left the intake center and stopped at the cafeteria for dinner. He ate ravenously and joyfully—until he saw Sev and Tito enter the dining hall together. It was a shock that quickly turned to humor as they settled in across the table with him.

"So I hear congratulations are in order?" Sev said.

"What are you two doing here?" Alex said.

"Having dinner," Tito said. "Why?"

"I thought you were dead," Alex admitted.

His friends burst out laughing, and while he felt chagrined, Alex couldn't help but join in.

"We're in the infiltrator program," Sev finally managed to say. "You were our first assignment."

"Our primary goal was to get to know you and make sure you weren't crazy," Tito said.

"Or a spy," Sev added.

"I wrote you a glowing report, by the way," Tito said.

"So...all that stuff about Master Sergeant Grossman wanting to kill you?" Alex said.

"All part of my role," Tito said with theatrical flair. "The talented young recruit slowly going insane."

"They do it to everyone," Sev said. "Don't take it personally."

"I don't know what's real and what isn't," Alex admitted.

"The mind games are pretty intense during basic," Tito said. "They have to be sure you'll pan out, especially in your division. There are a lot of high-tech secrets in the battle suits."

"So you didn't quit?" Alex said to Sev, then turned to Tito. "And you're not crazy?"

"Oh, he's crazy," Sev said.

"Like a fox," Tito replied.

"You made it through though!" Sev said. "Everyone's talking about it."

"About what?" Alex said.

"You don't know?" Tito replied. "Man, you got through basic in record time. Everyone's sayin' you're going to be some kind of ace in a battle suit."

"Yeah, keep it up and you'll be running this place one of these days," Sev said.

Alex stayed with his friends until they finished eating, although he was anxious to open his new PIL and get it all set up. Still, after feeling so alone on the base, it was good to have friends. Sev was much more talkative than she'd been while playing her role as the cool, calm, confident recruit. She and Tito were being groomed for work outside the company. Alex didn't know a lot about infiltrators. There were stories of course; spies were a popular fictional subject. And they had taught Alex a good lesson: not everything was as it seemed.

When they finished dinner, he hurried back to the barracks. He was alone in his room, as usual. Sitting on the bunk, he opened his new Personal Information Link. His first impression was that the device was very thin. It looked like a sheet of plastic, but when he ran a finger down the edge, the device lit up. Unlike a consumer model, the Flex PIL required Alex's company ID info. The home screen was where all the links to Ahzco's secure online entities were stored. There was plenty of storage on the device for other things too, like movies, games, books, and music. The home screen also had a link to his current status. It was a CDF app that showed where he was stationed, what his rank and division were, and other vitals for company records. Everything from blood type to DNA was kept by the CDF, and he had overview access to his own files.

There were company-specific apps, as well. Ahzco had divisions in various industries. Transportation, healthcare, entertainment, and education apps could link him to other sites where his employment earned him a discount. If he needed to get transportation to another planet, he could book it with companies that used Ahzco-manufactured vehicles and gave their employees special rates. If he was on assignment somewhere, he could look up what businesses and services had deals for Ahzco employees. But the most interesting apps to Alex were the banking and employee directory apps.

Messaging applications were numerous, and all charged nominal fees to users. Messages between worlds were the most expensive and oftentimes took the longest to go through. But Ahzco had a private messaging service for employees and their families. Alex opened the app, set up his account, and immediately searched for his father. Bruce Evans was listed as a senior mechanic on Skandia Seven. Alex immediately sent his parents a message. There were no fees for messages between employees, not even between star systems.

Alex also found Supervisor Cindy Purfoy on Helena Prime. He sent her a brief message as well, letting her know he had the PIL up and working. Finally, he sent a thank you to Vice President Loman Haley. Alex didn't really expect the senior executive to read it, but Alex had been taught that appreciation was something to value. Alex knew that he wouldn't be a private in the CDF, operating a brand-new Flex PIL, if the VP hadn't made an exception to get him into the program.

Once his correspondence was done, Alex checked the banking app. It took time to set up his secure profile and gain access to his account, but when he did, he saw a deposit waiting to be posted. The number was surprising: just over eight thousand standard credits. It was real money —not like the company credits that his parents had earned on NP8261—and it was more than he'd ever had before. A little over two thousand would be sent to his family, and almost a thousand more would be put into an investment account for his retirement—not that Alex could even contemplate leaving the CDF. His experience so far had been shocking, but also incredibly exciting. He was anxious to see what operator training was like and where his first posting would be.

He lay back on his bunk, relishing his good fortune. For the first time in his life he had money and a future, and everything he could hope for was within his grasp. It was such a shocking change from his dreary life on the Rock. It had only been a little over a week, but already his old life seemed like a dream.

Alex spent the entire next day exploring Sparta. It was a real town filled with businesses, restaurants, holo-theaters, virtual reality excursions, bars, and sports complexes. The Spartan Linx was a golf course at the edge of town. Alex didn't play—he'd never even picked up a golf club or tried to hit the small, glowing balls—but he walked along a raised concourse and admired the brilliant greens of the manicured fairways surrounded by the harsh red and browns of the planet's native desert.

Most of the businesses catered to CDF personnel passing through the town. There were plenty of specialty stores. Alex talked to more than one proprietor and learned that they had special licenses to sell and own retail establishments on Helena Prime. There were other cities around the planet, as well. Athens was the largest and home to the CDF's research, development, and testing division. Most of the personnel based there were senior scientists and engineers—wealthy individuals with families. Corinth was the training center for the technicians needed specifically by the CDF, and Thebes was home to Ahzco's sprawling munitions-manufacturing facilities.

Alex ate pizza for lunch and made notes on his Flex PIL of all things he wanted to try while he was in Sparta, but for the most part, as his father would say, he simply walked and gawked. He made two purchases other than food. The first was a new set of clothes. His fatigues were better than anything he'd ever owned before, yet he wanted something to wear that he felt really reflected his personality. There were several stores that sold clothing, and he saw a lot of options that he liked, but he eventually settled on real denim blue jeans and a tee-shirt with the KIX Beats logo. The look was vintage, but classic. His second purchase was more expensive: a leather aviator's jacket lined with sheep wool. It was heavy and warm. It made him feel good not just because of the way it looked, but because it was thick and expensive.

When he got back to the barracks that evening, he realized that he'd just had the best day of his life but had had no one to share it with. Still, he couldn't help but believe that finding someone to connect with was inevitable. It wasn't until he lay down that night that he remembered it was his birthday.

Chapter 30

Loman Haley took a private transport across town. He wanted to be far away from any prying eyes when he met with Ciara Prince. She had proven herself to be his best investigator, and if she had the information he needed, he planned to promote her.

The Raven was an antique bookstore where old-fashioned paper books could be bought or sold. It was also a hangout for book lovers and writers who loved to talk about stories, publishing, and famous writers of the past. The Raven sold strong coffee and had several sitting areas where people gathered and talked in hushed tones while others read and sipped coffee for hours at a time.

Loman wasn't a fan, but he appreciated the private nature of the establishment. There were no cameras in the The Raven, and the proprietor was sympathetic to Loman's needs. He knew his customers and could spot a lurker almost as soon as they walked through the door. The Raven was not the type of place where customers wandered in to browse; the books were all kept in shelves with security panels, and the cheapest book in the store—a tattered copy of an indie book called *Wizard Rising*—was over fifty-thousand standard credits. The customers were eccentric and private, which fit Loman's needs perfectly. He sometimes helped the proprietor ensure that a particular book being considered for purchase wasn't stolen. Loman had even invested in a book or two over the years. His collection included Robert Louis Stevenson's *Kidnapped* and a copy of Edgar Rice Burrow's *Jungle Tales of Tarzan*. They were both hardbacks, several times restored, and neither a first edition. Still, he had paid handsomely for both, which were kept in airtight display boxes. In Loman's mind, they were safe investments. The market for paper books was small, but the books would never go down in value and few people understood what they were worth. In a pinch, he could sell them and have enough credits to leave Arcadia and start a new life somewhere else.

He walked through the door and was pleased to see the store practically empty. The proprietor nodded from behind a long counter where he was reading one of the old books with white gloves on his hands. He carefully turned a page and returned his whole attention to the story. Loman went to the coffee bar, which was managed by an android that was older than some of the books. It was built to look like a human but failed miserably.

"May I help you?" the android said.

"Drip coffee, if you've got it," Loman said.

"Of course," the android said.

It slid along a track behind the bar. The robot had no legs—just a power base below the bar, so that a person would have to lean over and look down to see it. Loman did just that. The coffee bar was the one place a person could hide in The Raven, and Loman didn't want any surprises.

The android came back with a disposable cup of steaming coffee. Loman didn't really want the drink, but he wanted something to do with his hands.

"Cream? Sugar? We have over fifty flavors of—"

"No, thanks," Loman said. "Black's fine."

He waved his Ahzco ID over the payment reader. It chimed, and he slipped it back into his pocket. He was taking the coffee from the android when Ciara Prince arrived. Loman didn't hear her come in or even notice as she moved up silently behind him, but when he turned, she was there. Her dark hair was pulled tight across her head and tucked into the back of her bulky jacket. She had dark skin and soft features. Loman knew she could make herself either beautiful or completely forgettable, depending on what the occasion called for.

"Let's sit down," Loman said quietly. "You want coffee?"

Ciara shook her head. Loman led the way over to a cluster of overstuffed chairs. He sat in the corner with a clear view of the empty store. Ciara Prince sat beside him, and they leaned toward each other, not like lovers, but more like co-conspirators.

"The money trail's cold," Ciara said. "It was passed through several delivery services and currency exchanges. I traced it back to Oldman's, but all the big companies and most of the smaller ones have accounts there."

"So we're back to square one," Loman said. Refraining from pounding the arm of the chair he sat in. Instead, he turned the cup of coffee around and around in his hands.

"Not exactly," Ciara said. "I did some digging. The payments were sent by courier, through a small boutique firm that specializes in secure transfers. I've got an agent working one of the couriers as we speak."

"For what?" Loman asked. "They take a sealed package from one bank to another. They won't know anything."

"We know the trail they're using," Ciara said. "Whoever's behind the money probably won't switch that up. We'll know when the next payment goes out, where it goes, and who picks it up."

"Then we pick *them* up," Loman said.

"They may not know who the money's from," Ciara said, "but we'll know what they want."

It wasn't perfect, but it was a start.

"Who knows?" Ciara said. "Maybe we'll get lucky."

Loman didn't like counting on luck, but he only had four days left to find something for the board of directors. He needed tangible evidence.

"In other news, Zen Corp is denying any part in the raid on NP8261 or apex Perrin," Ciara said.

"That's not news," Loman said.

"But it is when it comes from the inside," Ciara continued. "Word is that sales of the disruptor drones have been stagnant. Whoever hit NP8261 did it using old tech."

"Something they had lying around," Loman said, raising his eyebrows. "Something they wouldn't miss."

"And that wouldn't easily be traced back to them," Ciara said. "The real question is: why hit NP8261 at all? Why Perrin? Neither affect our business."

"You think we aren't already considering that?" Loman asked.

"Of course you are," Ciara said. "But sometimes you can't see what's right in front of you when you've been looking so hard."

"Okay," Loman said. "What am I missing?"

"I don't know," Ciara said. "But if I were investigating, I'd look at what decisions you've made in response to those attacks."

Loman didn't respond. He sat still for a moment, contemplating what he'd done. After the attack on Perrin he'd sent a security team in, but it would take months to clean the air and water from the dirty bombs. No work could go on there, maybe for years.

In response to the attack on NP8261 he'd broken protocol and sent Alex Evans to Helena Prime to become an operator. He had met Evans in person and spent time with him. There was no way in his mind that Alex was a spy, but he needed to know for sure.

"I've got to make a call," Loman said.

"I'll just go powder my nose," Ciara said with a wink.

She got up and walked away. Loman watched her go. He couldn't help but feel his paranoia returning. The one thing he hated about his job was the need for constant suspicion. Even Ciara could be a double agent. She might be leading him on a wild goose chase away from whoever was really behind the attacks. He didn't know who he could trust, and that was a bitter pill to swallow.

He pulled his PIL out of the inside pocket of his jacket and activated it. Then he brought up his contacts and pressed the connect button for the head of his technical services group. A few seconds later, a man's face appeared on the screen. There were smudges on his cheeks —dirt or grease or some other solvent used in whatever project he was working on.

"Mr. Haley," the man said. "What can I do for you?"

"Do we have the report on the disruptors that hit our mining colony on NP8261?"

"There wasn't much left to analyze," the man said, "but I'll check."

"Put a rush on it," Loman said. "And get me a preliminary report ASAP."

"Yes, sir. Anything we need to look for in particular?"

"Just anything out of the ordinary," Loman said. "It could be important."

"I'll do it right now, sir."

"Thanks, Randy," Loman said.

He ended the call and glanced at his messages. He had other meetings to get to, and he wasn't getting what he'd hoped to get from Ciara Prince. There had to be a way out of the fog of mystery he was stymied in, but he hadn't found it yet. He got to his feet, returned the full cup of coffee to the bar, and met Ciara coming out of the restroom.

"Finish up with that courier," he said in a whisper. "I want to know the minute you're onto something."

She nodded. He gave her shoulder a soft squeeze before heading for the door. His time was running out, and he had to face the fact that he might not survive the corporate culling that would inevitably result from the attacks...and it wasn't the first time that he wondered if perhaps that wasn't the point of it all, anyway.

Chapter 31

Alex walked down the line, looking at the battle suits. He felt almost giddy. Some were bulky, like the AT Destroyer and the AR Valkyrie. The MP Patroller was much smaller, little more than an old-fashioned suit of body armor. Then there was FA Titan, which was more of a vehicle than a battle suit. It looked like a robot, only bigger and bristling with weapons.

He'd been allowed into training bay 5, home of Echo Company, before the other recruits had arrived for the day. Sleep had been sporadic, his excitement too high for him to rest well. Finally, after tossing and turning most of the night, he'd gotten up, dressed in his fatigues, and followed the directions that Supervisor Purfoy had sent to his Flex PIL. He was to meet his new training officer and join Echo Company. They were already a week ahead of him, but Purfoy's message assured him he would catch up quickly.

The door opened, and Alex walked around the Titan to see who was in the cavernous room. He was shocked to see a familiar face. He came to attention and saluted, waiting for his new training officer to acknowledge him.

"At ease, Private."

Alex relaxed but couldn't stop grinning.

"It's good to see you again," Chief McKinna said.

"You too, Chief," Alex said. "Really good."

"So, you made it through basic training," McKinna said. "And now you're joining us. I have to tell you, Alex. There may be some people who don't like that."

"Really?" Alex asked.

"You're the hotshot newcomer, and this is a competitive division," McKinna explained. "You'll take the day to familiarize yourself with the mechanized battle suits and meet your controller. Then you join the rest of the squad. It won't be easy, and I can't make allowances for you. It wouldn't help your standing with the rest of the squad if I did."

"I understand, sir. I'll do everything I can to make you proud."

"I'm sure you will," McKinna said. "Master Sergeant Gellar is going to give you the tour. She's knows her stuff, so pay attention. Tomorrow you get thrown to the wolves, and if you aren't prepared, they'll eat you alive. Accidents happen in operator training, Evans. Get your mind ready, and the body will follow suit. You read me?"

"Yes, sir," Alex said.

"Very good. I'll see you tomorrow," McKinna said.

Alex saluted, and McKinna waved a hand in front of his face before walking away. Alex watched him go. The chief was everything Alex wanted to be. McKinna could walk confidently into any situation—at least Alex imagined that he could. The man had wavy hair that was perfectly styled and a square jaw that looked just as good with a week's stubble as it did clean-shaven. His eyes were bright, his shoulders broad, and his self-assurance seemed unshakable. Meanwhile, Alex felt incredibly insecure. He had graduated from basic training, but that didn't mean he would make a good operator. The weight of the responsibility about to be placed on his shoulders felt overwhelming, and the fact that his squad mates might not want him was a devastating blow that was hard to come back from.

"So, you're the new ace," a woman's voice echoed through the room.

Alex looked up and saw a short woman with black hair, pale skin, and dark eyes. They seemed to bore right through him. She wore a long-sleeved, tight-fitting compression shirt and sweatpants. There were three chevrons and one rocker printed on the upper sleeve of her shirt, and just under her left collar bone was the name "Gellar." Once again, Alex stiffened into a salute.

"As you were, private. This is the CDF—we don't snap to attention every time a superior walks by," Gellar said. "It's time to get you suited up. We don't wear fatigues in our battle suits. Compression gear gives us a more tactile feel for the gear we're driving."

She showed him to a row of lockers. The one on the end had his name written on a strip of tape. Inside were five sets of compression pants and long-sleeved compression shirts just like the one Gellar was wearing, only with a single chevron on the sleeves and his name stenciled on the chest.

"Get dressed, then join me at the AT Destroyer," she ordered him.

"Yes, Master Sergeant," Alex replied.

When he returned, dressed in the tight-fitting garments, the Destroyer was open. The battle suit was in many ways a traditional mech. The upper portion looked like a human, only larger. The arms were like multi-tools, only instead of screwdrivers and Allen wrenches, the tools were various weapons that could be rotated into service as needed. There was a shoulder-mounted laser, and the lower portion of the suit was interchangeable depending on the need. The most common lower portion was a dual set of triangular tank treads, but there were also articulated spider legs that could climb steep mountains or even crawl up vertical buildings, wheels for hard ground, and others for swampy environments.

"First things first," Gellar said. "Get in and connect your INC. It might take you a few moments to adjust, so just take your time."

"Yes, Master Sergeant," Alex said, trying to sound serious. Yet he couldn't keep an excited grin from his face as he climbed up the triangular treads to the control seat.

The Destroyer reminded Alex of a clam shell. It was split up the sides, and the two halves angled back from each other. Inside was a platform seat. He climbed down, inserting his legs into control stirrups on either side of the seat. Just like the MP Defender he'd operated on NP8261, the Destroyer had a red activation button.

"Go ahead and press the activator," Gellar told him, "and you should feel the EM link."

Alex pressed the button, and the battle suit came to life with a gentle hum. He felt the link in his mind; it was like hearing the buzz of a bumble bee. He opened himself to the sound and felt the familiar connection. The buzz transformed from a sound to a feeling to a low rumble of power. Suddenly he knew things about the Destroyer. It was in standby mode, which made him feel naked and exposed. He wanted to bring it fully online, but he forced himself to wait. He could sense that the weapons weren't armed and that the unit had no munitions—it was almost like hunger or the feeling of an empty backpack slung over one shoulder.

"All right, now listen to my voice," Gellar said. "You're going to hear me through the Destroyer's internal speakers once you bring it fully online. Are you ready?"

"Yes, Master Sergeant," Alex said with gusto.

"All right, engage all systems."

Alex didn't know what to do, but he visualized the battle suit closing up, and it did. The low rumble of power increased in volume, and Alex could actually feel a sense of pent-up energy waiting to be released.

There were no screens inside the Destroyer. Every spare millimeter was filled with safety devices, including a gel padding that was fastened down on his head like a helmet. At first, the suit felt tight and suffocating. His initial instinct was to order it to open again, but he focused his mind. *It's safe*, he thought, *it's safe. People work in these suits every day.*

The darkness that had swallowed Alex as the suit closed began to transition as the INC fed information into his mind. Even though the suit's helmet was entirely opaque, images started to appear in his mind like he was imagining them; he saw the hangar where the battle suits were lined up and Master Sergeant Gellar placing a headset on. After a few seconds, the details became clearer. He could see, and with every passing second he felt less like a man inside a suit of armor and more like the battle suit itself.

Power, communications, life support, navigation, and fire control were all things he suddenly just *knew* about the Destroyer. He didn't have to read the information; the data was downloaded into his brain, almost as if he could feel it. It was so instinctual that he didn't even think of them as systems; they were a part of him now, as natural as knowing when to rest or eat. It was involuntary information that his brain sorted automatically and only brought to his attention as needed.

"Can you hear me, Private?"

"Yes I can, Master Sergeant," Alex said.

Information about the communication system flashed through his mind. He had three channels: command, company, and the Destroyer's external public address system. Master Sergeant Gellar's voice had come through the tiny speakers built into the padding by his ears.

Can you hear me, Alex Evans?

The new voice was like hearing his own thoughts, but he knew he wasn't talking to himself. For a moment, his mind was confused. It nearly made him feel sick. The voice wasn't coming from the speakers—it was on the command channel of the unit's communication system, and it came from his INC. The words just appeared in his mind, much like the information about the Destroyer's systems and the way Alex was able to see.

"Yes, I hear you," Alex said. "Who is this?"

Controller Nyx West, on the CDF Capitalism. We're in orbit over you now.

"We met," Alex said. "In the admin offices."

That's right. I've been chosen to be your partner, Alex. I'll help you control the MBS as well as give you direct orders during deployment.

"Okay," Alex said.

"Evans," Master Sergeant Gellar said. "Are you ready to move out?"

"Yes, Master Sergeant," Alex said with another thrill. He was excited to see what the battle suit could do.

"All right, you're going to move outside the hangar," Gellar instructed.

Opening bay doors now, Nyx added inside Alex's head.

The doors began to open, and sunlight flooded through the hangar.

"There's a practice course out there. Just head out and wait at the designated position. Then we work through some simulated exercises so that you can get a feel for the Destroyer's capabilities."

"Roger that, Master Sergeant," Alex said.

He saw Gellar step back out of the way, and he willed the Destroyer forward. He could feel the treads like they were his own legs. The mech rolled forward, turned smoothly, and accelerated as he headed outside the hangar. The training course was part track, part combat field with large obstacles that could be used for cover.

Designating starting point.

The coordinates were transferred to his mind, but not as a series of numbers. He simply *knew* that he was supposed to roll out to the far end of the course and wait between two tall, faux buildings. He let the suit go, rolling full-speed across the training course, and it felt good. It was like he had a new body with new capabilities, and he'd never been happier in his entire life.

Chapter 32

"All right, Ace, you made it into position. That's good," Master Sergeant Gellar said. "You're in a highly responsive battle vehicle. So, I'm going to give you targets for you to simulate fire with. We'll start with tracking lasers and stationary positions. Let me know when you're ready."

Alex, I control the laser on your shoulder. It's a short-range, high-energy weapon for emergencies. The rest of the weapons are under your control. I'm cycling up the long-range laser blasters now.

There was a vibration in the suit as the weapons on the arms of the Destroyer rotated into place. Alex lifted his arms. Just like in the MP Defender, the arms of the Destroyer had joysticks with multiple triggers. Red crosshairs appeared in his vision, tracking with the weapons as he moved them around.

"Wow, that's crazy," Alex said.

Don't depend on the aiming software too heavily, Nyx said. *It's better to use your instincts. Learn to point and shoot without giving it a lot of thought, unless you're aiming at a long-range target.*

The voice in his head sounded like his own, yet the words weren't his. Surprisingly enough, having met Nyx—even briefly—made it easier for his mind to begin hearing her words as they would sound. It helped to differentiate the voices in his head.

He activated the company channel simply by thinking about it. "I'm ready, Master Sergeant."

"Good man, here we go," Gellar replied.

Her voice sounded distant compared to Nyx's voice in his head, yet Alex knew that Master Sergeant was less than two hundred meters away, while Nyx was thousands of kilometers up in space.

A target rose up. It was so far away that it looked like the head of a pen, yet in Alex's mind it lit up with strange light, as if it were being highlighted on a computer screen. He pointed at it, the aiming reticle hovering around the small target.

"I can barely see it," Alex said.

You can use the Destroyer's telephoto capabilities, Alex. Just try to see the target.

He was looking right at the target, but he couldn't really see it. The stationary device was too small. He squinted his eyes a little, willing himself to see it more clearly, and suddenly his vision narrowed, as if walls had sprung up and formed a tunnel. Then, his vision actually zoomed in on the target until he could see it clearly. It was a simple, three-color target on a white background. Alex aimed his weapon at the red center and pulled the trigger.

A burst of light shot from the cannon on Alex's left side. He could see it as it streaked across the distance and impacted the target. It hit just outside the red center, in the yellow ring.

"Not bad," Gellar said. "Take another shot, then prepare for a medium-range, moving target."

"Yes, Master Sergeant," Alex said.

Target moving on your right, Nyx said.

Alex was still zoomed in on the stationary target. He took careful aim, then pulled the trigger. Almost immediately his vision returned to normal, and he could take in most of the training field at a glance. He saw a rolling target slowly moving across the field.

Switching your starboard weapon to auto-fire projectiles.

Using his right arm to aim and shoot was more difficult. He lifted his arm and pointed toward the moving target, but it was harder to keep it in the crosshairs. Pulling the trigger made a chugging noise, and he saw laser flashes mimicking projectiles. He fired three times. The first rounds flew high, and the second burst was behind the target. The third was ahead of the target, but the final few simulated rounds scored a hit.

"Good, now I want you to move," Gellar ordered. "Roll out slow, and head straight toward the hangar. I'll send targets to either side and maybe even behind you."

Alex was starting to sweat. Moving wasn't difficult, but his mind felt heavy, as if it were a waterlogged sponge. There were too many new things to comprehend and too much activity to keep up with. Nyx was helping, but he still felt slow and clumsy.

He started forward and was immediately joined by a target on his left side.

Target to port.

Alex turned his head but kept moving forward. He could feel the Destroyer's treads turning over the manicured grass of the field. The target, a faster-moving bullseye, was quickly racing toward the cover of a false storefront. There was no time to aim. Alex lifted his arm and fired on instinct. He hit the blue outer ring.

Switching both weapons to semi-auto, wide-pattern eviscerators.

Alex felt the weapons turning and caught sight of the target on his right at the same moment that Nyx warned him.

Target approaching from starboard.

His instinct was to stop and turn toward the danger. He raised both arms and fired. The smoothbore eviscerators fired tightly packed clusters of soft metal that separated as they flew. He hit the target with both shots, but it didn't stop moving.

"That's a simulated hit, Ace, but you need to keep moving before it crashes into you," Gellar said.

The Destroyer leaped forward, ripping up the turf with its powerful treads. Another target moved away from Alex. He had to aim high and let gravity pull his shots down onto the target, which was barely in range of the eviscerators.

Switching port weapon to thermobaric grenades. You have a target inside the building to your stern.

Alex turned completely around but continued moving backwards toward the hangar. He could see the target through the fake window on the second story of the building.

Aim low and take out the building.

Alex did what he was told, shooting through the first story with the grenade launcher. He heard the hollow-sounding shot, but the grenade was simulated. There was no explosion, but the target receded.

Alex turned back around and made his way into the hangar. Master Sergeant Gellar was waiting for him. She had a smile on her face and gave him a thumbs-up.

"Park it back in line, and shut it down."

I'll run diagnostics and see that it gets recharged, Alex.

Alex maneuvered the Destroyer back into line and then thought about the armor opening. It popped apart, and the gentle rumble in Alex's mind faded. The air in the hangar felt cool on his sweaty skin as he climbed out of the battle suit.

"You did excellent for your first run," the master sergeant said. "Do you need a break?"

"No, Master Sergeant," Alex said.

"Good. Let's move on to the FA Minotaur. You're going to love it."

The Minotaur was similar to the Destroyer. It had six wheels, each attached to heavy shocks. The weapon was mounted on a turret at the top. Unlike the Destroyer, the Minotaur was maneuvered by Nyx, leaving Alex to focus on operating the unit's weapons. Alex had been on excursions outside the colony on NP8261. Those little trips had been little more than joy rides, and quite often the pilot of the vehicle was reckless—but nothing had prepared Alex for racing around the training area in the Minotaur with Nyx in control. It wasn't that she was reckless, but Alex had never been in a ground vehicle that moved so fast, and to make matters worse, the INC made it feel as if she were controlling his own body. It took a few moments—and an effort of his will—to focus on the truth. No matter how it felt, he was in a mechanized battle suit. Nyx was controlling the suit, not Alex himself. Once he managed to let go of the need to control where he went and focused all his attention on firing the Minotaur's weapons, his marksmanship improved exponentially.

The next MBS was the All-Terrain Infiltrator, a hovercraft built for long-range operations. Starting and turning the vehicle took practice, and without a solid base, projectiles would rock the entire vehicle. The Infiltrator was mounted with laser cannons on either side that could rotate around to heavy projectile weapons when the craft was on the ground. They spent more time in the Infiltrator than the other suits, simply because Alex needed more time to adjust to piloting the vehicle. It was designed for hit-and-run missions on worlds with unreliable ground. And while it couldn't climb buildings like its sister craft, the Destroyer, it was much faster, especially over rough terrain.

They stopped for lunch, and Alex was grateful. Although the experience was thrilling, he was tired—not just physically, but mentally as well. Working the battle suits took all his concentration. Master Sergeant Gellar assured him that it would get easier. Most operators specialized in one type of suit, which they used exclusively wherever they were deployed. He knew the security force on MP8261 used the MP Defenders. Only the most talented operators were versed in all of the suits. Part of him wanted to show that he had what it took to be the best, but another part wanted to be able to master just one type of MBS. He could have a long, successful career without pushing himself mentally. He felt like he was in a fog, and while doing something completely physical, like eating a meal, helped, he was still worn down when he returned to the hangar.

"Ready for a real challenge?" Gellar said.

Alex wasn't sure he was, but he refused to let the master sergeant know that.

"Yes, Master Sergeant."

"The Asset-Recovery Valkyrie and the Fast-Attack Titan are both flyers," Gellar said. "Not everyone has the knack for piloting a craft in three dimensions. You'll start training on simulators, with your controller synced in with you."

She took him to a device that looked like a large barrel mounted on springs.

"This is a three-dimensional MBS flying sim," Gellar said. "It's not the same as flying, but it's pretty damn close. Get on board and clear the first five objectives, then you can have a break."

The fun was quickly dissipating, and Alex felt crushed under the weight of knowledge. He felt he needed time to absorb the knowledge he'd already gained—the last thing he wanted to do was forget what he'd learned—but he trusted that Master Sergeant Gellar knew best. If this was how other operators trained, so be it. If they could do it, so could he. He wouldn't give up until he succeeded.

Chapter 33

"You were right," Randy Fisher, head of the security division's technical team announced. He was a hologram in Loman's office, but the glowing recreation was so highly detailed that Loman felt like he was in the same room with the man. "Can't say why, but there's something strange about those disruptors."

"Strange how?" Loman asked.

"The armor's too thin, and their power supplies were overloaded."

"What's that mean?" Loman asked.

"It means they were no match for our operators," Randy said. "Normally they have heavy armor and lots of protection around the power supply. That's why there's not much left. Even a glancing hit to the power would cause them to explode—and without proper armor, they would mostly disintegrate."

"So the attack was rigged," Loman said, his mind racing.

"Looks that way. I mean, it's possible that they were refurbished units, but anyone smart enough to rebuild one should be smart enough to know that sending them out without proper armor and shielding for the power supply would make them easy targets."

"That's helpful," Loman said. "Great work, Randy."

"No problem. I'll send the official report along as soon as it's ready."

"Thank you," Loman said, switching off the holo-projector.

He sat back and sipped from his flask. Alcohol was his one vice, the one flaw he allowed himself to have. It didn't help him solve his problem, but it did take the edge off the stress he was under.

If the disruptor drones that had attacked NP8261 were rigged to blow, there could only be two reasons. The first and most tolerable was that whoever sent them didn't want there to be anything left to link back to them. It was a reasonable explanation, except for the fact that when they were on the ground they had attacked the operators, not the facilities. If they had wanted to hurt the company, why not go in with heavy armor and hit the buildings? It didn't make sense.

Unfortunately, the other reason was seeming more and more likely: that the entire attack was staged in order to get Loman to do something. Was it possible that Alex Evans was a double agent? His family worked on NP8261 almost his entire life. Yet it was possible that someone had gotten to him. It would explain how he'd managed to get into the Defender and use it against the drones. Someone could have been secretly training him all along, and the kid had just feigned ignorance. The only problem with that theory was that Loman had spent time with the kid. There was something about Alex Evans that made it hard for Loman to believe he wasn't genuine. If Alex had been older, he could have believed it. Years of training in infiltration and spycraft might have been enough to fool Loman, but Evans was just a kid—he was only just past his eighteenth birthday. Company files on his father and their family showed that he'd lived in the colony since he was a baby. There's no record of him ever leaving. Loman might have believed he was an imposter, but he'd seen the boy with his family. His mother would have known if the kid wasn't her own.

There was only one way to be sure: Loman had to go back. He had to sit in a room with Alex and ask him the hard questions. It wouldn't be good for building trust in a recruit that Loman had hoped would be the face of the CDF in the future, but he really had no choice. He pressed a button to activate the intercom to the administrative desk where Raz Gorman worked as Loman's gatekeeper.

"I'm canceling the rest of my meetings this week," Loman said. "I'll be off-world until Monday morning."

"Roger that, boss. Anything I can do for you?" Raz asked in his deep, rumbling voice.

"No, thanks. I just have to check on something."

He opened a drawer and slipped the flask back into its hiding place. If he didn't get some hard evidence, he was likely to be fired as soon as he got back on Monday. The board was scheduled to meet that morning. If he couldn't deliver answers, he would be relieved of all duties and perhaps even banned from his own office. He couldn't help but wonder what the next person might think when they discovered his liquid crutch. He knew he should stop drinking at work, but he didn't think he could do it. Maybe it was his way of saying that Ahzco didn't own him; he was the head of security, yet he could still break the rules.

Waving a hand at his computer, he activated the voice controls.

"I need a transport to the Helena system," he ordered.

The AI responded immediately. "The Helena system is closed by direct orders from Vice President of Security

Loman Haley. There are no flights going in or out of the Helena system."

"So book me a private transport," Loman said. "I'll make sure we can get in."

He snatched up his coat, checked his pocket for his PIL, then headed out of his office.

Ahzco had a private hangar at the nearby terminal with a private shuttle that could take executives up to the transit station in orbit without delay. An hour later, Loman was walking across the concourse of the space station toward a small, non-commercial vessel. He went through the airlock and onto the ship, which was filled with reclining chairs and a few bench seats. A steward greeted him and waved an ID reader over his Ahzco credentials.

"Welcome aboard, Vice President Haley."

"Thank you. Inform the pilots that I'm ready to go," Loman said. "The sooner the better."

Chapter 34

Alex stood at attention. There were twelve other privates lined up next to him. Most were short; Alex was the tallest. They were all trim, their hair grown out slightly longer than Alex's. There was an even split between boys and girls. Though they all stared straight ahead, he could feel the animosity radiating from them.

Chief McKinna and Master Sergeant Gellar stood facing the group. There was a long silence while everyone waited for the chief to speak. He was studying the group, waiting to see if they would say anything or do anything. The group seemed well-disciplined to Alex.

"As you probably know," Chief McKinna said in a soft voice that hid the unyielding expectations he had for the group, "a company of operators is usually twelve or less. Today, we have gained a thirteenth member of our squad. His name is Alex Chester Evans."

McKinna paused long enough for Alex to hear a few people snort or sigh. They had clearly heard of him, but he wasn't sure why he deserved such a response. He hadn't done anything to any of them. He'd never even met them before.

"By the end of the week, at least one person will have to go," McKinna said. "The slowest, the dumbest, the most annoying—it makes no difference. Even if we have to whittle the group down to just two or three. If you don't carry your weight, you will be left behind. If you fail to meet my expectations, you will be reassigned to toilet brigade. If you make a stupid mistake, I will personally beat the ever-loving hell out of you and send you home to your mothers in a wooden box. Am I clear?"

"Yes, Chief!" the line of operators in training shouted out.

"And I do mean anyone," McKinna said, looking straight at Alex. "I run a tight ship, and anyone who falls behind isn't worthy of wearing the battle suit. This isn't for the light of heart. Now mount up, we've got a three-day exercise and I'm ready to move."

Behind the group were four AT Infiltrators, four AT Destroyers on wheels instead of treads, and four FA Minotaurs. They were all ground-based mechanized battle suits, and as Alex turned around he saw that all were assigned to one of the other twelve members of the squad.

"You're in a Medic suit with me, Ace," Master Sergeant Gellar said.

Alex felt his heart drop into his stomach. He respected the medics. In a battle, the medics were tasked with getting operators out of damaged mech suits. A good medic could save lives, but it wasn't flashy or tough, at least not to Alex's mind. He wanted to be linked to a battle suit and sent to the front lines. It might have been hubris, but he couldn't deny his disappointment.

The AR Medic suit was more like close-fitting, hard-vacuum gear. It was part armor, part mobile medical bay. On the chest was a removable first aid kit. Both forearms were mounted with automatic trauma kits. A cauterizing laser was mounted on the left shoulder, and a robotic surgical arm was folded up inside a narrow pack on the back.

The AR Medic wasn't completely unarmed. On one hip they carried an Ahzco Personal Defense Laser Blaster.

It connected to the suit magnetically and could recharge using the suit's power supply. On the other hip was a combat dagger. Alex suited up and made sure he could move freely in the tight-fitting suit. He switched the pistol from his right hip to his left and made sure the dagger was snug.

"You haven't trained on the Medic suit, so listen to your controller," Master Sergeant Gellar said.

"Yes, Master Sergeant," Alex said.

He picked up the helmet. It was a full-face model but completely transparent. The helmet was snug around the back and top of his head and bulged out from his face. The bottom portion had a re-breather built in. The power switch was at the back of the helmet, and when Alex flipped it, the suit sealed. He felt his INC connect easily with the suit's computer.

"Morning, Nyx," he said.

Good morning, Alex. This looks like fun.

Alex wished he could be honest, but he didn't want to risk being overheard. He wasn't liked, and Chief McKinna's threat to kick someone off the squad by the end of the week surely hadn't helped his cause.

"All right, let's do a comms test," McKinna said over the company channel of their com-links. "Sound off."

The other recruits said their names and pronounced themselves ready. Alex counted, knowing he would go last. When his turn came, he spoke clearly.

"Evans, online," he said.

"Gellar, online," the Master Sergeant said, waving Alex over to the command cruiser.

Chief McKinna was already inside the big vehicle. It was the command post—the computer center that would run their simulations—and it was packed with enough food to feed the entire squad for three days. Master Sergeant Gellar showed Alex where to get onto a ladder at the rear of the vehicle. He climbed up and stood on a tiny platform, the ladder his only handhold. Gellar was on an identical platform on the other side of the ladder.

"Don't let go," she warned. "Things get bumpy once we're outside of town."

Alex calmed his mind. It didn't do him any good to worry. All he could hope for was to learn and earn his place in the company. If someone had to lose their place for him, then so be it. He didn't make the rules, and he wasn't trying to dash anyone's dreams. If McKinna wanted to kick someone out, it was his squad to command, and Alex could only do his job to the best of his abilities. Outside of that, he was as helpless as the other trainees.

"Let's roll out," McKinna said.

The command cruiser took the lead and led the squad through the streets of Sparta. It wasn't a large city, and most people didn't use vehicles in the town. He saw several people walking, but the convoy of battle suits wasn't an uncommon sight, and none of the pedestrians paid them any attention.

At the edge of town, the command cruiser slowed. It went off the smoothly paved streets and onto a rough desert road. Dust billowed out behind them, cutting off Alex's view. All he could see was the red cloud of dust and the red-painted stern of the big transport. Master Sergeant Gellar was barely visible.

"Any idea where we're going?" Alex asked Nyx.

About sixty kilometers into the desert. How's it look?

"I don't know," Alex admitted. "All I can see is dust."

We can see that up here, too. It's like the squad is hidden in a red cloud.

"So how does this Medic suit work?"

It's armored, so you should be safe enough. I'm guessing even if you fell off the back of the command cruiser, you wouldn't get hurt.

"Unless the rest of the squad runs me over," Alex said. "In this dust, they'd never see me."

Well, I guess I could warn them. The company frowns on controllers losing their operators. You wouldn't want me to look bad, would you?

"Oh, no," Alex said. "Anything but that."

She laughed. It was strange—hearing laughter in his mind was something he'd never experienced before. He had laughed plenty, but always out loud. He wasn't even sure if a person could laugh silently. It was the first thing that was completely hers, even though it was still in his head. He could hear the laughter, and it lifted his spirits.

Okay, well then, try and hold on. When you get called out, we'll have to open the battle suit to retrieve the operator. I'll transmit the emergency code for you, and you pull them free.

"So basically, after they get disabled in battle, I'm the first person they see," Alex said. "They're gonna love me."

Maybe not now, but in a real battle situation, they would die without your help.

Alex knew she was right, but he assumed that none of his squad mates would be thinking that way once the exercises started.

The trip across the desert took an hour. Alex was more than ready to step off the back of the command cruiser when it finally came to a stop. He and Master Sergeant Gellar stretched their backs and legs. Alex had to shake his hands to work out the soreness that clutching the ladder had brought on. Then Chief McKinna gave them orders through the earpieces built into the MBS. His voice was clear and unmistakable.

"Time for war games!"

Chapter 35

Chief McKinna split the squad into two groups and devised various exercises, from simulated battles to races to find hidden objects. For the entire first day, all Alex did was pretend to pull people from the mechs that were disabled in the game. It was frustrating and boring. He felt like a spectator, and Nyx was his only companion. It felt like he had an invisible friend. Having the freedom to talk with her via the INC connection to his AR Medic suit was the one bright spot in the day.

After watching several exercises, it soon became clear who was superior in the MBS. Ashton Timmons, who everyone called Ash, was fearless. She was in a FA Minotaur, which she drove like a racer. Speed and skill made her a force to be reckoned with, and when Alex was on her team it was obvious that the other trainees deferred to her. She was a woman with a strong will who felt that she was always right. Anyone who disagreed with her was quickly belittled and dismissed.

The best shooter was a boy named Oliver McGee. He went by the name Oggy and was a natural marksman. At first, Alex had expected the shooting—which was all laser simulation—to be easy. But shooting from a moving vehicle at a highly mobile target proved harder than Alex expected—not that he got a chance to try it himself, but he watched the exercises closely, trying to learn as much as possible.

There were patrol exercises, with one team setting up ambushes in the rugged hills near the camp where Chief McKinna had his control cruiser, and races across the vast expanse of desert. The sun beat down relentlessly, and while his suit kept his core body temp down, the transparent helmet seemed to intensify the sun's effects. At times, Alex felt like a bug being scorched by a giant with a magnifying glass. The only times he could forget his troubles were when he was called into action.

Nuk is down.

"I'm on it," Alex said.

He sprinted out across the desert plain, his breath puffing hard inside the helmet. From the study he'd done on the various mechanized battle suits, he knew that most AR Medics were dropped from the flying AR Valkyries. But in their exercises, he was forced to run out into the battle, find the downed mech, and go through the process of opening the suit to retrieve the operator.

Nuk was actually Nicolai Ukanovic. When Alex reached his MBS, a Destroyer, Nyx patched in the code that opened the vehicle. He climbed up and looked at Nuk, who was shaking his head angrily.

"What are you looking at?" Nuk snarled.

"Just checking to make sure you're okay," Alex said.

"Of course I'm okay. Oggy got a lucky shot on me, that's all!"

Alex lifted his hands to show he didn't mean any harm. "Just doing my job, man. Sorry."

"You don't know what it's like," Nuk snapped. It seemed that his anger was only growing. "When you open the Destroyer, it severs my connection to my controller with no warning."

"Look, I'm sorry, okay? I'm just doing what I was tasked with."

"Fine, you did it. Now leave me the hell alone."

Alex jumped from the side of the Destroyer. He felt bad for Nuk, but he knew the frustration was only temporary.

"Another happy customer," Alex said.

Good, 'cause you got another. Sly's down.

Alex couldn't say how he knew exactly which mech Nyx was talking about, but he was running before he even thought about where he was going. He knew Nyx must have sent the coordinates to him, and that his brain then translated the data into his thoughts, but it was still a mystery to Alex.

The mechs kicked up so much dust that it felt like Alex was running through a red fog. He could hear the MBS's still in action—the whine of the electric motors that powered them, the crunch of their hard wheels on the desert floor, the crackle of the tiny rock particles that were tossed across the ground as the vehicles slid into tight turns —but he didn't hear Oggy coming. Alex could just make out Sly's AR Infiltrator slumped down onto the ground straight in front of him.

Alex, stop, Nyx said calmly. *You're moving straight into Oggy's path.*

Alex stopped, his chest heaving from the run. He could hear something nearby in the cloud of dust, but he couldn't see it.

"Tell me...when he's passed," Alex said in between breaths.

Odd, Nyx said.

"What?"

When his controller spoke again, there was an edge to her voice. Alex was still getting to know Nyx, but there was an edge to the way she spoke that sent Alex into motion. The INC couldn't transfer emotion, but his brain translated her message into a warning cry.

Alex, move! He's coming right toward you.

Alex ran, dashing forward several steps, then veering to his right. Oggy's Minotaur appeared out of the cloud, and Alex had to dive forward to avoid being hit.

"What's he doing?" Alex said.

Trying to hurt you, Nyx replied, her voice calm again. *He changed course, Alex. It wasn't an accident. He's coming back around.*

Alex didn't question why Oggy would want to run him over. He was the outsider, with a reputation that might intimidate his fellow trainees. Still, he wasn't completely without recourse. He plucked the laser blaster from his hip and started running toward Sly's Infiltrator again. It was the only cover close by.

He's coming up from behind again.

"Tell me when he's close," Alex said. "I have to juke at the last second, or he'll just follow me."

I'm reporting him.

"No!" Alex said, his heart pounding in his ears as he ran. "Don't do that. It'll only make things worse."

Worse than trying to kill you?

"He isn't trying to kill me," Alex said. "He just wants me out of Echo Company."

He's almost on you. Go now!

Alex jumped sideways again, this time diving to his left. He hit the ground hard, but his armor absorbed most of the impact, and he rolled up on his knees. Oggy had already blown past Alex, but the rear of the Minotaur was still in sight. Alex squeezed off three quick shots, aiming for the rear wheels. He saw the flashes of laser light hit the dark tires just before the Minotaur disappeared into the dust cloud. The sound of the wheels locking up was unmistakable.

You got him!

"Lucky for us, the simulation doesn't take the power of this pistol into account," Alex said. "I doubt it would have made an impact at all otherwise."

I still think his behavior should be reported.

"That would eliminate one enemy but create ten more," Alex said. "I've got to find a way to win them over, and I don't think getting Oggy into trouble will work."

He trotted over to Sly's Infiltrator. Nyx sent the code, and the hovercraft opened. Sylvester Lassiter looked at him oddly.

"Did you just take out Oggy?" Sly asked.

"Yeah," Alex said.

"That's not your place, Alex. You're not a combatant."

Alex was shocked. Sly wasn't even on Oggy's team, but he didn't know who was friends with whom yet. It was obvious that getting into the good graces of the other trainees wasn't going to be easy.

Not the response I expected, Nyx said.

"No one cheers for you when they're all hoping you'll fail."

I'm not hoping you fail, Alex. Maybe you'll win them over, and maybe you won't, but from what I've seen, you've got what it takes to make a great operator. And I'm going to do all I can to help.

"At least I've got one friend," Alex said. He couldn't help but smile. "Who's next?"

Ice just went down. Looks like your team is going to lose again.

"Maybe that would change if they would put me in the game."

Chapter 36

Alex spent the entire day in the AR Medic battle suit. Other than stopping Oggy from running him over, he didn't engage in the battle simulations. That evening, they were all given time off to rest. As night fell, a hydro tank was brought out and lit. There was very little in the desert that would burn, so the hydrogen tank worked like a campfire. The heat of the day disappeared with the sun, and the night grew cold. No matter how the trainees felt about one another, they huddled close to the fire for warmth.

"You're doing well," Master Sergeant Gellar said. "The point of these exercises is to get you accustomed to the MBS's."

"I don't mind," Oggy said. "I like sports, and this is my kind of game."

"If only you could shoot and drive at the same time," Ash teased.

The good-natured, jovial spirit around the campfire was a nice change. Alex found that as long as he didn't engage anyone directly, they all managed to tolerate him. And it was helpful seeing who was friends with whom. Oggy and Ash were like team captains, and the group was split by gender. There were obvious competitions between the two sides, and after the day of war games it was looking like the boys were behind. Sly and Zeb had been taken out in every exercise, usually early on. Zebadiah Ben Goreski was a quiet, brooding boy who muttered under his breath a lot. From what Alex could tell, he wasn't used to not being the best. He was on the boy's side, but it was clear that he really didn't like Oggy or being the butt of most of the jokes.

The good times came to an abrupt end when Chief McKinna called Alex into the command cruiser. It didn't help that McKinna and Master Sergeant Gellar were using his initials as his nickname.

"Ace, you want to join me inside?" McKinna said.

It wasn't really a question, and he didn't wait for answer. Alex stood up, feeling every eye on him with more than a little animosity. The joking and laughter had stopped and didn't continue until he was inside the command cruiser. As he walked up the metal stairs and into the warm command post, he could imagine what his fellow trainees were going to say about him, but there was nothing he could do about that.

"Close the door," McKinna said.

Alex pulled the thin, metal door closed. Heaters were working to keep the interior of the cruiser warm. One side was filled with computers. A swivel chair was positioned to allow the user to control everything. A bank of monitors was powered off, but Alex guessed that they showed the desert from above.

Just behind the cockpit were two chairs and a small table. McKinna sat in one chair and waved at the other. Alex moved over and sat down.

"Not bad for your first day," McKinna said. "But I should have guessed you'd adapt quickly."

"Not much to it," Alex said. "I suppose the Medic suit does all the work if someone gets hurt."

"True that," McKinna said. "Still, you seem to have a knack for it. It might make a good specialty."

Alex didn't want to tell his chief that being a medic was the last thing he wanted. It was true, but he felt it was better not to make waves. There was too much at stake if he wanted to find a way to be part of the group.

"Still," Chief McKinna continued. "We better move you. I saw that you took out Oggy earlier today. I like to see my crews competing to be the best."

Alex nodded. It might have been the perfect time to bring up Oggy's aggressive behavior toward him, but Alex refused. He didn't need anyone else to fight his battles for him.

"I'm putting you in his Minotaur tomorrow," McKinna said. "We'll be doing escape and evade exercises —you'll love it."

"Yes, Chief," Alex said.

"Gellar says you've got talent. We'll see how you do tomorrow."

"Looking forward to it," Alex said.

It was true; he was excited about being able to actually take part in the exercises. But he knew that taking Oggy's MBS would solidify the animosity between them, and now the others might think Alex had complained to the chief about Oggy's efforts to run him down in the dust cloud.

"Good. I'll wake you an hour before sunrise. That's all the head start you're going to get," McKinna said with a grin. "If you can survive the day and make it back to camp before dark, I'll give you an extra day of liberty. If you get caught, you'll have to scrub battle suits while everyone else gets the day off."

Alex wanted to point out that by doing a good a job in the exercise, he would be separating himself even further from his squad mates. It was a lose-lose for him, but obviously that had to be McKinna's plan all along. Alex just couldn't figure out why.

"I'll do my best, Chief."

"I wouldn't expect anything less from a kid straight off NP8261. To be honest, I never thought I would get off that rock. Thankfully, when the VP came to recruit you, I managed to convince him to bring me along. Sometimes having someone familiar helps a person adapt."

Alex's mouth was dry, and he wasn't sure what to say. The truth was, he didn't know Chief McKinna any more than he knew the other trainees in the squad. He had spoken with the chief exactly twice, and one of those times Loman Haley had done most of the talking. All he could do was nod along, as if he agreed with everything Chief McKinna said.

"That was a dreary place. I don't know how you managed to survive growing up there. I was ready to leave as soon as I saw it," McKinna went on. Alex was starting to think his chief enjoyed the sound of his own voice. "But what choice do we have, really? For all I know, once we complete training, we might get sent right back there. We go where they say, do what they say, and if we're lucky and manage to live long enough, we get retired to some backwater planet with nothing to do.

"Well, enough rambling for me. You need some sleep. Go get some shut eye—I'll see that you're up in time to make a speedy escape."

McKinna got up and headed to the door. He flung it open and stepped onto the top step. Then he cleared his throat as he waited for the squad to quit talking and turn their attention his way.

"McGee, tomorrow you're in the AR Medic suit," the Chief said. "Ace will be in your FA Minotaur. Get some sleep, squad. We start tomorrow at first light."

McKinna stepped back, allowing Alex to leave the command cruiser. Alex could see the baleful glares from his squad mates but knew there was nothing he could do to change their minds. If he tried to say it wasn't his idea to take Oggy's MBS, they would never believe him. He walked down the steps and saw Master Sergeant Gellar getting sleep sacks from a hidden compartment in the cruiser's undercarriage.

Behind him, McKinna stuck his head out again and shared the agenda for the following day.

"Tomorrow we will be practicing an escape and evade exercise. If any of you manage to catch Ace, you'll all get an extra day of liberty." He paused to let the squad cheer for a moment. "And to the lucky SOB who takes him out, I will guarantee them a spot in Echo Company."

Alex had moved over to help Master Sergeant Gellar, but he heard the rest of the squad's excitement. Chasing him would be right up their alley, and getting rewarded for it was even better.

"Of course, if he evades you and makes it back here before dark, he'll get liberty and the entire squad will be on clean-up duty. So get some sleep. The search begins first thing in the morning."

He slammed the door of his command cruiser closed. Alex felt his hopes dwindling. Master Sergeant Gellar gave him a look that showed she had no sympathy for his predicament.

"Good luck," she said.

"Thanks," he replied.

He took a sleep sack and moved over by the battle suits. It was cold, and the stars above were tiny pinpricks against the black expanse of outer space. He unzipped the sleep sack, which was a thin body-length bag made for extreme environments. It was made of thin layers of heat-reflective material. With one side out, the sack would fill quickly with his body heat and keep him warm through the night. With the other side out, the sack would create a cooling respite from heat. He got into the sack and zipped it up to his neck. The bag was designed to enclose the user completely, but Alex wasn't ready to sleep yet. He stared up at the stars, trying to determine if any of the lights he could see were from the starship where Nyx was probably sleeping. He hoped she would be awake and at her station when he set out the next morning. The only sliver of light in the difficult situation he faced was the thought that he wouldn't be completely alone; he would have Nyx as a friend and as his controller. Together, they would deal with the extreme exercise Chief McKinna had stuck him with.

The fire was soon put out, and the only light was the stars. Alex thought the others were sleeping close together, but Master Sergeant Gellar ambled to where he lay, looking up at the night sky. She frowned at him.

"Why are you making things so difficult for yourself?"

"What?" Alex asked.

She stepped into her sleep sack and settled in nearby.

"Did you really think running to the chief would solve your problems?"

"I didn't," Alex said.

"You didn't tell him that Oggy tried to run you down?"

"No," Alex said. "That would only make the rest of the squad hate me even more."

"Huh," Gellar replied. "Well, I guess he just hates you for reasons of his own."

"I can't imagine why."

"You're from the same planet, aren't you?"

"He was the security chief on my home world, but I didn't know him," Alex said. He hadn't intended to share so much, but once he started, he couldn't stop. "I'd only met him twice. The CDF people didn't mingle with the locals too much. NP8261 is a single-colony world. My parents used to say that everyone knew everyone else, but that wasn't really true."

"Maybe he has a beef with your family?"

"If so, I don't know anything about it."

"Hey, he's an officer," Master Sergeant Gellar said, as if being an officer were something to avoid at all costs. "Who can say why they do the things they do? But he's pitting you against the squad, and you'll have to watch your six. I warned Oggy not to pull another stunt like he did today, but I can't protect you all the time."

"Thank you, Master Sergeant. But I'll be okay."

"Or you won't, but I guess either way you won't have to worry about it," she said with a chuckle.

Alex knew what she meant, and perhaps she thought it would encourage him, but it only made him shiver inside his sleep sack. The thought of what might have happened in the dust cloud was enough to keep him awake all night. But he knew he needed to rest; there was something fundamental about it. He had also eaten the instant meal from the small pouch despite the fact that it tasted like week-old soup. It was nourishment, and his body needed fuel. Sleep was difficult to come by on the cold, hard ground, knowing that his squad would just as soon see him dead, but he knew he needed to recharge. Even a few hours of sleep would go a long way toward accomplishing that.

"Sleep tight, Ace," Master Sergeant Gellar said. "You're CDF now. You'll just have to get used to people wanting to kill you."

Chapter 37

Nyx woke with a start. The alarm on her PIL, which was curled around her forearm like an electronic bracelet, was vibrating. She rolled out of her bunk and got dressed in the dark. There were almost four hundred controllers on the *Capitalism*. Most were partnered with operators in various stages of training or waiting for deployment. Some were running simulations and doing busy work while they waited to be paired with an operator. New controllers like herself fell to the bottom of the queue behind more experienced CDF personnel. She had recently met three controllers waiting for new operators after their previous partners had retired. Nyx had only just been paired with Alex Evans, and at first she felt incredibly lucky. But upon further reflection, the timing didn't exactly add up, and the fact that she had met him face-to-face only added to her belief that someone in the CDF had wanted them to be matched. She couldn't say why, and to be honest she didn't mind. Alex was talented, smart, and easy to work with. She had heard horror stories about controllers paired with operators who were too arrogant to take advice or too clumsy to advance in the service. Alex seemed like he had what it took to run any of the MBS's that were needed for a particular mission, and she was determined to make sure she did whatever she could to help him be a success. After all, his success was her success.

Once she was dressed, she hurried to the galley. It was extremely early in the morning down on Helena Prime, but time of day was relative on a star ship. The galley was open, and the automated food dispensers had selections for meals that ran the gamut from breakfast to midnight snack. She ordered a plate of eggs. Normally she preferred fruit, but her orders were clear: she would be at her station for a long time helping Alex on an escape and evade exercise. There was no telling when she might get time to eat again, so she chose something with protein that would keep her full longer.

She ate the eggs with a side of toast and a strip of bacon that was really just flavored protein. She drank orange juice, then filled a travel mug with hot coffee. The mug was powered, keeping the interior hot while the outside stayed cool to the touch. She also stuffed a meal replacement bar into her pocket. Eating while working with an operator was dicey, but she wanted the food just in case she needed it.

After gathering her things, she took the lift from the barracks up to the command level of the *Capitalism*. There were two large rooms filled with cubicles, one on either side of the ship's bridge. She found her small nook, set her snacks to the side, and brought her computer system online. Alex had not connected to an MBS yet, but it wouldn't be long. She propped her Flex PIL against the side of her monitor. It had the local time where Alex was on the planet below, along with the time of sunrise.

A light came on at her station, which was monitoring all the mechanized battle suits assigned to Echo Company on field exercises in the desert outside Sparta. One of the FA Minotaurs was coming online. She connected to it, knowing that Alex had been selected as the rabbit in the escape and evade exercise. A moment later, she heard his voice.

"Nyx?"

"I'm here, Alex. Good morning."

"Yeah, super early down here. How'd you sleep?" he asked.

"Well, thank you. And you?"

"As well as can be expected when you're sleeping on the ground in the freezing cold desert, knowing your whole squad hates you."

Tension suddenly gripped her body. She hadn't realized how bad things were for him, and that, in turn, made her worry that she wouldn't be able to help him. But his gentle, self-deprecating chuckle washed away her fears.

"We should get you moving," Nyx said. "I'm sending you coordinates to the starting point now. You have to get there, register, and then find a way back to camp without getting captured or killed."

"Piece of cake," Alex said.

For the next ninety minutes, she watched her primary monitor. It was a simultaneous feed from the Minotaur's camera, which was controlled by Alex's INC. Essentially, she saw what he saw. Her secondary monitor showed the top-down view of the desert from the surveillance satellite in geosynchronous orbit over the desert. She could zoom in all the way to about five meters above the ground. When Alex wasn't in his MBS, she could read the stenciling on his chest from the sat feed. Normally, she had company assets listed on the overhead feed so that she also knew where the other operators in Alex's squad were at all times, but she was denied that privilege for the escape and evade exercise. She only had visuals, with no computer assistance, which meant she could keep an eye out for any signs of the other operators, but that was all. Even her radar was offline. Basically, she could help him control the Minotaur and be a second set of eyes, and that was all.

"So I take it you've done this type of thing before?" Alex asked.

"Only sims," Nyx admitted. "This is my first real exercise."

"Sweet, we'll learn together."

The sun was up, and that meant the other operators were spreading out, searching for Alex.

"We'll have to keep an eye on your power," Nyx said. "It won't last all day if we aren't careful."

"You think it'll take that long?"

"The longer the better," Nyx said. "You don't want to get caught right off the bat, do you?

"No, that would be bad for me." Alex said.

"So, let's make sure that doesn't happen. You'll be at the checkpoint in a few minutes. In the meantime, I'm marking a few places that look good for hiding or ambushing the other members of your squad."

"That will make me so popular. Did you know that Chief McKinna is giving an extra day of liberty to whoever catches me?"

Another surprise. Nyx was beginning to wonder why Alex was being treated so differently—not that rewards were unusual in field exercises, but a full day's liberty seemed a bit excessive.

"What happens if you win?" Nyx asked

"I get the day off, and my squad gets stuck on cleaning duty that day."

Nyx frowned. That didn't seem right. It was like the chief was trying to alienate Alex even further. The thought crossed her mind that maybe being his controller wasn't good for her career. It might be better if she put some distance between them, but there was no good way to do that—and she had spent enough time with Alex to feel like he was a good person. The only thing she could do was be there for him, and if they got stuck with a lousy deployment, she could look for a transfer then.

"All right, I'm here. What now?" said Alex.

"Now the fun starts," Nyx said. "If the other members of your squad left at daybreak, they could be halfway to your current location by now. The problem for them is that they don't know where you are."

"So they're probably setting up a perimeter."

"Exactly—with scouts in all directions and enough distance from the camp that they can mobilize to your location once you're spotted and still have time to engage before getting too close to the camp."

"Not exactly a walk in the park," Alex said, "but if they're spread out like that, maybe we can slip past them."

"I wouldn't count on that. I can see your dust cloud even when you're moving slow."

"Okay, so stealth isn't the best tactic. And odds are good that Chief McKinna told them exactly where the checkpoint is."

"All right, then we need to flank them," Nyx said. "Head south—we've got plenty of time. We can swing around them and use the hills to the south of the camp for cover."

"There's less room to maneuver," Alex said doubtfully.

"It's a trade-off," Nyx replied. "In the open, they'll see you coming. In the hills, we can hide that dust cloud."

"Sounds like a plan."

It was a sound tactic—unless, of course, the rest of the squad anticipated it. In that case, she was leading Alex straight into a trap. She zoomed out of the satellite feed and then back down closer to the camp. There was no sign of movement and no tell-tale dust clouds. She moved the feed over, searching for signs of the squad, but there was nothing. The sun had been up for an hour, and the hunters were in position. Her heart sank a little. If the rest of the squad was hidden, how could she help Alex?

Maybe it would be better if he failed. She tried to feel good about that outcome. If Alex was captured or killed, the rest of the squad would be rewarded. But the more she considered it, the more she realized that it would only pit them against Alex more. The only way for him to win their respect was if he earned it by showing them how good he really was. And for Alex to be at his best, she needed to be at her best. One way or another, she had to make sure he put up a good fight.

Chapter 38

Alex was being hunted, and he felt it. It was an entirely new sensation. He had been afraid many times in his life, but they all seemed trite compared to being hunted. He was in no real danger that he knew of—it was a game, just a field exercise—but it felt more like his life was on the line. Perhaps it was because the stakes were high or because he knew the people chasing him bore him ill will—whatever the reason, he was concerned.

The first two hours had him racing across the desert. It was a good way to acclimate to the Minotaur. It was a fast-attack battle suit that felt more like a vehicle. The Minotaur had six wheels and could accelerate to well over a hundred kilometers an hour. But the real strength of the Minotaur, as Alex saw it, was the suit's ability to accelerate. He could go from a full stop to over forty kilometers per hour in just under a second. It wasn't faster than a laser blast or even a projectile weapon, but it was faster than most people could aim.

Hold on, Nyx warned. She was the voice in his head, and while they were creeping along through the foothills to a rugged mountain range, she was his eyes as well. *I've got movement. Three klicks due north of your position.*

Alex held his breath, as if that would help hide the battle suit and keep the red dust from billowing up around him. He was used to dust. His home world was a rock with almost no soil—just dust that blew constantly and clung to everything. But the dust on Helena Prime was different. It settled quickly enough, but any movement along the ground puffed it up into the air in a red cloud. Alex wished they were on a planet with grass and heavy soil. It would have made his job of sneaking back to the camp much easier.

It's a Destroyer.

"Any idea who's in it?" Alex asked.

Negative. I have no reading on the other members of Echo Company.

Alex already knew that she couldn't track them, but still it would have helped to know who was there, waiting for him to stick his head out.

"I can't just stay here," Alex said.

The Destroyer's moving, Nyx explained. *Let's see if it drops down off that hill.*

The waiting was the worst. The tension seemed to build up around him, suffocating him inside the battle suit. It was a fully encased MBS—no part of Alex was exposed. Thick crash padding pressed in against his body from every side. He could move his arms, which controlled the weapons system, and there were several millimeters of space in front of his face, but the tension made the suit seem unbearably confining.

He worked through his mental exercises as he waited to find out what the Destroyer would do, reminding himself that this was a training exercise. His goal was to be the best fugitive he could be—to make the job hard on his squad mates. If he was caught, so be it, but he wouldn't make it easy on them.

It stopped. Probably on overwatch. From what I can tell, that's the tallest hill around.

"So, what options do we have?"

You can run for it and hope that Destroyer can't hit a moving target. It just got into position, so there's a chance we're at the end of the line. We might be able to slip around it, moving fast, and get back to the camp.

"As soon as I move, he'll call in reinforcements," Alex said. "And the hills will make it easier to target me. There's not much room for evasive maneuvers."

The other option is a long-range strike, but that's an incredibly hard shot: three kilometers and an elevated target.

"We can roll up the hill," Alex offered. "You take the controls. Go as slowly as possible."

I have navigation. Switching the turret to rocket-powered grenades. Good luck.

Alex felt the Minotaur moving and had to fight the urge to retake control. It was like the battle suit was moving on its own. He rotated around so that he was looking behind him. Dust was rising, but only a meter or so before drifting back down.

It's noticed us. All the Destroyer's weapons are trained in our direction.

"Keep going, nice and slow."

What if it fires first?

"I'm guessing whoever is in that Destroyer has his laser weapon ready and is waiting for us to creep over the crest of the hill. But it can't hit us unless it can see us. So stop before you get to the top."

This was a mistake. The controller will have seen us and called in backup.

"Then we'll take them out, one at a time," Alex said.

It took them almost ten minutes to creep up the hill.

"All right," Alex said. "This should be good."

Elevation difference is eight meters. You are 2.7 kilometers from target. Sending telemetry information to you now.

Alex couldn't see the Destroyer, but because they were doing a field exercise, that played in his favor. The shot was difficult—right at the edge of the rocket-propelled grenade's range—but as long as Alex followed the computer's recommendation, it couldn't help but register a hit.

"Here goes nothing," Alex said.

He pulled the trigger on his joystick. The Minotaur rocked a little, as if an actual grenade had been launched.

That's a hit! You did it! That Destroyer is incapacitated.

"All right—one down, eleven more to go," Alex said. "How are we looking?"

It's clear. I'm zooming out. If that Destroyer called in assistance, we should be able to see the dust cloud.

"Fine," Alex replied. "I'll move us closer."

All it took was willing the Minotaur to move, and it did. The sensation was different than walking or running, but the command seemed the same. He didn't think about the battle suit moving, he just thought of where he wanted to go. They trundled over the crest of the hill, still moving cautiously. Alex caught sight of the Destroyer. He couldn't tell anything about who was inside. Then he moved down between the hills, and the Destroyer was out of sight.

In the valley between the foothills, Alex turned away from the Destroyer. He wanted to continue moving around the camp. Odds were high that the other controllers were searching for him. He needed a place with cover and a clear escape route.

Three incoming MBS's, Nyx said. *Northeast of our position, about fourteen klicks out.*

"Roger that," Alex said, having just spotted a hilltop with a large boulder at the summit. "Let's creep up that hill and tuck in behind that boulder."

You'll still be visible. There's no place to hide. We should try to outrun them.

"The odds aren't in our favor if we run," Alex argued. "And that boulder won't hide us, but it will make us difficult to target."

He rolled the Minotaur up to the top of the hill. The boulder was slightly wider than the battle suit and almost as high as the turret. Alex rotated the gun back and forth, making sure he was clear of the rock if he needed to fire.

This doesn't make sense.

"Perhaps not in a conventional fight, but remember we can see them coming, and they're hemmed in by the hills."

Meaning?

"Meaning we can target them using the computer," Alex said. "Three quick shots right at the edge of our effective range. We're stationary—that gives us an edge. You take control of navigation. I'll calculate the targets once we know how they're approaching."

Nyx didn't respond right away, which left Alex feeling like something was wrong. When she did speak, her words were clipped. It was still his own voice that he heard, but her diction was decidedly her own.

It's too risky. We should make a run for it.

"We will, but not yet. Trust me, Nyx. We can do this. Plot us a course out of the hills and back to camp. Make it a looping approach. If there are more of them closing in on this location, we need to keep them from cutting us off."

Again she didn't reply, and he had to trust that she was doing as he asked. Alex didn't know if she outranked him, or if protocol dictated that he should defer to her wishes, but he had a feeling that he was in the perfect spot to strike the hunters. He just needed to draw them in.

They're splitting up.

"We knew they would. Show me where they are."

His vision faded, flickered, and then changed. He was suddenly in the air, looking down at the hills. He could see his own Minotaur at the bottom of his field of view. The approaching battle suits were moving toward his position along the valleys of three different hills.

"What's their range?"

Five kilometers and closing.

"Good, calculate shots here, here, and here," he said, focusing his mind on parts of the valley ahead of each of the Minotaurs.

You'll be in range of their weapons, remember.

"Yes, I remember," Alex said.

He couldn't tell if she was angry or nervous. He could feel fear throbbing inside his throat, making it hard to swallow. The trajectory of the first shot came into his mind, and he aimed carefully, waiting for the target to drop into his trap.

Alex fired. The computers running the simulation calculated the rocket-propelled grenade needed 2.6 seconds to reach the targets. In that tiny window of time, the Minotaur fired at Alex.

That's a hit. One MB—

She stopped in mid-sentence, and Alex feared that they'd been hit.

It impacted the boulder. That was too close.

Alex was swiveling to his next target. He fired, then aimed at the third. The second Minotaur went down without firing a shot, but the third changed course and Alex missed. It fired back as the operator raced up the hill. Alex saw flashes of light shooting toward him. He fired again, aiming on instinct alone. It was a miss. Fortunately, the shots coming at him from the third Minotaur were either hitting the boulder or soaring high.

"Go now!" Alex said.

The battle suit shot down the hill and out of visual range. Alex lobbed another grenade toward his opponent, but it missed.

"Switch the weapon to auto-projectiles," Alex said. "Whatever has the best range."

Switching the weapon to fifty-caliber alloy slugs, fully automatic discharge. At least we took out three of them.

"We're not out of the fight yet," Alex declared. "Head up the next hill."

Will be exposed.

"So will they."

Chapter 39

Alex's Minotaur shot up the hill and actually went airborne for a second. As the battle suit tilted down, Alex saw his chance. He pointed his weapon at the other Minotaur that was just cresting a hill of its own. For that split second, its turret was still pointed up and couldn't target them. Alex squeezed the trigger and let the Minotaur's automatic weapon roar. Tiny flashes of light raced across the space between the two warriors. Some hit the dusty hill and others flew wide, but just as the Minotaur brought its own weapon to bear, it took several hits.

It all happened in a flash. Maybe two whole seconds had passed, but Alex doubted it. The other battle suit was lost to sight as it fell down the hill, careening around the craggy base and into a straight stretch.

I can't believe you just did that.

"Did we get it?"

Yes…how? The odds were astronomical.

"Did you ever play video games?"

Chess, Mah Jong, Solitaire, and an old math game called Mine Sweeper.

"Didn't you play anything from this century?"

My parents said nothing useful came from playing games. I read a lot.

"There are a lot of shooting games," Alex said. "Sometimes you just shoot as fast as you can. They call it spray and pray."

It's a good thing lucky shots count.

"You can say that again."

So what now?

"Now we make a run for it."

It may be too late for that. We're down to a quarter of our power. If you go racing toward the camp, I can't promise you won't run out of power.

"If we go slow, they'll catch us," Alex said. "Speed is our only advantage."

Maybe...

"What are you thinking?"

Nyx didn't reply right away, and Alex was frustrated. He had taken out three of his closest rivals, and yet it seemed they were no closer to victory.

The Minotaur can deploy solar panels to recharge the power supply. I think, if we move to a position where we can recharge for a while, then we could make our run for the camp.

"But that will give the rest of the squad time to get between us and the camp," Alex replied.

True, but they're down to just eight MBS's still in action.

"Eight to one—not great odds," Alex said.

That's why we pick a good place to wait on them. There's no cover, and we have to be in direct sunlight to use the solar panels, but we might even the odds a little before we run for it.

"Do you have a place in mind?"

I'm looking. Keep moving north, but keep your speed steady. We can't afford to waste power.

"Roger that, steady as she goes. How much time do we have left?"

Eight hours until sunset. That's enough to get the power supply up to half a charge with a couple hours left to reach the camp.

As Alex trundled along, he scanned for any signs of movement. Perhaps it was paranoia, but he felt like the other members of Echo Company might pop out from behind the rugged hills at any moment. It was really Nyx's job to watch for danger, but she seemed far away while he was in the danger zone.

I found it. The perfect spot. It's got cover and a good view of the approaching valleys. I'm sending you the coordinates now.

Alex had no idea how the INC chip worked with the brain, but he suddenly knew where he was going and how to get there. It wasn't like having directions through a large city, but more like he needed to go northwest for eight kilometers to reach a certain spot.

"Any sign of the others?"

Negative. Seems like they're holding back.

"Probably setting a trap closer to camp."

That thought hung between them. Alex had to admit that he never really had much hope. The entire squad was hunting him, and they knew where he was going. Once they discovered where he was, it wouldn't be hard to watch him and set up an ambush. They also had the luxury of just keeping him from the camp. Once the sun set, they would win by default.

"They should build some sort of camouflage into these suits," Alex said.

Agreed. Under different circumstances, we could wait until night and let darkness cover our tracks.

Alex found it interesting that Nyx said "our" tracks instead of "your" tracks. She wasn't in any danger, and yet she was identifying with him.

"So, what's it like being a controller?"

Pretty much like you'd expect, Nyx said. *We train pretty much all day long. I've been waiting for an operator for a few months now.*

"What's your station like?"

I'm in a little cubical with three display screens. I've got one set on the satellite feed, one that sees what you see, and one that's keeping track of the Minotaur's systems. For instance, I know that your starboard middle tire is at thirty-one PSI while the rest of the tires are thirty-two.

"So, it's a little like a video game," Alex said.

No, it's not a game. Your life is at stake. If I make the wrong call, you could die. I take that very seriously.

"Well, that's good to know," Alex said. "I'm not expendable?"

Absolutely not. Once we get paired with an operator, we work together for the rest of our careers. Assuming you don't retire early.

"Or get vaporized by a disruptor drone?"

I can't protect you, Alex. But I don't think of my life as being separate from yours. It's why I joined the CDF. I want to make a difference, and I'm really good at this.

"I didn't mean to imply—"

I know, I'm not angry with you. It's just that I'm really passionate about this job. The executives all think the INC makes you superior, and in some small ways it does. But I think what really sets the Ahzco CDF apart is that every operator has a controller. It's like two people doing one job. Two minds, four eyes—it's an unrivaled synergy unlike anything humanity has ever done. Warfare hasn't changed in thousands of years, until now. And I'm part of that. I get to participate, and maybe make it better.

"Wow, you really are passionate about it."

Aren't you?

"I guess," Alex said, "in some ways. I'd be lying if I said I had a lot of other options before joining. But I like the idea of making a difference. I want to protect people who can't protect themselves."

What was your life like before you joined?

"Boring," Alex said. "NP8261 is a level-three world. My dad works for the company. They sent us there when I was just a baby. It was a company town, most of it under the surface. A lot of rough people—miners, mostly—with no real hope of life ever getting better."

Sounds depressing.

"It was. I tried to get into a technical school, but I'm not very good with written tests. So when the CDF offered me a shot, I jumped at the chance."

Nyx was quiet for a moment, and Alex couldn't help but feel like she was probably disappointed. She was smart and ambitious. He guessed that she probably had a lot of things she could have done, but she wanted to make a difference in the CDF. Then they paired her with a country bumpkin who got in by the skin of his teeth.

It's odd that they matched us up, Nyx said.

Alex felt his heart drop into his stomach. He hated disappointing people. Tears burned his eyes, and he wanted to tell her that she could find another operator, but he knew it wasn't her choice to make.

There were several controllers with more experience.

"I'm sorry," Alex said.

For what?

"That you got stuck with me."

Alex, that's not what I'm saying.

He felt a spark of hope, but he was sure she was just trying to make him feel better.

Think about it, she continued. *It's no coincidence that we met that day in the admin office. And I've never heard of controllers meeting their operators before being matched. It's unusual, and the brass doesn't do things without a purpose.*

"What does that mean?" Alex asked.

I don't know. But you're not just another operator. And I'm not just any controller. I'm not saying we don't have some kinks to work out, but we're working pretty well together—a lot better than I would have expected this early in our partnership.

"We make a good team."

Yes, we do. An usually good team.

"You don't think it's just luck of the draw?"

Highly improbable.

"Someone's watching out for us, maybe."

Grooming us for something, would be my guess, but I have no idea what it might be.

Alex rolled up to the coordinates Nyx had set for him. He had a good view of the surrounding land. They were near the edge of the foothills, and there was more space between the hills. Anyone who tried to attack him would be visible and open to his fire from an elevated position. The Minotaur was surrounded by a jumble of boulders. It looked almost like someone had stacked them up for just that purpose. Behind them, there was an old stream bed. If they had to make a run for it, they could flee to the stream bed and race away with barely more than their turret showing above the crumbling banks.

"I'm in position," Alex said.

Good. Deploying solar array. A few more hours, and we should be good to go.

"In the meantime, try to find the rest of the company," Alex said. "When we make our move, I want to know what we're getting ourselves into."

Chapter 40

Loman walked into the command center of the Transit Resupply Orbital Yard, or TROY, space station. It was the center of all the CDF's activity in the Helena System. Loman thought again about the bomb on the freighter that had failed to reach its explosive potential. If the saboteur had set off that type of device on TROY, it would have been devastating to the entire CDF, leaving Ahzco vulnerable.

The command center was a large, crescent-shaped room, with administrators and supervisors manning computer stations in descending rows. There were huge, holographic displays on the curving wall that made it seem like the room was open to space. In one direction lay Helena Prime and all the ships in orbit around the planet. In the other directions were the various lunar bases where the CDF had training facilities.

"Attention!" Colonel Bixby shouted in a loud, gruff voice. "Commander on deck."

The administrators at their stations started to rise up.

"As you were," Loman said. "Colonel, you have something for me?"

Bixby waved toward a bank of video displays. "Echo company is running field exercises. I've already ordered a transit to pick up Private Evans, but they're in an escape and evade simulation. Evans is the rabbit and cut off from communications."

"So we have to wait," Loman said, acutely aware that his time was running out.

If he was at fault of bringing Alex Evans into the CDF, then it wouldn't matter how much time he had. He'd be fired forthwith, and rightly so. But if the attack on NP8261 wasn't about Evans, then Loman had to find out who was behind it and why. Waiting to speak to the new recruit only made him irritable.

"He's on the move again," Bixby said. "If he can't return to their camp by nightfall, which is in ninety-seven minutes, the exercise will end."

Loman could see the FA Minotaur trundling across the desert on one display. Another showed the camp. The command cruiser was at the top of the screen, and two rows of MBS's waited to intercept and destroy Alex.

"Eight to one," Bixby said. "Not great odds, but he's out of time."

"Maybe he'll surprise us," Loman said. "The kid's got a knack for this stuff."

"Yeah, I read his file," Bixby said. "Four disruptors is impressive even for a fully trained operator."

Loman didn't bother mentioning that the entire attack on NP8261 was most likely staged. He had read the reports on Alex, too—including Supervisor Purfoy's footnote that included her suspicions that he was more than he seemed. What Loman couldn't figure out was what made Alex so good. He had fought in a battle suit without the INC. He had adapted to the mental link faster than anyone in CDF history. And after a quick scan of the situation, he seemed to be using one of their most advanced battle suits like an old pro.

"He's the only operator in a fast-attack-class MBS?" Loman asked.

"Actually, there were three others," one of the administrators helping with the display said. "He took them out already."

"Three Minotaurs?" Bixby asked, not bothering to hide the surprise in his voice.

"And one AT Destroyer," the admin said.

"That's impressive," Loman said.

Loman and Bixby settled in to watch the exercise unfold. Alex was still nearly ten kilometers from the camp when he came to a stop. The dust kicked up by his Minotaur puffed out over him until it was hard to see the MBS.

"Why's he stopping?" Loman asked. "Trying to decide what to do?"

"Or maybe he's figured something out," Bixby said.

Alex started forward again, but instead of moving straight toward the camp, he began to make long, angling zig-zags, like a sailing ship tacking back and forth. It was soon clear what strategy he was employing. A southerly wind was blowing his dust past him and toward the camp —and a large, thick cloud of dust was now rolling toward the two ranks of hunters, their prey lost in the swirling, red dust.

"I can't see him," Loman said.

"I think that's the point," Bixby replied. "The other trainees can't see him, and neither can the controllers helping them."

Loman shook his head. He couldn't believe that a kid barely out of high school could devise such an effective plan.

"Whose idea was it?" Loman asked. "Can we tap into their communications?"

"Just one second, sir," the admin said.

A second later, a speaker hidden among the display screens picked up the conversation between Alex and Nyx.

"It's working," Nyx said.

"Good, let's hope we're lucky and they aren't," Alex replied.

"Movement!" Nyx said with an urgent tone. "They're moving to intercept."

"Can you track their positions?"

"Only if they don't alter course once they enter the dust cloud."

"How many?"

"Just the Infiltrators. All four are moving toward you. Six kilometers and closing."

"Copy that. Let's switch to lasers."

"Laser cannon is online. Transmitting Infiltrator courses to you now. Good luck, Alex."

"Yeah, now we get to see if your trick with the dust works."

Bixby turned to Loman. "I guess that answers your question."

Loman nodded but didn't take his eyes off the screen. All he could see was the dust cloud, moving slowly like a mini sandstorm, and the four Infiltrators racing forward, the hovercrafts kicking up even more dust to join the maelstrom.

"I wonder who's giving the orders down there," Loman said. "They should have spread out and tried to catch him in a crossfire."

"Escape and evade exercises are usually team-led," Bixby said. "Turner, can you tap into their feed as well?"

"Yes, Colonel."

As soon as the Infiltrators were down to only one kilometer from the dust cloud, they started shooting their laser cannons—but the lasers sucked battery power and ran the risk of overheating during rapid fire. Standard fire rate was one blast every two seconds.

"They're shooting, Alex," Nyx warned.

Alex didn't respond, but a laser hit the Interceptor on the right side of the screen. The operator in that MBS cursed as the power shut down and the hovercraft dropped to the ground.

"Good shot," Nyx said.

As she was speaking, another blast took out the next Interceptor in line. The last two were just entering the dust cloud when Alex took out the third.

"His strategy is working," Bixby said.

"Her strategy, but yes," Loman said. "It's working."

"I'm down," said a frustrated trainee.

There were no more flashes in the dust cloud. Everyone gathered around the bank of monitors, waiting to see what would happen next.

"Spread out," came a male voice. "Start shooting. Give it everything you've got."

"That's a trainee," the admin sitting at the controls to the observation console said. "His name is Oliver McGee, a private from the Es Qudar system. He's got high marks from Chief McKinna."

The three destroyers began shooting. Lasers and soft-alloy projectiles flashed across the open space. They were still five kilometers from the dust cloud, and Alex was somewhere inside the haze. Their shots fell short, but the dust was beginning to settle. Loman could make out geometric shapes in the cloud that he assumed were the battle suits. One was moving forward slowly.

"They've opened fire," Nyx warned Alex.

"I can hear it," Alex replied. "How much time is left?"

"Forty minutes, maybe less," Nyx said. "What do you want to do? Circle around?"

"I don't know," Alex said. "I think the best way is for you to take control of navigation. Start circling wide, like you're going to go around them. Once they move, race back at full speed, but right at the edge of laser range. If we get any closer, they'll use their auto cannons and we won't be able to dodge that much firepower."

"Kid knows his limits," Bixby whispered.

Loman just nodded, completely absorbed by the battle on the ground.

"We'll dart in and out of range," Alex said. "Maybe we'll get lucky."

"Either way I'd call this a win," Nyx said. "You've taken out half the squad all by yourself."

"Not me," he replied. "Us. I couldn't have done any of it without you."

Bixby grunted. Loman guessed he was moved by Alex's humility, but Loman couldn't help but wonder if it was all just a ploy.

"All right," Nyx said. "I have navigation controls. Swinging wide."

"Wait until they start moving to intercept to turn back," Alex said. "They'll have trouble shooting and driving at the same time."

Dust began to boil up from inside the cloud. For a moment they lost sight of Alex's FA Minotaur—until it shot out of the sandstorm at almost full speed. The admin hit a few keys and brought up the Minotaur's systems on a side screen. Loman saw they were down to a quarter of their power supply. The readout also showed distance to their objective at 5.2 kilometers. The Minotaur had more than enough power. It could circle around the objective six or seven times at full speed and not run out of power, as long as Alex didn't go crazy with the laser cannon.

"They're moving!" Nyx said.

"Turn back," Alex said, already rotating the turret on the Minotaur.

The battle suit turned into a rolling, dusty slide. When the wheels finally caught traction, the Minotaur shot back the way it had come, angling so that it was moving closer to the AT Destroyers near the camp.

"He's coming back," Oggy shouted, his voice distorted over the speaker system and making it hard to understand.

The lead Destroyer kept plowing ahead, but the other—caught in the dust trail of the first—altered course. They turned south, looking for a target. The first started shooting long laser strikes that faded out before reaching the Minotaur. The operator in the Destroyer was a poor marksman, and most wouldn't have hit the moving battle suit even if it had been in range. Loman caught himself tensing as they closed toward one another. Alex had yet to fire.

"What's the maximum range of those lasers?" Loman asked.

"3.89 kilometers," Bixby said without looking away from the monitors.

"Distance between targets?" Loman continued.

"4.4 klicks to the nearest Destroyer," the admin said.

"He's a cool customer," Bixby said.

Loman agreed. But was Alex *too* cool? Was it possible that the kid was just a prodigy and not some kind of super-spy or saboteur? Loman watched as Alex fired the laser cannon. His first shot was just short and in front of the Destroyer. Loman thought at first that it was a poor shot. Maybe his nerves had gotten to him. But then he realized that Alex was testing the range with the first shot, and his second hit the mark.

The Destroyer shut down suddenly, dust rising up around it. The operator inside let loose a string of foul curses that made Bixby chuckle.

"One down, two to go," the Colonel said.

"Mr. Haley, the transport you ordered is inbound. ETA six minutes," the admin said.

"Very good," Loman replied, just as the second Destroyer began blasting away.

"We're still outside their range," Nyx said.

"Keep moving closer," Alex said.

The Destroyer stopped moving, but it was clear that targeting Alex in the Minotaur, which was moving at full speed, was too difficult for the operator. The shots were all wide and short.

"Going in," Nyx said.

The Minotaur juked sideways, and Alex fired a single laser blast at that very moment. It took the Destroyer out.

"Great shot," Nyx said.

"Turn toward the camp," Alex said.

She jerked the Minotaur into a sliding turn. Alex rotated the turret quickly. The Destroyer, with its two-gun arms, could only bring one to bear. It fired wildly, spraying the air lasers substituting for projectiles. Alex fired back, his own shot going just wide. The Destroyer was desperate and turned too quickly, spinning past its target and then trying to turn back, but Alex's second shot was on the money.

"He did it," Bixby said. "I can't believe it."

"It's amazing," Loman said. "Almost too good to be true."

"Well, he was facing trainees, after all," Bixby said.

"I want him on his way here now," Loman snapped. "We've wasted enough time."

He turned away from the monitors and didn't pay attention to the looks of surprise on the faces of Colonel Bixby and the other admins who had watched the final showdown in the desert outside Sparta.

Chapter 41

Oh my gosh, Alex! That was amazing.

"Stop," Alex said.

He felt completely deflated. There was some joy in having defeated the other trainees, but the truth was that it only left him tired. The sun was almost down, the Minotaur was low on power, and all Alex wanted was to be done with the entire exercise. Unfortunately, he couldn't roll into the camp victoriously. He was less than a kilometer from the target coordinates, but between the Minotaur and the finish line was Oggy.

The last remaining member of Echo Company stood calmly in the AR Medic suit. In his right hand, which was hanging down at his side, he held the personal defense laser pistol. The weapon's range was only a couple hundred meters. Alex was still in weapons mode. His laser cannon was pointed right at the sole survivor of the escape and evade exercise. And while Alex was too far away for Oggy to hit him with his pistol, the truculent trainee was well within Alex's range. In fact, Oggy was standing right in Alex's aiming reticle.

The Minotaur rolled to a stop.

You have navigation controls, Alex. We're 0.87 kilometers from the camp. Twelve minutes remain until sundown.

"Okay," Alex said. "I've got it."

What are you going to do?

"I don't know yet," Alex admitted.

He had proven himself, if not to the other trainees, then certainly to Chief McKinna and Master Sergeant

Gellar. And he had earned the right to win the exercise. The truth was, there was probably nothing he could do to win Oggy's respect. But he still felt the need to try.

"Power down the weapons," Alex said.

He turned the turret away from Oggy until it pointed behind him.

Laser is powered down. All available energy is channeled to locomotion.

"Roger that," Alex said. "And thank you, Nyx. This was an incredible experience—one I'll never forget."

What are you going to do?

"Finish the exercise."

Alex angled the Minotaur slightly, aiming to go around Oggy.

He might shoot you.

"I expect he will," Alex said with a sigh. "But it's up to him. I deserve to be here. I've proven that now. But if he wants to hold onto some imagined grudge, I won't stop him from doing that, either."

Alex was within range of the laser pistol, and Oggy still hadn't raised it. The look on the trainee's face was unreadable. There was anger, but also disbelief—and, Alex hoped, a tiny bit of respect. He went slowly to within five meters of Oggy and stopped.

We're three hundred meters from the camp, Nyx said softly.

Alex didn't answer. He was looking at Oggy, but the other boy wouldn't so much as turn his head to look at Alex in the Minotaur. Alex gave him a few more seconds, then rolled on. A transport was coming in for a landing, kicking up even more of the red dust while the sun slid down into the horizon. Only a rim of golden light remained, but it was more than enough time to reach the camp. Alex didn't have to ask to know that he had enough power. He had made it. He had won.

Suddenly, without warning of any kind, the Minotaur went black.

"What the..." Alex said. "Nyx, did we run out of power?"

There was no response. "Nyx?"

Nothing. The musical hum of his connection via the INC to the Minotaur ended, and the armor split apart around him. Cool, dusty air wafted in, but Alex could feel the heat from the sun radiating from the desert floor. He hoisted himself out of the battle suit and climbed down to the ground.

Oggy was walking toward him, the pistol clipped to his hip and his helmet under one arm. Alex looked at him with disbelief, but Oggy avoided his gaze.

"Evans!" Master Sergeant Gellar barked. "Get over here! On the double!"

Alex turned and jogged the last fifty meters to the camp. He couldn't believe that Oggy had shot him in the back, not when he'd given the arrogant trainee a chance to end the exercise with honor. He knew he would never forget the experience, or the fact that no matter what the future held, he would never trust Oggy again.

"You're being called up to TROY," Gellar said as Alex trotted up to her. "Get on the transport."

"What about the training exercises?" Alex asked.

"When the brass calls, you answer, no matter what," Gellar said, stepping close.

"Do you know what's going on?"

"Only that you've been sent for. There's nothing about this that I would call normal, so watch your back, okay?"

Alex nodded. Gellar slapped his shoulder. "That was a hell of an exercise, Ace. You'll make a great operator. Any company would be happy to have you."

"But not everyone," Alex said, glancing back at Oggy's stony face.

"They'll come around. I've seen it a hundred times."

"Thanks, Master Sergeant," Alex said, feeling a little better.

"Go—don't keep the shuttle waiting."

He snapped off a salute, which she briskly returned, then jogged over to the transport. A sergeant with a scanner was waiting at the door.

"You Evans?"

"Yes, Sergeant," Alex said.

"ID"

Alex held the card out to the sergeant, who scanned it. The device beeped, and the sergeant nodded. "Okay, Private. Get strapped in. We're going up fast."

"Yes, Sergeant," Alex replied.

They both stepped into the small cabin, and Alex saw Chief McKinna sitting nearby. He nodded at Alex. "Good job on the E and E. Took you longer than I expected, but you got it done."

Alex wondered if he should mention the fact that Oggy had shot him in the back, but decided from the tiny smirk on McKinna's face that he already knew. In fact, something told Alex that McKinna had probably told Oggy to do it.

He sat down in a comfortable chair, his stomach growling and his mouth dry from the long day in the Minotaur. The seat swelled up around him, inflating to hold his body firm in the cushions. The shuttle lifted off and rose up well over a hundred meters on repulsors alone. The engines kicked in, and Alex felt his body pushed back into the seat cushions. He closed his eyes. The cabin was dimly lit, the planet dark below them. All he wanted was to sleep and let the stress of the day drain away into oblivion.

Chapter 42

Loman was waiting in a small observation room. Bixby leaned against the frame of the door. The wall between the observation room and the interrogation room was completely transparent from Loman's side. He knew that inside the room, the walls were all glossy white just like the floor, the ceiling, and the table. The only thing that wasn't glossy white was the chairs. They were dull gray, unpainted metal chairs that were built for discomfort and to make a subject nervous.

He would be lying if he were to say that he felt no guilt about bringing Alex Evans to TROY for an investigation, but there was nothing else he could do. Loman had serious questions, and he needed answers desperately. If Alex could shine even a shred of light into the mystery of the attacks on Ahzco properties, it would be worth it.

"Sir, we have the reports on Bruce Evans and his family," an admin said, handing Loman a data tablet.

"This is everything?" Loman asked. "Including a timeline of what they've done and who they've spoken with since arriving on Skandia Seven?"

"Yes sir, it's all there. Nothing seems amiss, sir," the admin said. "They've settled into life in their new home, and Bruce has begun work. His supervisor is pleased to have him."

"Fine, thank you," Loman muttered.

The admin left the room, and Colonel Bixby sighed. "You really think this kid is a spy?"

"I think it's possible," Loman said.

"You'll probably break him in the interrogation," Bixby said. "It would be a damn shame to lose such a natural operator."

"You think I don't know that?" Loman snapped, his voice loud in the little room. "You think I didn't have plans for him? That I didn't think he could have been the future of the entire division?"

Bixby held up his hands in surrender. "I'm just saying, it's a shame."

"Desperate times call for desperate measures," Loman grumbled. "Someone is trying to ruin everything the company is doing. You're no closer to finding out who's behind it all."

"I found the girl," Bixby said.

"But not who she's been working with," Loman said. "A body doesn't help us. The work crew would have found her when they went to make repairs."

"It's got to be a rival corporation," Bixby said. "If they can take you down, whoever replaces you will be swamped for weeks trying to learn the job."

"That's a good theory, but it doesn't make any sense," Loman said. "If this were about money, they would have hit us where it hurts."

"Losing that colony ship didn't hurt?" Bixby said.

"Yes, of course it did," Loman replied. "But the other attacks have been—"

"Distractions, maybe," Bixby replied. "Something to throw us off the scent."

A voice came over an intercom and interrupted the conversation. "Vice President Haley, the shuttle is docking now."

"Thank you," Loman said, looking hard at Bixby. "We'll know soon enough."

"The freighter is ready to make the trip," the colonel said. "The repairs are made, and the crew is back aboard."

"You've vetted them?"

"Yes, sir. They all check out," Bixby said.

"And the colonists?"

"We're still doing interviews and running background checks. We've got twenty-two new employees and sixty-eight that were transferring from other stations."

"We'll have to take them separately, anyway," Loman said. "But it would be good for all of us if one just happened to be dirty."

"It's hard to believe," Bixby said.

"No one is immune to greed," Loman said. "Desperation is a pretty strong motivator, too."

A display monitor flickered on, and both men looked at it. The image showed several operators in MP Patroller suits. The Patroller suits were heavier than Medics, but basically the same minus the medical components. Instead of a knife, they carried stun batons, flex cuffs, and blasters with both stun and kill settings. They were short-range weapons made for spaceships and stations where a projectile or strong laser could compromise the hull. The suits were white and gray, and the operators looked intimidating standing outside the airlock.

When the door opened, Alex walked through. He seemed surprised but didn't resist. Loman hadn't really expected him to; there was nowhere to run on a space station, and TROY had plenty of security personnel. Most were in transit, but a fugitive wouldn't last long. The picture changed to show the six Patrollers escorting Alex through the hallways.

"You going to let him stew a while?" Bixby asked.

"There's no time. And I only have one card to play," Loman replied.

"What's that?"

"His family," Loman said. "I've got an order to have them all detained written up and ready to send. I'll let him read it, and if he doesn't play ball, I'll push it through."

"And if he's innocent?"

"Again, if you have a better idea, I'm all ears."

Bixby looked down. Loman knew the colonel had come up through the ranks. Maybe he was empathizing with Alex too much. Alex was a valuable operator, but no one was above the wellbeing of the company. Something strange went down on NP8261, and Loman had to know what it was and who was behind it. That was the priority—not Alex, and not even Loman himself, for that matter.

The door to the interrogation room opened and Alex stepped in. One of the patrollers pointed to a chair and told him to sit. Alex obeyed. There was a look of complete shock on the young man's face, and Loman knew in his gut that Alex had no idea what was going on. But he had come too far to turn back now, and he had no other options.

"Let's do this," Loman said, "and get it over with."

"Yes, sir," Bixby muttered.

Loman understood the man's disgust at the situation. And Bixby wasn't used to taking orders since becoming a colonel, but his sense of duty was strong. He led the way into the interrogation room.

Chapter 43

Alex was scared. He'd never been in trouble with the law, but he recognized the Patroller suits and knew what they were used for. The operators had been professional and showed no emotion as they escorted him through the space station, but it felt as if he were being arrested. The room they took him to was clearly an interrogation room—he'd seen enough holo-films to know that. They hadn't used flex cuffs or their stun batons like they had during basic training, but the fear he felt was just the same.

It crossed his mind that perhaps everything that had happened from the time he joined Echo Company had been a test of sorts, just like the mental stress exercises Master Sergeant Grossman had put him through. He felt a little foolish at the thought of how belligerent the other recruits had been toward him, not to mention how Chief McKinna had treated him. The thought gave him some relief and a twinge of frustration. He didn't like the mind games, but he told himself there was surely a reason for it.

The door opened, and Loman Haley stepped in. Alex wondered if Loman was really even the vice president of security, or if he was just another actor pretending to be the executive. Alex had to force himself not to frown.

"Alex, I'm here to talk to you about the attack on NP8261," Loman said.

"Has there been another attack?" Alex asked.

"No," Loman said. "But we've learned some things about the attack you were involved in. Now, I've dealt with in you in good faith. I even helped your family, remember?"

"Yes, sir," Alex said, his hands squeezing his knees under the table.

He tried to calm his mind and focus on the truth, but he didn't know what that was anymore. Was he even in the CDF? He couldn't say for certain.

"So I'm going to ask you one time to tell me everything you know about the attack and who was behind it. If you refuse, then I'm going to have to—"

The door suddenly opened, and Chief McKinna stepped in.

"What's the meaning of this?" Loman said. His face was turning red, and there was a level of anger in his voice that Alex had never heard before. Alex put his hands on the table and slid his feet back so that if he needed to, he could spring up from the uncomfortable chair he was sitting in.

"Colonel Bixby, get Chief McKinna out of here right now!" Loman bellowed.

"No, he's not going to do that," McKinna said, pulling a small but viscous-looking weapon from his pocket. He pointed the weapon at Loman.

"Make this quick," Bixby said.

"Don't tell me what to do," McKinna snarled. "I've waited a long time for this, and I won't be denied."

Alex felt as if the room had been flooded with hot air. Sweat popped up on his scalp and down his back. The fear was palpable; he could see it on Loman's face. If this was another exercise, Alex couldn't understand his role in it.

"It's called a Heartstopper," McKinna said.

He pulled the trigger, and what looked like blue-white electricity snapped out from the tiny barrel. It hit Loman in the chest. He cried out—a terrible scream that made Alex flinch. The electricity snapped and popped across the executive's body, which shook hard as he dropped to the floor. McKinna just laughed, and Alex felt the sweat roll down his back.

"Whoo, ain't that a bitch, Loman?" McKinna said. "You see, this little beauty was intended to be a stun gun, but it doesn't really stun you so much as shock you."

Loman was whimpering on the floor.

"Evans, get him up," McKinna ordered.

Alex didn't move.

"Don't even think about it, Private, or you'll be next," McKinna said. "Do what we tell you, and you can catch the first ride back to that stinking rock we found you on."

"No," Alex said. "You're just going to kill me."

"We can do that now or later, kid," Colonel Bixby said. "But let me just tell you what your friend Loman was about to do to you." He leaned over the table and looked Alex in the eye. "He had an order of arrest written up for your parents and that cute kid sister of yours. He wasn't content to just interrogate you—he was going to have your family split up, tortured, and probably killed if they were lucky."

"He's worse than the bugs that eat dung," Chief McKinna said. "He sends people out to die just so he and his bigwig friends can make more money. He isn't worth dying for. Do what we tell you, and we'll assign you to the security division on NP8261. Who knows, you might even get transferred to a level-two planet one of these days, if you can keep your mouth shut."

Alex felt torn. The news about his parents had rattled him. He felt sick and shaky, but when Colonel Bixby put his hand on the pistol holstered at his hip, Alex got slowly to his feet.

"See there, a man of reason and some intelligence," McKinna said, "despite being brought up in the armpit of the galaxy. Don't worry, kid, the security hangar on the Rock ain't so bad. You'll see."

Alex stepped around the table and bent over Loman. He was shaking his head, and tears were in his eyes. If this was a test of some sort, the vice president was really selling it. Alex took hold of Loman's arm and helped him up. The executive was shaky on his feet, and Alex slid the other metal chair over for him to sit on.

Loman nodded at him, a way of saying thank you, perhaps—Alex couldn't be sure. He backed into the corner and watched the other two men. McKinna looked insane. There were veins standing out in his neck and on his forehead. He stared straight at Loman with intense hatred.

"Why?" Loman managed to say.

"You don't even know, do you?" McKinna snarled. "You've killed so many people, you can't even keep track."

"New Persia," Colonel Bixby snapped. "The attack on the Shar Dar Corporation."

"You weren't part of that operation," Loman said, still trying to catch his breath.

"No, but Ella Ferguson was," McKinna said. "She was a controller. They shouldn't have even been in danger."

McKinna's voice was getting louder. He leaned down, screaming in Loman's face.

"But you didn't care about that, did you? You sent them in without intel, and there was a whole squadron of Askars training in the Mecca system!"

"It was a tragic mistake," Loman said. "Our intelligence was bad."

"Just a mistake?" McKinna snarled. "A mistake? I loved her!"

He drew back his hand to hit Loman, but Colonel Bixby grabbed his arm and pulled him back.

"You can't do that," Bixby said. "You leave a mark on him, and no one will believe he died of a heart attack."

"You should have let me take him on NP8261," McKinna said. "I could have taken my time."

"And everyone would have known what happened," Bixby said. "We've worked too hard to throw it all away now."

"So that's what this is about?" Loman said.

Alex could see blood on his teeth and guessed that Loman had bitten his tongue when McKinna shocked him with the little pistol.

"You want my job?" Loman continued.

"I don't just want it," Bixby said. "I deserve it. You're a fool, Loman. All you care about is the damn profit and loss statements. You've forgotten that there are people in the CDF whose lives depend on your decisions."

"I do what's best for the company," Loman said.

"You do what's best for the bottom line, and to hell with everything else," Bixby said. "All you care about is the money."

"That's not true," Loman said. "You don't know what I have to put up with."

"Do you think we care about what you have to put up with?" McKinna snapped.

"I know it's hard," Bixby said sarcastically. "Sitting up in your ivory palace on Arcadia, trying to decide what to have for dinner while people are fighting and dying for the company you claim to care so much about."

"They call this the Heartstopper because if you get hit three times with it, it stops your heart," McKinna said.

There was an eerie calmness to his voice. Loman shook his head and held up his hands to ward off the blow, but there was no stopping it. The little gun spit out the electrical charge, and it shook Loman's entire body. The scream he made was so horrific that Alex felt his stomach churn, and he thought he might be sick. Loman toppled over onto the floor and lay there weeping. A strong odor filled the little room, and Alex realized it was urine. Loman Haley, Vice President of Security for Ahzco, had wet his pants.

"What a pathetic worm you are," McKinna shouted down at him.

"This is taking too long," Bixby said.

"The pistol has to recharge," McKinna snapped. "Stand him up, Evans. I want to look into his eyes when he dies."

Alex moved slowly. He didn't want to be involved. He didn't want to touch Loman, but he didn't have a choice. If there was a way out of this awful fix he'd found himself in, he hadn't discovered it yet. And time was running out.

Chapter 44

"Do it!" McKinna barked at Alex. "Get that sick bastard back on his feet."

Alex stepped over to Loman, who was weeping and moaning. He felt sorry for the executive, but he didn't know what to do to help him.

"I'm sorry," Alex whispered.

Loman looked at him with such desperation that Alex felt near panic. Then his lessons from Master Sergeant Grossman kicked in. He knew that being afraid would only keep him from seeing his options. He needed a clear mind if he was going to find a way to help.

He reached under Loman's arms to lift him up and felt something hard inside a hidden pocket of the VP's jacket. Alex didn't have to tell Loman to stumble—the man could barely hold himself up—so when Alex let go of him just short of getting the VP's legs straight, he wobbled for a second, then dropped. Alex caught him, and this time his left hand went inside Loman's jacket. As he pulled him back up, he removed the metal object. Alex had no idea what it was, but he could feel that it was metal, and there was liquid inside it.

"All right, step away," McKinna said, "or I'll shoot you, too."

"I'm moving," Alex said.

But instead of stepping away, he turned suddenly and threw the metal flask toward Chief McKinna. He had intended to hit the furious chief in the face and follow up with a punch or kick, but McKinna raised his gun hand to protect his face. The flask hit the gun, which went off. The electrical discharge hit the flask, then bounced back and hit McKinna. At the same instant, Alex launched himself at Colonel Bixby, who was fumbling with the strap on his pistol.

Alex lowered his shoulder and slammed into Bixby. The colonel was knocked back into the door, which rattled with the impact. McKinna had dropped to the floor, screaming in pain. Alex snatched up the metal chair and whirled it down in a chopping motion, just as Bixby pulled his pistol from the holster and was starting to raise it toward Alex. The chair hit the colonel's forearm. There was an audible snap; the gun went off and then dropped to the floor as Bixby screamed in pain. Alex clenched his fist and hit the colonel right on the side of his chin. An icy tremor raced up Alex's arm, but Bixby dropped to the floor, his body stiff for a moment, then went limp as his eyes rolled back in his head.

McKinna, finally regaining control of himself, raised the Heartstopper at Alex. There was nothing he could do to avoid the shot. McKinna pulled the trigger, but nothing happened; the pistol needed to recharge. Alex kicked it from McKinna's shaking hand and then dropped the heel of his boot down on the chief's face. McKinna's head was slammed back onto the floor as blood gushed from his nose. He moaned and turned onto his side, away from Alex, who snatched up Bixby's laser pistol and pointed it at him.

"Don't," Loman said in a shaky voice. "Don't kill him. We need him. We need to question both of them."

He coughed, and Alex looked over. The VP was holding his side. At that moment, the smell of burned flesh reached Alex. There was a black wound in the flesh between Loman's fingers. Alex saw charred bits of fabric from the suit coat.

"It's not too bad," Loman said. "He got me in the love handle. Nothing but fat there. Did me a favor, really."

Alex could see by the sweat sheen on Loman's pale face that the man was in bad shape. Alex bent down, grabbed Bixby, and pulled him out of the way. Then he tried to open the door, but there was no handle.

"You need a...a spec..."

Loman slumped over. Alex was afraid the VP was dead, but he set his fear aside and started searching Bixby's body for something that would open the door. He found a bulky device in the colonel's coat pocket as he began to come to.

"Move and I'll kill you," Alex said as he stood up.

The device looked like a door handle. He touched the door with it and felt a magnetic connection. He turned the handle, and the door swung open.

"Help!" Alex shouted.

The patrollers weren't far away and came running.

"The vice president's hurt bad," Alex said. "And these two—"

He never saw the stun baton as it touched his body. He went rigid, then the world went black.

When he woke up, there was a pain in his side and a lump on his head, but he was otherwise unharmed. He was in a medical bed with rails on either side, much like the one he'd woke up in after the surgery for the Implanted Neural Controller chip.

"The hero awakes," said a familiar voice.

Alex looked over and saw Loman Haley in the next bed over. He had several wires coming out of the neck of his medical gown, but otherwise he looked okay.

"What happened?"

"Sorry about that, but the patroller saw you with a pistol and used his stun baton," Loman said. "I didn't see it, but they told me when I came to."

"How long was I out?"

"About ten hours," Loman said. "But you needed some rest after the day you had."

"Are you okay?"

"Oh yes, fine, thanks to you. I thought that was the end of me, until you sprang into action. I've never seen anything like it."

"You've never seen a fight before?"

"I've never seen anyone who knows so instinctually what to do in a fight," Loman said. "How'd you know my flask would reflect the charge from that awful gun McKinna had?"

"I didn't know," Alex said. "Didn't even know what it was."

"You mean it was an accident?"

"I meant to hit him in the face with it," Alex said.

"You are a lucky SOB, but I'm even more so. You saved my life, Alex."

"I just did what I had to do," Alex admitted. "They were going to kill me, too."

"Maybe, maybe not. Bixby's pretty convincing."

"Was what he said true?" Alex asked.

"Yes and no," Loman admitted. "I knew something was wrong with the attack on NP8261. We checked the disruptor drones and found that they had been tampered with. It made sense that the attack was really just a chance to get you off the planet and into the CDF."

"Me?"

"Well, I admit I jumped to a conclusion there. I should have suspected that McKinna was the real culprit, but I thought his years of loyal service exempted him from being a threat. You, on the other hand, were a complete mystery."

"I'm nobody," Alex said. "How could I have gotten drones dropped on the colony?"

"I was hoping you'd tell me that."

"Were you really going to have my family arrested?"

"I was really going to threaten you with it," Loman said. "But no. We had your family checked out. They're doing fine on Skandia Seven. They spent the last week buying furniture for the new house they're buying and getting your sister squared away at the Bowing Academy."

"I want to see them," Alex said.

He hadn't meant it as a request. He was hurting and out of sorts. There may have even been a painkiller in his system. But Loman just laughed.

"Of course you do. And you can. In fact, you can do whatever you want, Alex. You saved my life. You want to retire to a tropical planet and lay on the beach for the rest of your days? I'll make that happen. You deserve no less."

"No," Alex said, sitting up in the bed. A wave of dizziness hit him, and he had to hold onto the bed rails until it passed. "I want to go back to my company."

"Echo Company?" Loman said. "We're probably going to break that group up. There's no telling what Chief

McKinna did to them. They'll have to start their operator training over again."

"Don't split them up," Alex said. "That's my squad."

"You're sure?" McKinna said. "You'll have to wait until you graduate to see your folks."

"I can wait," Alex said, laying back on the soft pillows. "That's what I want."

"Then that's what you'll get, Alex," Loman said. "I don't think we've solved the question of who was behind the attacks on our vessels. Bixby rigged the second one to put pressure on the board of directors to fire me. But there are still bad people out there in the galaxy, people who don't want Ahzco to succeed. And there are hundreds of thousands of employees who need our protection. If being an operator is really what you want, I couldn't be prouder."

"It's what I want," Alex said.

Chapter 45

Alex was up. Loman had been taken from the room and sent back to Arcadia on a medical vessel. The doctor informed Alex that he had hit his head on the floor when the patroller stunned him, and they kept him in the med bay for a couple of days to make sure there was no lingering damage. The last order of business was to test his INC to make sure everything was functioning properly. Alex was so used to the rumble and whine of EM waves from the machines around him that he hardly noticed them anymore.

He walked down the corridor and into a room. There was an INC-compatibility machine, just like the one he had been tested on in Sparta. He powered it on and synced immediately. After a few moments, it was clear that he could operate everything with no pain and no loss of function to the chip in the back of his head. When he powered it down and walked out, expecting to find the doctor, to his surprise there was a visitor waiting for him.

Nyx stood in the corridor. She had on fatigues, which were all gray and white. Her hair was growing out, but Alex recognized the light in her eyes instantly. Seeing her made his heart leap a little bit.

"Alex," she said. "Are you okay?"

"Yeah," he said. "What are you doing here?"

"I'm here to check on you," she said. "Everyone is talking about what happened. It's unbelievable."

"Tell me about it," Alex said. "I lived through it, and I still can't believe it."

"They're calling you a hero," she said with a smile. "But I already knew that."

"Nah, I just did what I had to do and got lucky," Alex said.

She took his arm. "Do you have time to get something to eat?"

"Sure," he said. "But the doctors haven't released me yet."

"Good, then you don't have to rush back down to the planet," she said with a grin.

"I'm supposed to report back with the results of the INC-compatibility test."

"You will," she said. "But first, we eat. It's my treat."

They were an interesting pair. She in gray and white fatigues, he in red and brown. The station was full of CDF personnel, but most were officers and very few wore fatigues. They slipped into a bistro, and people began to recognize him. Several people came over and shook his hand. Alex tried to downplay what happened, but he also felt good about it. He hadn't been lying when he told Loman Haley he was just trying to survive or that hitting McKinna with a flask had been a lucky accident. But an unarmed private who was barely out of basic training had overpowered two armed veteran officers, and that was an impressive feat. It didn't hurt to see the look of admiration on Nyx's face whenever people congratulated him, either.

"I'm surprised you weren't promoted to some cushy post on a vacation world," Nyx said when their food came.

"The VP offered," Alex said. "But I told him I was right where I wanted to be."

"You're kidding, right?"

"No," Alex said. "I want to be an operator and work with you."

"It's an honor," she said.

"No—it's a perfect fit," Alex said.

She blushed just a little, her golden skin turning a rosy shade of red. They talked about family and the future. Alex didn't really care where he was deployed, but Nyx was hoping for a carrier post.

"That way, we'll be on the same ship," she said.

"And I could see more of you," he said with a smile.

"That's what I was thinking."

"Then that's what I want, too. Maybe I could make a call to the VP."

"Really?" Nyx asked.

Alex shook his head. "No, unfortunately not. I mean, he knows me, but I have no way of contacting him. Maybe he would take a message from me on the company net."

"Don't push it," Nyx said. "We'll find a way."

"Yeah," Alex said. "We'll find a way. I like that."

"Are they assigning you to a new company?"

"No," Alex said. "I'm going back to Echo."

"Really? Even though Oggy shot you in the back?"

"Yeah, that needs to be sorted out. I don't want to run from it."

"But you don't have to put up with it," Nyx said. "You deserve better than that."

"Maybe," Alex said. "But I wasn't supposed to be in the CDF at all. I feel like I cheated somehow just to get in."

"That's crazy," Nyx said. "You've more than proven yourself."

"I just don't want any more special treatment, you know? I want to feel like I've earned my way."

"I get it," Nyx said. "And I have no doubt that things will work out."

There was a look in her eye that made him feel like she was talking about more than just his squad—and he knew he wanted to see that look in her eyes for the rest of his life.

Chapter 46

Loman walked slowly off the lift and into the lounge deep underground. The entire board of directors was waiting for him, but the mood was subdued. No one was making jokes about him being late this time around.

"Let's get started," Chairwoman Faulk announced.

Loman saw a few sympathetic nods as he shuffled into the room. Since turning fifty, his body was more reluctant to bounce back from injury or stress. The electric shocks had sapped him of energy, and falling to the ground twice had left him sore and bruised. Then there was the laser pistol shot. It had fortunately hit the fleshy part of his side and not some vital organ, but the soreness was intense. Yet putting off the BOD was even more painful.

They all filed into the boardroom. Loman sat gratefully into one of the large executive chairs. It took him a moment to find a position that relieved the pain of the long trek through the building. Loman hadn't even been to his home or office yet. As soon as the medical transport released him, he'd taken a shuttle down to Arcadia and made his way to the board meeting.

"We are all pleased that you survived your ordeal in the Helena system," Lynn Faulk said, but from her tone she sounded anything but pleased. "Have the assailants given us the information we seek?"

Loman cleared his throat. "Not everything, but it's early in the process. They have confessed to the attacks on NP8261 and the freighter bound for Creedence Three."

"And the attacks on Perrin and the colony ship?"

"As of yet, they have shed no light on those deplorable acts," Loman said. "But we have leads and are continuing the investigation on numerous fronts."

"That is disappointing, Vice President of Security," Faulk said. "I had hoped for more from you."

"Well now, hang on," CEO Ian Gentry spoke up. "Getting that information nearly cost Loman his life. I think we're moving in a positive direction. The freighter taking the gear to Creedence Three is en route as we speak."

"We've incurred some losses, but we're still trending toward a profitable quarter," Chief Financial Officer Mary Shapario said.

"The security around our supply chain has increased," Walt Grummons said. "I'm confident that we're prepared for an attack."

"The attack on me was personal," Loman said. "Chief McKinna blamed me for an operation in the New Mecca system nearly a decade ago that went horribly wrong. And Colonel Bixby wanted my job. We've been looking for an enemy behind these attacks—and we all know that there are numerous corporate and private groups that would love to see us fall—but I am beginning a thorough review of all Ahzco employees. The danger from within may be far greater than that from without."

"Eloquent, but hardly believable," Faulk said. "I'm afraid you sound rather paranoid, Mr. Haley. As chairwoman I feel obligated to relieve you of your duties. In light of the attack on your person, what you need is rest and recovery."

"That would be a mistake, madam chairwoman," Loman replied.

There was a burning sensation in his stomach, and he could feel his legs trembling underneath the table.

"The doctors have cleared Vice President Haley to return to his duties," Ian Gentry said. "I don't think removing him would be in the best interests of the company."

"We'd be giving whoever attacked us exactly what they want," Mary Shapario added.

"If you replace me," Loman said. "You'll spend a year trying to get the new VP up to speed. We'll be vulnerable, and our enemies will know it."

"We have new products launching in the next quarter," Gentry said. "Without strong sales, we might see a dip in stock prices."

"Not to mention that people won't believe we're a safe company to work for or invest in," Mary Shapario said.

"You make compelling arguments," Lynn Faulk said.

She looked down at her PIL, but not before Loman caught a hint of a smile on her lips. He wanted to curse, but the board of directors meeting was not the time or place to show weakness. Faulk hadn't really wanted him replaced at all. She had something else in mind, and he had given her the perfect opportunity to implement it.

"It seems replacing Loman is not the best route to take at this time," Faulk said. "The attack on his life has brought to bear the fact that having one person in charge of each division is a weakness that our enemies can exploit. Therefore, I propose a restructuring of the senior executives."

An immediate, physical response was not surprising. Eyes went wide, several members of the BOD pushed back from the table, and some looked sick. They were faithful employees, each at the height of their respective divisions, and the chairman of the board was talking about restructuring—which was really code for shuffling the existing directors out and new directors in. What Faulk wanted was a corporate takeover, a coup of sorts. She had the power, but simply firing the directors would result in horrible press and a massive drop in stock prices. A restructuring would be news, but boring and perhaps even confusing to most investors. She could push out anyone who opposed her agenda and bring the others so tightly under her control that they would do whatever she wanted.

"We need two, perhaps even three people at the head of every division," she continued. "In case something happens to one of us, the others would stand ready to continue operations without interruption."

"And perhaps you have ideas for something happening to us?" Ian Gentry said. "This is too much, Lynn. You're pushing for too much change."

"Am I? Well, it only seems prudent. You said yourself that if Loman were to step down—a very real possibility, I might add, in light of his recent troubles—that we would be vulnerable."

"More people in the upper echelons of each divisions will make us slow," Walt Grummons said. He was the VP of logistics and knew a lot about how the company functioned. "It will water down the decision-making process."

"We'll get less done," Mary Shapario said. "I can almost guarantee a decline in profits."

"A decline in profits would almost certainly necessitate a change of leadership," Faulk said, and Loman saw the hints of a smile on her face again. "I propose that you begin the process of designing a new executive structure that shares each director's responsibilities. I'll listen to your proposals when we meet again next month."

The meeting ended, and Lynn Faulk and the rest of the scary six left the board room.

"She's pushing us out," Ian Gentry said quietly.

"But why?" Walt Grummons asked. "The company is doing great. What more could she hope for?"

"It's about power," Loman said. "She wants unfettered power over the company and all our resources."

"Doesn't she have that already?" Gentry complained.

"Not really," Loman said. "The company is still run by committee. I think she's looking to wield all the power herself, to be seen outside the company as the woman with all the resources of Ahzco at her complete disposal."

"She's a megalomaniac," Shapario said.

"So what do we do?" Gummons asked.

The directors all looked at Loman. He wasn't the CEO, but he was head of security, and they were all afraid. Unfortunately, so was Loman. But an idea was starting to form in his mind—he just needed a little time and a lot of luck.

Chapter 47

Alex stepped off the shuttle, feeling light inside. His lunch with Nyx had been fun. No, more than that, it had been exciting, and he was looking forward to seeing her again. Hopefully sooner rather than later.

There were three people waiting when he stepped off the shuttle. Master Sergeant Gellar was no surprise. She stood next to Master Sergeant Grossman and Supervisor Purfoy. Alex immediately came to attention.

"As you were," Purfoy said. "Welcome back."

"It's good to be back," Alex said.

"Hell of a thing up there," Master Sergeant Grossman said. "You have the unique distinction of having given not one, but two superior officers the ass-whipping they deserved."

"That's not the action that we should be focused on," Purfoy said.

"He saved the VP," Master Sergeant Gellar said.

"Yes, and his heroics have been in the best tradition of the CDF," Purfoy said.

"I was lucky," Alex said. "I wasn't thinking about saving anyone but me."

"Every operator I know will tell you that luck is just as important as anything else when it comes to combat," Grossman said. "We're damn proud, Evans."

"Yes," Purfoy said. "We wanted you to know that we are proud of what you've done. You've proven yourself to be an excellent operator."

"Ready to head back to Echo Company?" Gellar asked.

"Yes, Master Sergeant," Alex said, feeling a little relieved. All he wanted was for things to get back to normal.

"You get some liberty," Grossman said. "Come find me. I'll buy you a drink."

"And if you ever need anything," Supervisor Purfoy said. "Don't hesitate to ask."

"Yes, Supervisor Purfoy. I appreciate that."

"I suppose you can call me 'Soup' now," Purfoy said. "All my friends do."

Alex smiled.

"Let's go, Private," Master Sergeant Gellar called from a transport nearby. "It's time to get back to your training."

Alex saluted again, then jogged over to the transport. It was an open cab hovercraft. He climbed in beside Gellar, and they zoomed away on a cushion of air. It felt good to be back in Sparta. The town was beginning to feel like home. Alex enjoyed breathing fresh air and seeing the clean streets and colorful landscaping.

They drove onto the campus for operator training and straight into the hangar for Echo Company. There were more battle suits lined up and simulators against one wall. There was also a group of sofas in a square under a banner that read "Echo Company."

Master Sergeant Gellar stopped the transport, and Alex climbed out.

"Go join the others," she told him. "The new CO should be here soon."

"Yes, Master Sergeant," Alex said.

The walk from the transport to the sitting area where the rest of the squad waited was more difficult than Alex expected. The rest of the trainees were waiting for him. He stopped just outside the square of couches.

"Welcome back," Ash said. She slid and waved at an open seat.

"Heard about the attack up on TROY," Sly said.

"And that you could have had your pick of any assignment," Nuk said. "Why come back here?"

"Maybe because he wants to make sure we all bow and scrape to make him feel like the big man," Oggy said with a sneer. "I say he got lucky. And don't forget, the brass had him up there to question him."

"Give us a break, Og," Ash said.

"Yeah, man, I think Ace is okay," Sly said.

Alex could tell from the look on Nuk's face that he wasn't so sure. And Oggy didn't try to hide his complete disdain.

"I came back because this is what I want to do," Alex said. "I want to be an operator, and I want to be part of this squad."

"That's the heart of every great operator," a voice boomed.

Everyone turned and saw an officer approaching. He was tall with wavy hair and chiseled features. Instead of fatigues, he wore an aviator's jumpsuit. Alex and all the rest of the trainees jumped to their feet.

"Officer on deck!" Master Sergeant Gellar shouted.

They all stood at attention.

"Have them fall out, Master Sergeant," the officer said.

"You heard the man," Gellar barked. "Line up for inspection."

Alex and the others hurried out and stood side-by-side, their bodies stiff and their heads held high.

"Every operator has to want it," the officer said, "just as Private Evans has pointed out. You have to be willing to fight and die for the person on your right and on your left. You have to trust that your brothers and sisters in arms have your back. That's what makes a good squad of operators. We are the best-trained, best-equipped warriors in the galaxy, but you can lean too heavy on the tech. The most valuable weapons a warrior has are his mind and his fellow operators.

"My name is Chief Landry, and I am your new commanding officer. I don't care what you've done in the past or what you've learned. I've been given the express order straight from the top brass to whip you into the best squad in the CDF, and that is what I fully expect to do. We will be physically, mentally, and experientially better than every other squad, period. I don't expect it to be so, I demand it to be. If you can't cut it, there are other outfits in need of operators who will settle for just getting by. That attitude won't cut it here, I guarantee you. And I will say this one time, just for the record: no one is getting any special treatment. Past heroics have no bearing going forward. Evans, we all know what you did, and I'm proud to have you on my squad. That said, if you don't pull your weight, I'll cut you without a second thought. That goes for every one of you. This is a meritocracy—only your abilities will see you through. Understood?"

"Yes, Chief!" Alex and the rest of the squad all shouted in unison.

Alex couldn't help but smile. He loved being part of a squad, knowing he was going to be an operator. It might be true that he was given special consideration for joining the CDF, but he had earned his place and would continue to do so in the future. He couldn't ask for anything more than that.

"All right people, today we learn to fly," Chief Landry said. "Welcome to the fast-attack battle suit, Titan. Built for any environment, she is the ultimate MBS in the galaxy and we're going to specialize in operating the Titan for special deployment. Master Sergeant Gellar, the squad is yours."

"Yes, Chief Landry," Gellar said.

She waited until he had walked away before turning to the squad and smiling.

"Who's ready to have some fun?"

Author's Note

Dear Reader, thank you so much for joining Alex on his adventure in CDF. The story continues in Carthage Prime, which will be published in early June. Don't forget to follow me on Facebook and Instagram or sign up for announcements on my website

http://www.tobyneighbors.com/contacts.html

www.ingramcontent.com/pod-product-compliance
Lightning Source LLC
Chambersburg PA
CBHW031024260626
47153CB00017B/2022